FIRE & HEIST

FIRE & HEIST

SARAH BETH DURST

CROWN
NEW YORK

Text copyright © 2018 by Sarah Beth Durst
Jacket art copyright © 2018 by Stuart Wade/Diligence Studio

All rights reserved. Published in the United States by Crown Books for Young Readers, an imprint of Random House Children's Books, a division of Penguin Random House LLC, New York.

Crown and the colophon are registered trademarks of Penguin Random House LLC.

Visit us on the Web! GetUnderlined.com

Educators and librarians, for a variety of teaching tools, visit us at RHTeachersLibrarians.com

Library of Congress Cataloging-in-Publication Data
Name: Durst, Sarah Beth.
Title: Fire and heist / Sarah Beth Durst.
Description: New York : Crown Books for Young Readers, 2018. | Summary: As Sky Hawkins, a were-dragon, faces her first heist she discovers secrets about her missing mother, the true reason her boyfriend broke up with her, and the valuable jewel that could restore her family's wealth and rank.
Identifiers: LCCN 2018010531 | ISBN 978-1-101-93100-4 (hardback) | ISBN 978-1-101-93101-1 (glb) | ISBN 978-1-101-93102-8 (epub)
Subjects: CYAC: Dragons—Fiction. | Shapeshifting—Fiction. | Stealing—Fiction. | Secrets—Fiction. | Fantasy.
Classification: LCC PZ7.D93436 Fir 2018 | DDC [Fic]—dc23

Printed in the United States of America
10 9 8 7 6 5 4 3 2 1
First Edition

FOR DAD AND MARIE

CHAPTER ONE

Gold.

Symbol *Au*.

Atomic number 79.

Dictionary definition: "a yellow malleable ductile metallic element."

You could say my family is obsessed with it. For my mother's fortieth birthday, my father commissioned a grand piano with 24-karat gold keys. The entire piano is covered in gold leaf and is the tackiest instrument ever played. He tried to smash it with a hammer after she disappeared, but my oldest brother talked him out of it. So he satisfied himself with sealing the double doors of the music room shut.

All of which only partially explains why I was stuck on the chandelier in the foyer, dangling upside down and hoping that the chain holding the chandelier wouldn't break.

I'd planned to spend this Saturday night out, with the

goal of healing my shattered heart. You see, according to our family stories, back in the Dark Ages when we both hunted and were hunted, our ancestors used to console themselves after being thwarted in love by gorging on elk carcasses, telling stirring tales of heroic exploits, and burning all their ex-lovers' belongings—and occasionally the ex-lover himself. So I'd decided that I'd go back to my roots by eating buttery popcorn, watching an action movie with no romance whatsoever, and then burning old mementos of my ex-boyfriend Ryan on the barbecue grill.

Bringing Gabriela (a non-wyvern who sits next to me in Modern Wyvern History class) so I wouldn't be alone—my old friends ditched me when Ryan did—I'd bought my ticket and a tub of popcorn, but I couldn't do it. Just couldn't. I'd fled the theater, abandoning Gabriela and the popcorn but taking my mementos—a Valentine's Day card that played the chicken dance, a strip of photos from a carnival photo booth taken on Santa Monica Pier during a trip to the California Stronghold, and the perfect replica (in miniature) of a talon, cast in gold, on a matching gold chain that Ryan gave me for my birthday only a few weeks before he decided to end years of friendship and several months of enthusiastic kissing. I wore the necklace home, tucked under my shirt, over my stupidly sentimental heart.

I was looking forward to moping in an empty house—you know, sighing loudly, singing off-key to depressing music, and wearing pajamas inside out because you're too sad to reverse them—without any commentary from any of my brothers. All of them have zero tolerance for a proper sulk, and they're impossible to avoid, even though our house is enormous, with six bedrooms and eight bathrooms. (Don't ask me why so many bathrooms. My brother Liam, one of the twins, claims one of our grandfathers was enamored with the idea of indoor plumbing—apparently they didn't have it back Home and he was a recent exile. Liam said our illustrious grandfather had even purchased gold bathroom fixtures, then immediately panicked about thieves and hid them. So underneath the floorboards in one of the six bedrooms, there's supposedly a stash of solid-gold toilet handles. I looked for them one summer but no luck. It's possible Liam was lying. He likes to mess with me.)

Anyway, I came home, let myself in, kicked off my shoes, reset the locks and perimeter alarms, and then raided the refrigerator for leftover Chinese food. Taking a container of lo mein, I was walking up the back staircase to my bedroom when I heard the faint tinkle of breaking glass from the front of the house.

Midstep, I froze.

I ran through the possibilities: someone dropped a glass (impossible, since no one was home), a knickknack was precariously perched and fell on its own (possible, since we have a *lot* of knickknacks), or a thief was breaking in (unlikely, since the alarms hadn't sounded). I was certain it was the middle option, but we've been raised to be paranoid, so I clutched my lo mein and raced the rest of the way upstairs to the security room.

My feet were silent on the plush carpet. Stopping in front of the door, I pressed my finger on the ID pad. It didn't unlock. I tried another finger. Still no click of recognition. Beginning to worry, I tried the doorknob, and the door swung open easily.

Inside, all the security TVs showed static.

The lo mein slipped from my fingers. It hit the floor, and the noodles scattered across the carpet. Lunging forward, I slapped the master alarm.

Silence.

No red light. No siren.

I picked up the phone. Also silence. And there weren't any cell phones in the house. We don't use them. They're too easy to hack and track.

I knew exactly what I was supposed to do: get to the safe room, triple-lock the door, and stay there until Dad came home and I heard the all clear. We'd drilled this dozens of times. Over the years, my brothers and I had stashed all our favorite snacks and games in the safe room to entertain us during the longer drills. But this wasn't a drill, and my brothers weren't home. So I did something stupid. Standing in the security room, noodles around my feet, static on the screens . . . I lost my temper.

My name is Sky Hawkins. You may have seen my family name in the newspapers or on TV. Wyverns, distantly related to King Atahualpa (who saved the Inca Empire), Sir Francis Drake (a pirate who was knighted by the queen of England), and that guy who started the California Gold Rush and also the guy who stopped it. Billionaires who lost half our fortune in an investment scam. Socialites whose mother went missing in the midst of the scandal. And me, the youngest, the debutante, whose boyfriend publicly dumped her in the wake of the mess, during the last Wyvern Reckoning. It's been a rotten month, and I did *not* want to add "estate robbed" to the list of things that went wrong.

When I lose my temper, I don't explode; I shrink in. The world narrows down to me and whoever or whatever has wronged me. It feels as if time slows, and everything looks bright and sharp. *Tunnel vision*, my father calls it. My heart beat faster. Adrenaline pumped through my veins. But I felt calm, as if the past and future had fallen away and all that existed was this moment, with me upstairs and the intruder (or intruders) downstairs.

Scooping up my chopsticks (because any weapon is better than none), I moved down the hall toward the front staircase. My steps were still silent. The carpet's thick, and my feet were bare. At the top of the grand staircase, I stopped and listened.

No footsteps. No voices. No more breaking glass.

These stairs could squeak if you didn't know exactly where to step, which I did, thanks to plenty of practice sneaking midnight snacks. Creeping down the curved staircase, I scanned the foyer. Only a few lights were on, spotlights on my father's favorite statues of our more illustrious ancestors. Shadows crisscrossed the tile floor. The windows on either side of the vast front door were intact, and the door was still locked, triple deadbolts.

Keeping to the shadows, I slipped across the foyer to the dining room. No intruders. No broken windows. Crossing back, I peeked into the front sitting room—again, no sign of entry. I then checked the door to the basement, but the lock was untouched. Odd. Very odd. The intruder knew our systems and how to disable them. Given that, he or she most likely knew the layout of the house, as well as which rooms had the most valuables. But the thief hadn't emptied the china cabinet with the gold plates or gone for the wine cellars, which led to the vault, and he hadn't visited any bedrooms for any personal jewels. He'd chosen the front of the house, which had the foyer, the dining room, the front sitting room . . . and the music room.

Mom's piano.

No way was I letting anyone steal that.

Dad always says that executing a heist is like a chess game: you plan for every contingency, and you have backup plans. Stopping a heist, though, is entirely different. You have to improvise.

I hate improv.

Carefully, quietly, I slipped across the foyer and pressed my eye to the keyhole. At first, all I saw was the piano itself, gleaming in the moonlight. I thought of Mom, practicing Bach, note after note, while my brothers blasted their competing music from their rooms. I liked to sit on the couch by the window, doing my homework, listening to her. . . .

A black shadow slipped in front of my view. I drew back.

Heart thumping, I forced myself to look again. I needed to know what I was up against. This time, I saw them: three men, dressed all in black, their faces hidden. Two were lifting one side of the piano; the third was shoving a platform with wheels under one of the legs. I ducked down.

Three men.

One, I could handle.

Maybe two, if I were clever enough.

Not three.

Think, Sky, I told myself. *Think fast.* The men were lifting the piano onto wheels. That meant they planned to take the entire thing, which meant they couldn't leave via the windows—much too narrow for a grand piano. They'd have to open the doors that Dad had sealed shut. If I could hold them here, just until someone else came home . . .

—6—

Spinning around, I scanned the foyer. Statues, vase with flowers, mirrors on wall . . . By the door, there was a pile of mail, plus my brother Tuck's fishing supplies. It was his newest hobby, after his failure at beekeeping. (Seriously, Tuck? Beekeeping?) I beelined for them. No fishing rod, but the box held tackle, copious amounts of fishing line, and a hideous plaid hat.

Behind me, I heard a hiss. I turned to see a line of char on the music room door. It spread, inch by inch, top to bottom. Dad had melted the hinges, so the thieves were carving their own way through.

Grabbing the fishing hat, I booked it to the door and hung the hat over the knob, so it would block the view through the keyhole, and then I worked fast: taking the fishing line and weaving it between the bases of the statues and the legs of various end tables. Goal was simple: slow the thieves.

The line of char now was all the way down one side of the door and proceeding to the right. Blue smokeless flame licked at the ash. It looked like a blowtorch, but I'd bet a wheelbarrow full of gold that these weren't ordinary human thieves and this wasn't any kind of torch.

These men were like us.

Wyverns, aka were-dragons, aka distant descendants of the (extinct) mighty dragons of old who once dominated the skies of Home.

In other words, these men were dangerous.

Now would be the time to hide in the safe room. Still, I hesitated. The fishing line might trip them (best case) or slow them (second-best case) for a few minutes, but it wouldn't stop them. If only I could sound an alarm . . .

I had a thought, the kind that feels like there's a cartoon lightbulb over your head.

All the security alarms were on the same computerized system. But we also had ordinary battery-powered smoke alarms that my father cursed at whenever the batteries ran out and they started to beep. We had no need for high-tech ones—we aren't afraid of fire, only theft. There was one on the ceiling of the foyer, next to the chandelier.

Running up the stairs, I climbed onto the railing. The chandelier was only a few feet from me, close enough to change the lightbulbs. The alarm was a few feet beyond it. Grabbing one of the golden arms of the chandelier, I stepped on. It swung under my weight.

Shifting, I inched closer to the alarm. Now I only had to trigger it. I needed something to set on fire. I reached into my pocket for the chopsticks.

You can do this, I told myself. Breathe. Stay calm. Center yourself. I tried to remember the lessons that had been drilled into me: Draw the flame from your center, think of warmth, believe in the heat. And dream of flying free through the sky in your true form, on your own wings, the sun on your scales, the world beneath your talons.

Pursing my lips in an O, I breathed out a tendril of fire.

The tiny flame landed on the chopstick and then died.

Below, the wood of the door creaked. *Block it out*, I told myself. Focusing, I breathed, trying to summon more fire. The flame seared up my throat and out my mouth. It shot onto the chopstick, and the chopstick caught fire. Leaning forward, I stretched out my arm, holding the fiery chopstick so that the smoke rose up toward the sensor.

As the ash crumbled, the door began to fall. The men

caught it before it crashed. Carrying it back into the music room, they set it aside, leaving a gaping hole. They began to wheel the piano into the foyer. The first man was walking backward, and his ankles hit the fishing line. He lost his balance and fell, pulling the line with him—and yanking down the statue of Sir Francis Drake that it was tied to, which pulled over the end tables. Thief, statue, and tables all crashed down. The vase of flowers shattered, spraying shards of glass across the tile.

And the smoke alarm began to wail.

My fingers slipped, and I dropped back, hanging from my knees, upside down, from the chandelier. Swearing, two of the men tried to help the one who had fallen as the front door to the house slammed open. A familiar figure filled the doorway.

My father put his hands on his hips. "You are all idiots," he proclaimed. "Give me one good reason why I shouldn't disown you all."

Below me, the three thieves snapped to attention.

Oh, no, I thought.

"Clean up this mess and meet me in my office," Dad said. "And get your sister down from the ceiling. We are not monkeys; we should not act like them."

All three of my brothers looked up at me. Dangling upside down by my knees, I waved at them and managed a weak smile.

CHAPTER TWO

I HAVE THREE BROTHERS: Liam, Tuck, and Charles (never Charlie). All older. Charles is nineteen, with investment-banker hair and carefully cultivated muscles. Liam and Tuck are eighteen, fraternal twins—Liam is the one with fashion sense and a swagger, and Tuck likes to wear a fedora. I'm the baby at sixteen. People used to say my mother kept trying until she got a girl. My brothers used to say she should have quit while she was ahead. They didn't say that anymore. In fact, they didn't mention her at all, because silence, repression, and denial are healthy ways to deal with family problems.

When we were younger, I used to follow them around like a puppy dog. They'd climb onto the roof; I'd climb onto the roof. They'd sneak into a humans-only club; I'd sneak into a humans-only club. They'd rob a jewelry store; I'd . . . well, watch mostly. Dad had firm ideas about when it was age appropriate to embark on a life of crime.

I didn't know it was ever age appropriate to try to rob yourself.

"Anyone want to explain why you were trying to steal Mom's piano?" I asked.

None of them answered. Instead, they removed their masks and glared at one another, as if they could shoot fire out of their eyes. (We can't. Just out of our mouths.)

"Liam." Charles had mastered the art of inserting the maximum amount of disapproval into two syllables. It was a skill that came with being the oldest and most responsible. He'd started acting like a miniature adult around the time he discovered his four-year-old sister tasting his special birthday dinner to check if it was okay, because I'm thoughtful like that. Also, I was curious what venison pizza tasted like. (For the record, it tastes weird.)

"I checked!" Liam said. If Charles is the most responsible one, then Liam is the least. Mom used to say he'd forget his head if it wasn't attached. In response, he once bought some plastic heads from a wig shop and left them around the house where she could find them.

"Obviously not well enough."

"She'd left!" Liam cried. "Movie started at seven-fifteen, ninety-minute run time, plus previews. After that, she'd planned to be out back at the grill." He'd taken notes on my plan? I didn't think anyone was even listening when I told them about it, especially Liam, who rarely took anything I said seriously. Or anything anyone said seriously. No one had even said our traditional "Bye, have fun storming the castle" when Gabriela had swung by to pick me up. "Everyone left, exactly as they were supposed to. I did the sweep, came in to disable the cams, exactly as planned." Liam was the family's expert on all things with wires. He loved fiddling with anything electrical or explosive. As a little kid, he was constantly accidentally blowing up the TV. You know, as one does.

Still dangling, I felt my head begin to ache. "Guys, I can tell we all have a lot to talk about, but would you mind helping me down first?" I crunched myself up to grab the arms of the chandelier. My sweaty fingertips touched the metal, then slipped, and I swung back down. *Ow.* Also, the smoke alarm was still beeping loud enough to echo inside my skull.

"*You* should have seen her come home," Liam said, poking Charles in the shoulder. "If you were in position, how did she get by you? Tell me that." He poked again. Poke, poke, poke.

Charles caught his finger.

"Ow."

Charles let go. "Tuck needed help with the window," he said, his voice reasonable, as if of course nothing could ever be his fault. In Charles's case, age also came with a large dose of superiority. As the oldest brother, he was the crew leader for all their schemes.

Tuck kicked the glass shards from the vase toward the center of the room, into one pile. "You didn't need to break it. Three more minutes and I would have had it melted," he muttered. Tuck was always convinced he could conquer any task with just a few minutes of effort. After that, he usually lost interest. But he was the best of the three of them with flame—that was due to natural talent, though, not practice. He wouldn't have had any problem incinerating that chopstick.

"You couldn't maintain the heat," Charles said.

"You didn't give me a chance." Muttering again. He was going through a mumbling stage, Mom had said. Dad was always hollering at him to speak up.

"You had chances," Charles said. "This wasn't amateur hour. We needed perfection. Everyone had to be on their game. If you couldn't perform, then I had to replace you."

"Seems like the only one off their game was you, Charles," Liam pointed out. "You left your post. You let her slip past you. You broke the window, instead of letting Tuck melt the glass, which was probably what alerted her."

Charles, in addition to being the oldest, was also the strongest, due to the amount of loving attention he paid to his biceps. He used that strength to loom menacingly as he argued. "I was not the one who—"

I cut into their argument again. "Hello? Up here?"

They ignored me, again. Instead, they kept hurling accusations at one another until they were standing nose to nose in the middle of the fallen statues and broken glass. Smoke was beginning to curl out of the corners of Liam's mouth, and Charles's hands had curled into fists. Tuck just looked like he wanted to hide under a table.

Brothers can be such idiots.

Stretching my arms out, I began to swing. The chandelier creaked but swayed with me. I reached my arms toward the railing, as if I were a trapeze artist preparing to leap to the next trapeze. My fingertips grazed the wood. I swung back, then forward. The chandelier creaked louder. I heard the plaster in the ceiling crack and had the fleeting thought that this was a bad idea—then my hands grabbed onto the railing as, simultaneously, the ceiling gave way. I clung to the railing as the chandelier dropped. A foot down, the wires caught it.

All three brothers looked up.

I scrambled over the railing. The chandelier now hung by its wires only, like a loose tooth. The ceiling around it was cracked.

All three of them, in exactly the same tone of voice, said, "*Sky!*"

And I took that as my cue to leave.

Scurrying down the hall, I hurried to the security room. It occurred to me that even though my idiot brothers had failed to steal the piano, they *had* succeeded in shutting off all our security systems—which meant we were vulnerable to any non-idiot thief who decided to visit us tonight. It also meant that since it was my brothers' work, I might be able to figure out how they'd done it. If they'd shut it off in the software, it could be a relatively simple fix. I knew the codes too. If Liam had rigged something with the hardware . . . that could be trickier. Regardless of what my brothers did in the foyer, it was the height of stupidity to leave the entire security system down. Stepping over the spilled lo mein, I walked into the security room.

My father was already there, on his back, underneath the desk. The screens still showed static.

"Hand me the electrical tape," he said without any kind of preamble.

I located the roll of tape on the table, next to the pens, and handed it to him. I should have guessed he'd be here. Dad was security obsessed. It was kind of unavoidable, given who and what we were.

He took it, grunted thanks, and said, "Let me guess: you got yourself down without any help and came straight here to reset the security system, rather than staying with your brothers to clean."

I hesitated for a moment, wondering what was the correct answer. Since the only options were the truth and an obvious lie, I opted for truth. "Yes?"

He waved the tape at me, scolding with it. "Don't question. Answer. You need to learn to speak with conviction. No crew will ever follow your lead if you don't project confidence. Try again."

"Yes, Dad. I swung myself off the chandelier and then ran here."

"You broke the chandelier."

It wasn't a question, but I figured it was safer to answer anyway. "Yes."

He snorted, either in amusement or disapproval. I voted disapproval. He hadn't laughed in weeks, not since Mom had left. "And you left your brothers with the mess."

There was only one answer to that too. "Yes."

"Hit the reset," Dad said.

I flipped a red switch off, then on. The computers whirred as they rebooted. I pushed the power buttons on all the screens. One after another, they blinked back on. Very nice. My brothers might have their specialties, but Dad is good at everything. In fact, I'd yet to find anything he wasn't great at. He set an impossible bar for all of us, which explained many of my brothers' issues. Not me, of course. I have no issues. *Except for a broken heart*, I amended.

"Check the phone."

I lifted up the receiver. No dial tone. "Not yet."

Grunting, Dad fiddled with more wires. His body was blocking my view. Squatting, I tried to get a better look at what he was doing. "You're blocking the light," he complained.

"Teach me?" I asked.

"You don't need to know this."

In addition to protecting the house, Dad liked to protect me. It drove me crazy when he refused to tell me things that my brothers clearly knew, supposedly for my safety. I didn't know if it was because I was the youngest or because I hadn't led my first heist yet or what. For our kind, leading your first heist is a major milestone, even better than learning to talk, walk, or do long division. "If I'd known how to do this, I wouldn't have needed to dangle from the ceiling, and the chandelier wouldn't be broken," I pointed out.

He considered that for a moment, then waved me under. I scooted underneath the table with my father. Lying on my back, I looked up at the rat's nest of wires. It was the closest I'd been to my father in probably years. We aren't a physically affectionate family. My mother used to hug me about once a year, usually on my birthday, and I couldn't remember the last time my father hugged me. He smelled like smoke. Not cigarette smoke, but forest fire smoke. Pine smoke, the kind that makes you think of winter, even though it's spring. I always loved that smell. Made me feel safe.

Dad pointed out the different wires, explaining the pitfalls in trying to bypass a security system. Liam had cut them in a certain order, one that wouldn't trip the redundant alarms in place to prevent someone from disabling the system by cutting them. But with an unfamiliar system, you'd be better off hacking the software. You never knew when someone might rig their hardware to a bomb. Cut the wrong wire, and *boom*. He worked quickly, stripping the wires and twisting them together. "Later tonight, I'll replace all the wires, but this temporary fix will get the system operational again."

"What if someone gets in while we're restoring the system?" I asked.

His hands stopped moving. There were shadows on his face, but I thought I saw his cheek twitch. A smile? A frown? I couldn't tell. At last, he said in his gruff voice, "I don't say this often enough, but I am proud of you, Sky."

I felt a rush of warmth, and now it was my cheek that twitched. Just a little dust in my eye. "You're using a spell," I guessed. Spells cost gold, both to purchase and to use; we prefer to rely on human security systems, but I knew my father kept a few on hand.

"Yes, of course."

"Then you knew I had come home."

He smiled, a very rare sight. I stared at his lips, curled within his beard. "Yes, of course," he said again.

"But you didn't warn them."

"This was their test."

I was tempted to smile too, but then I thought of the mess in the foyer with the statues, the vase, and the chandelier. At least the statues hadn't fallen on top of my brothers. "They're angry with me."

"They're angry with themselves," he corrected.

"And me."

"And you."

I sighed, then wondered if this new proud-of-me dad would be open to an actual conversation. "They're always angry these days. Everyone is."

Dad resumed work on the wires. His big hands were quick with the delicate strands. He shifted from one computer to the next. "It is a difficult time."

I took a deep breath. "Can you tell me—"

"No," he cut me off. "It's better if you don't know."

"Like the security system? Dad . . . the more I know, the safer I am."

He now looked sad. "That is very much untrue. And the older you get, the more you will understand how very much untrue that is. There are many things that I wish I could unlearn about the world. Keep your innocence as long as possible, Sky. It's a precious thing."

"I'm not a baby anymore," I said. "And she—"

"Enough."

Charles might be able to imbue a name with disapproval, but Dad is the master at filling a single word with a wealth of meaning. That word had sadness, anger, and everything else lumped into it. I changed tactics. "Why were Charles, Liam, and Tuck trying to steal the piano? It's too recognizable to be pawnable. If they wanted it just for the gold, it would have been easier to dismantle it in the room then head out the window."

"That was the test. Entire piano."

"Why?" I asked. "When exactly is that situation going to come up?" As far as I knew, not many people owned gold grand pianos.

His hands quit moving. "They needed a distraction from tomorrow."

"What's—" I stopped myself. How could I have forgotten? Tomorrow. Mom's birthday. "Oh." It wasn't quite an answer. I didn't see how stealing Mom's piano today could make tomorrow easier, but it clearly made sense for my father, and he just as clearly didn't want to talk about it. But I had one more question that I wanted to ask, one I hadn't dared ask since the day she disappeared. Today, though, he was proud of me, so perhaps I could dare . . . "Do you think she's still alive?"

"Yes."

I exhaled. He hadn't ever implied that she wasn't, but I'd been secretly worrying. No one had told me much when it happened. Mom had been off on a mission that was supposed to dramatically increase our wealth—you know, the usual. But then something had gone wrong. Or more accurately, she had done something wrong. And she hadn't come back. And just like that, the whole family was disgraced.

I couldn't help thinking: If she was still alive, why hadn't she come back or sent word or made contact of any kind? Didn't she care about us? "Does she need help?" I asked.

"No."

I wished I could force him to tell me. Surely the truth couldn't be as bad as all the various scenarios I'd conjured up, most of which involved my mother dead, hurt, trapped, or subjected to horrible science experiments in some human supremacist's illegal laboratory. Whatever she'd done, we could fix it together, couldn't we? Like the security system. We just needed to know which wires to mend. We were a formidable family. I'd always been told if we stuck together, there was nothing we couldn't do. And now I wasn't even supposed to ask questions.

I thought of Ryan and how I'd thought we were a for-midable team too, through thick and thin and all of that. I'd counted on us being together forever. Even used to day-dream about our wedding day—the whole stupid wedding dream, complete with a marshmallow-fluff dress and a bou-quet that matched the table arrangements, as if this was anything I'd normally care about. Emma and Emily, my best girl friends (or *former* best girl friends), had already dubbed themselves my co–maids of honor. All Ryan and I had to do was stick together another few years. Instead, we'd quit just shy of eight months. Well, sixteen years, really, but less than one of them spent on kissing terms.

I'd known Ryan since we were both in diapers. Not that I remember that. But I've seen pictures. I'd had pigtails. He'd had an adorable potbelly. Our families used to summer together in the California Stronghold, one of the wyvern-run states. The two of us learned how to swim together, and how to evade doing chores. I remember holing up for hours and hours in secret hideaways that we'd find on the beach, creating elaborate games and practicing breathing fire. We even had a secret alcove on his family's estate here in Aspen, tucked behind the gardens at the top of a cliff. It had a view of the mountains and a lake. That was where I'd first kissed him, age six, a peck full on the lips. He'd wiped it off.

When I was eight years old, I decided I was going to marry him. I was careful not to tell him, of course, since everyone knows boys can't be trusted with secrets like that. I did inform my parents, in case they wanted to make ar-rangements. They weren't interested. Our kind likes to do arranged marriages, mainly to make sure the genetic pool stays strong enough to keep the were-dragon traits but not so inbred that we end up born with scales instead of human skin. Since Ryan is only half were-dragon—his mother is human—and I'm full, I thought it would make sense for everyone if he married me.

Mom hated when I used the word "were-dragon" to describe us. "We're wyverns," she used to say. "Be proud of it. You can trace your heritage back generations, to before our family's exile from Home." But ever since I first heard about werewolves, I've loved the word were-dragon. It describes us nicely, plus it has a neat double-meaning with the word "were." Our ancestors *were* dragons. And now we're *were*-dragons—humans capable of turning dragon.

Or dragons capable of turning human.

Semantics.

Of course, the fact is that no wyvern had transformed into a dragon since Sir Francis Drake sank the Spanish Armada with his dragonfire in the 1500s. Our shapeshifting skill was lost generations ago. But all of us had training in the useful art of breathing fire. And we were all pretty much fire resistant, which is an awesome plus when it comes to fresh-baked cookies. No need to wait for them to cool. Or use oven mitts. Just go straight for the still-in-the-oven cookies. And no worrying about scalding the roof of your mouth either. We're rated up to about 2,000° F. In other words, we can toast a marshmallow on a finger, but a blowtorch would hurt us. (Average propane torches burn at 3,600° F, and oxygen-fed torches routinely reach up to a searing 5,000° F. You get to know these fun facts when you're born with literal firepower.)

We also, as I mentioned, all really love gold. And that was what made it so odd that Dad had chosen the piano as my brothers' target. Dad may have wanted to smash it, but he wouldn't want that much gold to leave the property. "What were they going to do with the piano once they stole it?"

"What would *you* have done with it?" Dad asked.

I wouldn't have tried to steal it in the first place. There were lots of other more portable valuables around our property. Plus that was Mom's piano. But Dad wasn't looking for that answer. "Stripped the keys and turned them into necklaces to wear on special occasions."

"I will give you a necklace. Six ounces, gold," Dad said in a decisive voice. "You deserve it for your work today."

I thought of the chandelier. He hadn't seen the ceiling yet. Plus I knew he liked those statues, and several of them were most likely damaged. The vase was certainly beyond salvaging (though it wasn't gold so he might not care). "I made a mess."

He sighed. "Your mother made a mess. We are simply doing the best we can with the pieces that she left behind." He pushed himself out from under the desk and stood up. Around us, the screens were now showing different views of the house, including the foyer. Tuck was sweeping the broken glass into a trash can, and Charles and Liam were pushing the Sir Francis Drake statue back up onto his pedestal. Charles had taken off his shirt, because he likes his muscles the way a toddler likes his teddy bear.

"Do you hate her?" I asked. "Is that why we aren't trying to find her?"

"Emotions have nothing to do with it," Dad said. "Believe me when I say that it is for the good of the family." I wanted to ask more, but his tone was final. "You don't need to come to my office while I speak with your brothers. You should go, help yourself to . . . popcorn, isn't it?"

I nodded and wondered how he knew. I didn't think he'd been paying attention either when I'd talked about my plans for tonight, or that he knew it had been exactly one month since Ryan had stood in the middle of all the wyverns gathered for the ritual of the Reckoning—including Emma, Emily, and all the wyverns I thought were my friends—and denied me. "With lots of butter."

He almost smiled again, which would have been the second time in a single conversation. He used to smile all the time and laugh, a big booming guffaw that echoed through the house. Mom had taken that with her, when she left. But then the smile faded, and he was as serious as a shadow again. "You need to forget that boy exists. And forget about your mother. They betrayed our trust, and all that is left is to move forward."

I looked into his eyes, up because he's nearly two feet taller than I am. "Are you? Moving forward, I mean. Can you forget?"

Dad studied me, as if he were deciding what answer I was ready for. I wished I dared yell at him to just tell me what he wanted to say! "Of course not. But that doesn't stop me from wanting better for you. You did nothing to deserve any of this."

I felt a lump in my throat. My father *never* showed vulnerability. He was as solid as the walls of a vault. "Do you want . . ." I swallowed.

He waited for me to finish.

". . . popcorn? I can share."

"Thank you," he said gravely. "May I have a rain check?

I have work to do and sons to scold." Shocking me again, he kissed the top of my head and then strode out of the security room.

Turning, I watched him on the cameras as my stoic, always-strong father paused alone in the hallway and wiped his eyes with the back of his hand.

CHAPTER THREE

BREAKFAST THE NEXT MORNING was, shall we say, tense. I wished I'd stayed in my room and polished off the rest of the popcorn, rather than allowing myself to be tempted by the lure of Tuck's made-from-scratch pancakes. (I love pancakes. I am deeply suspicious of anyone who doesn't love pancakes.) Dad sat at the head of the table, and my brothers and I sat on the sides.

Mom's seat wasn't just empty; it was totally gone.

The first breakfast after she disappeared, I'd come down, seen her empty chair, and burst into tears. Dad had promptly removed it, which was arguably worse—I'd cried harder. Now I simply didn't look at the empty spot. None of us did. Or at one another, because eye contact could lead to conversation, which could lead to *feelings*, and no one wants those. Especially not before noon.

Tuck breathed on a plate and crisped a few strips of bacon. He passed it to Liam, who passed it to Charles, who passed it to me. One was left by the time it reached me. I drowned it in maple syrup and decided bacon was worth the awkwardness. I also took another pancake.

Midway through the pancake, Dad broke the silence, because that's what he does. "Liam, I need you to buy a new protection spell from Maximus. Extra fire resistance up to 3,500 degrees, liquid form so we can mix it in a paint, for the foyer. Take Sky with you."

"But Sky—"

"Did it sound like I wanted a debate? Sky knows how to behave herself." He leveled a look at me. "Sky, you're to let Liam take the lead. Your role is observation only. Maximus is touchy—ever since he lost his wife, he has been increasingly erratic. But he's one of the few wyvern wizards who will still deal with us, so we're stuck with him. Both of you, try not to alienate him."

I stuffed my mouth with blueberry pancakes so I wouldn't say anything to accidentally change Dad's mind. My brothers *never* let me come on family business. I couldn't help being a little excited about this. First Dad had showed me the security system, and now he was sending me out to meet a wizard. For observation only, but still it was a start.

Humans have known about wyverns since King Atahualpa revealed our existence in 1533, but the fact that a few of our kind are also wizards is a closely guarded secret. (Honestly, though, you'd think more of them would have guessed. Merlin, for instance, hadn't exactly kept a low profile.) Anyway, allowing me to observe a bargaining meeting with one was a big deal. It meant that Dad trusted me.

Liam shot me a look. I could tell he'd rather be accompanied by a Gila monster than bring me along. I wanted to say it wasn't my fault that (a) no one had told me they were being tested and (b) no one had noticed I'd come home. It was, granted, my fault that I hadn't followed procedure and gone to the safe room, but so far no one had pointed that out, probably because it was obvious that Dad didn't disapprove.

Charles was refusing to meet my eyes at all, pretending that I didn't exist, which I thought didn't match his oh-so-mature attitude. And Tuck was shooting me glares in between stuffing his own mouth with pancakes.

Maybe enough maple syrup would lighten all of their moods.

Or maybe they were just looking for someone to blame for everything that had gone wrong over the past month.

I knew who I blamed.

Mom.

And Ryan.

Whatever she'd done had turned everything upside down for us. She should've taken us into account. Family first. She shouldn't have left us to deal with the mess she created.

And Ryan should have stood by me. He turned his back on me when I needed him most, because his family asked him to. Like all our other so-called friends, they didn't want to be associated with our disgraced name. When push came to shove, he chose them over me.

Mom hadn't chosen family first, and I'd lost.

Ryan *had* chosen family first, and I'd lost.

It would have been nice if everything we were going through could have united my brothers and me, instead of splintering us apart.

We finished our breakfast in silence, and then split up to finish dressing. Liam met me in the foyer. He was wearing a long trench coat over a business suit, and he'd slicked his hair into a style I like to call "fashionable hedgehog."

Liam doesn't like it when I call it that.

"Nice hair," I said.

"Don't," he warned.

"You used to have a sense of humor."

"Yeah, and that table used to have a vase."

My brothers had finished cleaning the foyer. All the statues were back on their pedestals, all traces of broken glass had been swept away, and the table that used to hold the vase was empty. Looking up, I saw the chandelier had been reattached and the ceiling had been patched with spackle.

A year ago, there would have been a brand-new chandelier and a brand-new vase. I know, I know, poor little rich girl. The world's smallest violin is playing, and all that. But the vase and the chandelier were just two more reminders that we'd not only lost half our wealth but also our place in society, all of our friends, the majority of my parents' business contacts, and of course Mom. So, yeah, excuse me for letting the lack of things bother me. Lately, walking through the house felt like poking a bruise over and over again. Everything made me think of her.

Outside, there were other obvious signs that our finances were not what they were before our disgrace. Our fleet of classic cars and race cars had been reduced to one for everyone in the family with a driver's license, which was everyone except me. (I'm an excellent driver but a lousy parker.) The best showpieces had been sold off. Again, I know, no sympathy. But you try losing your mother and still being grateful to have kept a car or two.

It's possible I'm a little angry and defensive about all this.

Liam hopped into his Ferrari and didn't wait for me to buckle myself in before slamming on the gas and roaring out of the garage. Squealing to a stop, he waited for the gate across the driveway to open, since he didn't want the car sliced like cheese if he tried to ram his way through. I buckled my seat belt and, since I've driven with Liam before, double-checked it. The radio was on, loud, howling a song about a guy burning with love for a wyvern girl, pun intended. The bass thrummed through the leather of the car seat so that I could feel it through my thighs and back.

"You know it's not my fault," I said.

"What?" he said.

"Not my fault!" I said louder.

"I know."

"Then stop blaming me."

"I'm blaming myself."

"Feels like you're blaming me. Can I turn this down?" I reached for the volume control. He smacked my hand and then peeled through the open gate. I was knocked backward by the sudden acceleration.

I used to get along great with Liam. He liked to laugh, and I was fine with being the punch line of his jokes, so long as someone was paying attention to me. Worked out well. When we got a little older, I used to try to turn the tables on him. Sometimes I succeeded, like the time I hid a snakeskin in his bed so he'd think he was able to transform and had molted in his sleep, and he liked laughing about that just as much as he did when the joke was on me. But like my father, Liam hadn't laughed in weeks.

We all needed something to go right, for a change.

"Where are we going?" Maybe I could get him talking about something else. It would be nice to have a normal conversation so this entire trip wasn't tense.

"We're visiting Maximus, like Dad told us to."

"Where? And who's Maximus? Come on, Liam, info. If you want me to behave right, you need to tell me what to expect."

"Maximus's a jewelry guy—at least that's his public face. He owns Maximus's Fine Jewelry and Estate Treasures. He's also a wizard. Not a great one, but he does know how to make a few spells very, very well. Whatever you do, don't call him Dumbledore."

"Why would I call him Dumbledore?"

Gravely, he said, "You'll want to know that I told you not to. It's like telling someone not to think about a pink elephant. All you can picture is a pink elephant."

"Then why tell me?"

"I like to mess with you."

And for an instant, I thought, *Maybe things can be normal.* But before I could think up some witty response, Liam stomped on the gas.

Spinning the wheel, he squealed around a turn, and I slid against the car door. And then he spun the wheel the other way, and I slid back. Unfortunately, the road from our house has a lot of turns. Fortunately, it wasn't winter, so I didn't have to worry about Liam hitting any ice. It was barely spring, and the leaves on the trees were curled up, about to pop open into proper leaves. Stubborn patches of old snow still stuck to the sides of rocks. They were pocked with dirt and barely resembled snow. Looked more like dryer lint.

By the time we reached downtown Aspen, there were no more traces of snow, and I felt vaguely nauseous, which I suspected had been Liam's ploy to keep me from wanting to chat more.

I scanned the street, on the lookout for any of my former friends—we used to hang out downtown together all the time . . . laughing at not-particularly-funny in-jokes, mocking whatever human TV show we were currently binging, eating nachos, trying (and, in my case, failing) to char the nachos with our fire breath . . . you know, teen stuff. But I didn't see anyone I knew.

Liam parked, sliding the car in between two SUVs. When he shut it off, the radio shut off too, and the silence felt loud. "Let me take the lead," he said.

"Dad already said that."

"Yeah, but I know how you get. You always think you know best. You don't. You aren't as smart as you think you are, Sky."

I blinked at him. "Ouch." Where had that come from? I knew he was mad about the fishing line—he'd been the one to trip—but seriously?

Rubbing his eyes, he grimaced as if he wanted me to think he was rude because he was overtired, not because he hated me. "Look, let's just try to get through this."

"I didn't think spending time with me was such awful torture." Getting out of the car, I told myself that I was *not* upset by anything he said. He was in a bad mood, and he was taking it out on me, because he could. He couldn't take it out on Charles—Charles would never allow it. Dad was out of the question. And Tuck was Liam's twin. I was the easiest and safest target. I understood that it wasn't personal and that he didn't mean it. Still, I was getting very tired of everyone using me as their dumping ground for whatever excess emotion they were experiencing. I missed Mom too.

I wished for the millionth time that I could call Ryan. In addition to being good at the whole kissing thing, he'd been my best friend. Yes, I'd fallen for my best friend, the nice guy, the one you aren't supposed to notice but is secretly there all along, except I'd noticed him from the very beginning—it had just taken a while for him to admit he'd noticed me back. He hadn't wanted to risk ruining our friendship by saying anything, and neither had I.

We both had other friends, obviously—Emma, Emily, Jake, Topher, Rosario, Carlos—but they were more hanging-out-with friends, not share-the-dark-secrets-of-your-soul friends. You don't get many of those in a lifetime. Ryan was mine.

When we finally kissed for real, though, it hadn't ruined anything. It had made everything a thousand times better. I knew I'd found the love of my life. My soul mate.

His family had taken that from me—and he'd let them. Straightening, I walked toward the jewelry store. Liam hurried out of the car, beeped the lock, and matched my pace.

"Sorry, Sky. Rough night last night. You didn't know what we were up to. If any of us had bothered to fill you in, that never would have happened."

"Yeah, I thought of that."

"You were supposed to be out."

"I was. I came back."

"Why?" he asked.

He sounded genuinely interested, and I wished I could talk to him about *feelings* stuff. But even in the best of times, that wasn't our relationship. I used to talk about feelings with Ryan, and of course with Mom.

I stopped walking.

Of all of us, I'd been closest to Mom. Could that be why . . . "You know I wasn't involved, right? Mom never gave me any hint. I don't know where she's gone, or why. Or what happened, beyond the fact that whatever she did was so bad that everyone hates us for it."

Grabbing my arm, Liam propelled me along the sidewalk. He shot glances at the random tourists. "We don't talk about this out in public."

"We don't talk about it at all. Ever. And that's stupid."

"Not now, Sky."

He was right. Even though I desperately wanted to have this conversation, including telling him what an idiot he was for not talking to me, for blaming me, for whatever it was he was feeling toward me, this wasn't the place. Anyone could overhear the Hawkins kids arguing in the street and leak it to the tabloids.

Even a month later, humans obsessed with wyvern gossip (yes, it's totally a thing—some people love movie stars, some drool over their favorite baseball heroes, and others latch on to wyverns as their "celebrities" of choice) were still salivating to know details about our family's fall from grace. There were so many conflicting stories about what had led to our expulsion from the upper echelons of wyvern society. The most persistent rumor was that my mother had stolen millions and then lost it all in an investment scam.

And I had to admit it was possible. Whatever had happened was certainly all about gold. Nothing else would have excited our kind so much.

Liam halted in the middle of the sidewalk.

And I saw him. Ryan. My Ryan.

He looked exactly the same as he had the last time I saw him, which intellectually wasn't a surprise since I last saw him at school less than a week ago before April break began, but still I thought he should be gaunt and withered from lack of me. Instead, he looked . . . well, he needed to comb his hair. Bits were sticking scarecrow-like in various directions. Also, he had brown socks with black shoes, because he has the fashion sense of a platypus. But it was his eyes that I stared at most of all. Big, brown, with lashes that would put mascara companies out of business. His eyes transform him from doofy-boy-next-door to movie-star-mixed-with-your-favorite-teddy-bear.

"Sky," he said, or breathed. Or maybe I just imagined him saying my name.

"Hi, Ryan," I wanted to say. Cool, calm, collected. Instead, I didn't say anything. I couldn't get my throat to work. I felt flooded with memories: climbing trees as kids (he'd burned our names into the bark), the first time we held hands (under the table at an otherwise boring brunch), the time he gave me all of his ice cream when I dropped mine (a sign we were destined to be together).

"You look great," he said.

"Thanks," I said, and mentally kicked myself. I'd rehearsed what I'd say to him if I saw him about a million times. I would be sophisticated and suave. Make him see that he hadn't hurt me. Make him remember what he missed. Instead, I said, *Thanks*.

He stared at me more.

I stared back.

It was awkward. Very awkward. Like, naked-at-school awkward. Except worse. I felt like I was missing both clothes and skin, and my heart was laid bare to the wind and birds, just waiting to bleed out.

He lowered his eyes and quit looking back at me. "Uh, I have to . . ."

"Run away?" Liam suggested.

At that instant, I wanted to hug my brother.

Ryan flinched. "Sorry?"

"You should be," Liam said. "You could have stood by her."

"I didn't have a choice," Ryan said.

I snorted, loudly. "There's always a choice."

"Sky . . ." He stopped, but he looked as if he wanted to say more. In his eyes were everything I'd wanted to see in them: regret, sorrow, pain. Maybe he hadn't wanted to break up with me. Maybe he'd had a reason, a good reason.

Maybe I was right to still hope.

And I waited for him to continue, to apologize, to explain, to drop to his knees and beg my forgiveness. But he didn't. Instead, he said, "You're wearing my necklace. I mean, the one I gave you. Not mine. But I gave it to you. So it's yours now." He winced. I used to love the adorable awkwardness that came out when he was nervous. Still did love it. It made me want to wrap my arms around him.

My hand went to my throat. The gold talon dangled

there. I'd put it on again this morning without thinking about it. Touching it, I had the urge to say "finders keepers" and flee. Instead, I said, "It looks good on me."

"It does," he agreed.

More staring.

Liam sighed so loudly that I could practically hear his eyes rolling.

I wanted to ask Ryan if he missed me. I wanted to yell at him. I wanted to say a million things that I never had the chance to say. Also, I kind of wanted to pummel him for putting me through this without any shred of an explanation. But we were in the middle of the sidewalk, and more and more people were stopping to stare. A few snapped pictures. Grabbing my elbow, Liam propelled me away, toward Maximus's jewelry store.

"It would have been a bad idea to punch him in public," Liam told me. Despite our recent communication issues, he still knew me well enough to guess my thoughts.

"My life is full of disappointments." I kept my voice light, even though I wanted to rage and cry and scream and howl at Ryan to face me, come back, and talk to me!

"Save your revenge for another time," Liam advised as he guided me to the shop door. "There will be other moments, ones that won't backfire on us."

I liked that he said "us," as if we were still a team. But he was wrong about my wanting revenge. All I wanted was an explanation. Well, not *all* . . .

As we went inside, Liam flipped the "Open" sign to "Closed" and locked the door. Standing next to a diamond ring display, I tried to stop my brain from endlessly replaying the unsatisfying conversation. I focused on the rings: the stones in the rings were nice and sparkly, but the gold was muddy. It wasn't the 24-karat that the label claimed. A wizard should have known that.

Actually, I had no idea what a wizard should or shouldn't know. I'd never met one, though I'd heard of them. Their spells were fueled by gold and, as I understood it, drew from our natural abilities, such as causing and resisting fire. The security spell that Dad had used last night was supposedly based on detecting our ability to breathe fire, calling to the nascent embers within us—in other words, it was a wyvern detection spell.

Glancing out the window, I saw shoppers and tourists. No Ryan.

What would he have said if we hadn't been out on the street, if we'd been alone? We hadn't spoken since the Reckoning. He hadn't called or emailed or even tried to check on me.

"Sky, you okay?" Liam asked.

He didn't sound like he really wanted to know. It was a "suck it up and pay attention" kind of tone.

"We trust this Maximus?" I asked softly.

"We don't trust anybody who's not family," Liam answered just as softly. He then plastered a smile on his face as a very handsome, very tall, and very dark-skinned man strode through the back door.

"Liam! Delighted to see you!" He smiled, and it was as if a spotlight shone on him. He appeared to be mid-twenties, though sometimes it's difficult to tell with our kind, with more muscles than a jeweler should have. His voice was rich and low, like he should be recording movie trailer voiceovers. He didn't look or sound anything like Dumbledore.

He looked as if he'd walked off the set of a perfume commercial.

Liam clasped Maximus's hand. "Maximus, I'm pleased to introduce my sister to you. Sky, this is Maximus, an old friend of the family."

"Not so old as all that." He flashed his overly magnificent smile at me, and I did *not* roll my eyes, which I knew would make Dad proud. Clearly, Maximus was aware he was absurdly gorgeous.

As Maximus continued to ooze charisma at me, Liam cleared his throat. "I'm here to buy from the special collection."

"Of course you are. Shall we get down to business?" He pulled out a chair for himself and for Liam. When he went to fetch an additional one for me, Liam stopped him. "She's only here to observe," my brother said.

Thanks, Liam, I thought, but I stayed by the rings with their subpar gold.

"Very well," Maximus said. He redirected his movie-star smile toward Liam. It felt like a spotlight shifting aim. "I'm sure you'll understand why, but I have to renegotiate a few of the minor details of our transactions. Lately I've been getting a lot of pressure to break off relations with your family. Hate to do that, given our history, but I will need to compensate for any loss of opportunity you're costing me."

"Frankly, I *don't* understand," Liam said, his voice still friendly. "My family's personal problems don't have anything to do with our business here. This is purely a monetary transaction. Now I have some lovely things for you this time." Reaching into his coat pocket, Liam pulled out a black velvet bag. He opened his hand and poured the contents onto his palm.

A necklace, a bracelet, and two rings.

All of them were Mom's.

"You can't!" The words burst out of my mouth.

Both men looked at me. Maximus seemed interested. Liam was frowning. I felt my face flush red. I knew I was only here to observe, and I knew that the fact that Maximus hadn't gotten a chair for me was significant; I wasn't supposed to be part of the conversation. Wyvern protocol was clear. I should have stayed silent. But selling Mom's jewels! On her birthday! Liam turned to Maximus. "What Sky is trying to say is that these items have significant sentimental value to our family, as well as intrinsic worth, and we won't part with them easily."

"Ahh, I see. They belonged to *her*, did they?" From his expression, I expected him to lick his lips, rub his hands together, and cackle maniacally. Maybe he wasn't a movie-star hero, I thought; maybe he was a villain.

"That wasn't a fact that I intended to share, but yes." Liam shot me another look, and I couldn't tell if it was a real glare or a staged one—it was possible I'd helped his cause. Leaning forward, he began bargaining in earnest now, asking for spells in exchange for the jewels. He bargained hard, emphasizing the emotional importance and the whiff of scandal attached to them, which would be a great selling point for Maximus.

It took all my self-restraint not to grab Mom's jewels out of Liam's hand and run for the door. What right did Liam have to sell Mom's jewelry? How could Dad have approved this? They were hers! She'd gathered them, hoarded them, maybe someday planned to pass them on to me. I knew that necklace. She'd worn it at her throat with her blue silk dress. And those rings—I could picture them on her fingers. I thought of her hands, detangling my hair, helping me wash away early attempts at wearing makeup, turning the pages of a magazine as we had breakfast together. And now we were selling off her things. It felt obscene and final. . . .

It occurred to me that maybe this was why Dad had told me to come along. He never did anything on a whim, and I wasn't here to help Liam. Maybe he thought this would help *me*. Give me some closure. Help me move on.

He was wrong about that.

All it did was make me angry.

As I stared at the jewelry, Liam's and Maximus's voices faded to a buzz. A plan. I needed a plan, to take control of my life, to make things right. But how? My hands were clenched. I felt my heart rate increase. I felt as if my skin were tingling—like the moment before your fight-or-flight reflex kicks in—and I looked out the window . . .

And saw Ryan.

He was kicking a can across the street, as if casually, but looking at me the entire time. He stepped into the alley beside the store, and then he leaned back out and looked at me again. A month ago, I would have laughed at his lack of subtlety. Now I couldn't remember how to laugh. His message couldn't be clearer:

He wanted to talk.

CHAPTER FOUR

As I STARED OUT the window at the alley where the love of my life and destroyer of my heart waited for me, it occurred to me that I had three options:

1. Ignore him.
2. Wave back so that he *knows* I'm ignoring him.
3. Sneak away from Liam to rendezvous with Ryan in the back alley and risk having my heart broken again.

As Liam lifted Mom's sapphire necklace into the air to show off its sparkle, I thought a little extra heartbreak sounded a lot less painful than sitting here listening to them haggle over Mom's treasures. I interrupted, "Where's the bathroom?"

"In the back," Maximus said. "Use the air freshener. And if you touch anything outside the bathroom, I'll chop your hands off." He smiled pleasantly, and I tucked my hands behind my back to show my obedience as I scooted out of the showroom.

You'd expect the back room of an upscale Aspen jewelry shop and/or a secret wizard store to be classier than the back room of a generic truck stop, but no. Junk cluttered metal shelves, paint cans and paper towel rolls wedged between stacks of velvet jewelry boxes. Sweat-soaked gym clothes were piled on top of a safe, and a half-eaten lunch lay on a table. The only nice thing was a framed photo of a woman with platinum-blond hair and a movie-star smile that matched Maximus's—presumably his late wife. I hurried through with zero desire to touch anything and found the back door, marked "Emergency Only." After checking it for an alarm, I pushed it open and slipped outside into a narrow alley between Maximus's shop and an art gallery.

The alley was cleaner than the back room, with a neat row of bins that split the trash into paper, plastic, glass, aluminum, organic, and so on. Next to the bin for plastic was Ryan.

"Sky!" He rushed forward, then stopped when he saw my expression.

Knocking a rock into the door so it wouldn't close behind me, I walked toward him. I was not going to show weakness. He'd humiliated me as well as broken my heart. "You wanted to talk to me?"

He flinched at my tone. "Yeah."

"Okay. Talk."

He swallowed once, twice. "How have you been?" He winced. "I mean . . . I know . . . Well, I don't know. Are you okay?"

I crossed my arms. "No."

He looked down. Scuffed his shoe.

"Are you okay?" The question left my lips before I thought about whether that was an appropriate question for me, the wronged party, to be asking. I wasn't supposed to care what he felt anymore. He'd hurt me; he'd lost the right to my feelings. "Never mind. Don't care."

"I'm fine."

"Good." He didn't seem fine. He was pacing, back and forth, in the alley. I watched him, wondering what words were going to burst out. I knew what words I wanted to hear.

"I was watching some surveillance tapes . . ."

Okay, those were *not* the words. "For fun?"

"For you."

Oh. "Really? Of me?" Could he miss me? Was that what he was trying to say? He *should* miss me. We'd been insepa-rable for years. "Is that supposed to be romantic? Because it borders on creepy—"

He cut me off. "Of your mother. On the night she dis-appeared. She shows up on our surveillance tapes, breaking into our house."

I felt my jaw drop. Approximately six billion questions crowded into my head all at once, but the loudest was *Why, why, why?*

"And I know what she was trying to steal."

Opening my mouth, I tried to form at least one coherent question.

But Ryan answered before I could speak. "A jewel. There's a jewel in our vault. It's supposed to be"—he spread his hands, to indicate the jewel was basketball size—"very valuable. So valuable the council doesn't even know we have it."

My head felt as if it were a bottle of soda that someone had shaken vigorously. "She broke into your family vault?"

"Yeah, and she went straight for the jewel." He exhaled as if the words themselves had been fighting to get out of his mouth. "I wanted to tell you as soon as I discovered the tapes—but my father's monitoring the phone and my emails. I've been hanging out downtown for the last three days, hoping you'd show up somewhere and I'd be able to talk to you. Sky, you don't know how badly I've wanted to see you, to know you're okay, to explain why—"

I barely heard him—my head was buzzing, trying to digest this news about my mom. I'd known she was out on a heist. I simply hadn't known the target. "So my mother was last seen at *your* house. . . ." I tried to ignore the panicky butterfly feeling.

Taking a step backward, Ryan waved his hands as if to ward off my words. He actually seemed afraid. Of what? "I don't know what happened to her. The feed from the security cameras cuts out before she reaches the jewel. It's just static."

"Someone must know what happened! She was in your house! Your parents—"

"Don't ask them. Trust me. You can't ask them. They won't talk, and you'll lose your chance." His gorgeous eyes were wide. Earnest. *Scared*, I thought. He got that look when he talked about his parents sometimes. He lived in fear of disappointing them—I often thought it was because he was an only child, their heir, their everything. It was a lot to live up to. But this . . . it seemed like more.

"What do you mean? Ryan, why are you telling me this? My chance to do what?"

He looked at me and said softly, seriously, "To steal it."

Staring at him, I felt my eyes fill with tears until he and the alley and all the ridiculously specific recycling bins blurred in front of me. And then I was crying.

I hadn't cried when Dad broke the news about Mom.

I hadn't cried when my family's so-called friends rejected us.

I hadn't cried when Ryan turned his back on me.

But now, now, I began to sob. Ugly, shoulder-heaving sobs, as if my entire face had become a faucet. I wiped my face furiously on my sleeve. It didn't help. And then Ryan was there, his arms around me, and I was crying into his shoulder.

I knew I should push him away—he hadn't apologized or explained or said anything about us. But *Mom* . . . He stroked my hair and suddenly I didn't care about anything that he'd done in the past month. He was here with me now.

His voice muffled by my hair, he said, "I can't stay. My parents can't know. . . . But can we talk tonight? Ten o'clock, where we used to meet?"

Crying so hard that I began hiccupping, I nodded.

He kissed the top of my head and murmured something that *sounded* like he'd said, "I love you, Sky." But Ryan had never said those words. Drawing away from him, I blinked hard to clear my tears enough to see his expression. . . .

I was too late, though. He fled the alley.

The nice thing about having an emotionally stunted brother with poor communication skills is that he didn't ask any questions when I returned to Maximus's shop with an obviously tear-streaked face. He finished his bargaining, and we walked out of the jewelry store without speaking or looking at each other and got into the car. The radio blasted as Liam pulled out of the parking spot and sped away.

Leaning my head against the window, I gazed out at the mountains beyond the shops, restaurants, and condos. This time of year, the chairlifts were motionless, and the trails were mowed paths of yellowed green between clumps of trees. The aspens with their white trunks were stripes against the dark evergreens. A hawk circled high above the pines. Mom loved these mountains in early spring. She said it made her feel as if the Rockies were keeping secrets. In a few weeks, all the flowers and leaves would burst out for everyone to see, but now was the season of secrets, when everything beautiful was hidden under the veneer of left-over winter—and then she'd usually burst into singing "The Sound of Music" at top volume, because she knew it embarrassed my brothers. They're fun to embarrass. Or they used to be.

A month of moping, of hiding, of shame. I was sick of it.

And Ryan had just offered me a way to end it, if it was true.

Liam took the turns as fast uphill as he did down, and I jerked forward against my seat belt as he spun into our garage and slammed on his brakes. He was out of the car before I could say a word. I followed him into the house but slowed outside the music room.

The remnants of the door had been hauled away, and all that remained were the divots in the frame where the hinges had been. Dad would seal it up again soon, but for now it looked almost like it used to, with the piano sparkling in the sunlight.

It was wrong. All of it, a million times wrong. Selling Mom's jewelry, stealing the piano, sniping at one another all the time—as if we could erase our shame from every-one's memory by erasing our memory of her. *I won't do it*, I thought.

And that was the moment when a switch inside me flipped.

You know how sometimes in life, you can look back on a moment and know that this, *this*, this was the instant when everything changed? I felt, in that moment, as if I were outside myself, looking in, and knowing that from here on, everything would be different.

My feet walked forward and stopped in front of the piano. Sitting down, I lifted the keyboard cover. I laid my fingertips on the gold keys, felt the dust on the smooth sur-faces.

I didn't intend to play. But my fingers pressed down on the high E, then D-sharp, then back to E, and again and again until it rolled into B and I was playing "Für Elise" from memory, the way I used to do for Mom, to prove that I did practice sometimes. She used to say it was the whiniest song that Beethoven ever wrote—the melody sings "Why oh why oh why . . ." and it felt perfect right now. Leaning into the piano, I let my fingers fly through the insistent runs. The melody demanded, driving forward. I heard footsteps in the foyer, but I didn't stop, and then more footsteps on the stairs. Closing my eyes, I played from memory, crescendoing the "Why oh why oh why," drilling my fingers into the keys, until Dad barked, "Enough!"

I lifted my fingers and raised my foot off the pedal. Reflected in the gold piano, I saw my father and three brothers, distorted in the sheen.

"You won't play that again," Dad said.

I didn't answer.

"We thought she was back," Tuck said, his voice quiet.

"She's not coming back," Dad said. "She made her choices."

What choices? I wanted to scream at him, but I knew he wouldn't answer. Thanks to Ryan, I had enough of my own answer: she'd tried and failed to steal a jewel. "And what about our choices? What are we choosing? Yes, she left, but we're still here." Standing, I turned to face my family, what was left of it. "We're still Hawkinses, no matter how many sapphire necklaces we sell or doors we seal shut."

Dad exhaled so hard that bits of smoke swirled out of his nose. I automatically took a step backward—Dad's flame can hit a target nearly a football field away—and thumped against the piano keys. They clanged discordantly. "Of course. But now isn't the time—"

"Yes, it is! It's exactly the time to reclaim who we are!" Seeing my brothers' expressions, I realized I was shouting. At Dad. When he was already angry. I clamped my mouth shut.

Charles spoke. "Sky, you don't understand—"

I cut Charles off. "It's not so complicated to understand. Dad, you always told us that a dragon without a hoard is nothing. If we want to restore our rank at the next Reckoning, we need a new hoard." It was so supremely logical that I was amazed no one had said it before.

To Dad, Liam said, "This is my fault. I should have had her wait outside while I bargained with Maximus. She was upset about the jewelry—"

"Yes, of course, I was upset!" I was shouting again. But it wasn't just about Mom's jewelry. "We have a wrong to right. A mission to complete! And instead, we've just been moping around here, licking our wounds."

Liam and Tuck exchanged glances—the kind of glances that only twins can exchange, with layers of meaning embedded in each twitch of the eyebrow. I was fairly certain that this glance meant they thought I was being irrational. But I wasn't irrational. I was right. I'd never been more right about anything in my entire life.

I fixed my gaze on each of them. "Admit it: if we finish what Mom started, the invitations would start coming again, the press would worship us, and the other wyverns wouldn't treat us like we're scum on the bottoms of their shoes." All of them looked uncomfortable. Tuck was eyeing the window as if he wanted to jump out of it and run away across the lawn. "Steal something significant, and we can start acting like a family again."

Dad sighed again, this time without smoke, and he seemed to deflate. His shoulders sagged forward, and the lines in his face seemed to deepen with more shadows. He looked surprisingly old, which wasn't a word I ever associated with my father. "Sky, we can't. You don't understand what's at stake. What your mother tried . . . If we failed, we'd risk losing what we have left. I'm not willing to risk that."

"But if we don't fail, we gain back all we lost." *And maybe even Mom*, I thought, but I didn't say it out loud. It was such a fragile, beautiful hope that I didn't dare put it into words. But maybe, maybe, if we retraced her steps, we'd find answers. Maybe we'd even find her. If I had that jewel, I could at least bargain for news of her.

"Stop it, Sky," Charles said. "The answer is no."

My fingers itched to play "Für Elise" again. Why oh why oh why?

"We will fail," Dad said.

"Not if we work together," I said. "All five of us. We'd be a formidable team."

He shook his head. "You don't even know what she was attempting—"

"She was trying to steal from Ryan's family," I interrupted. "Some kind of jewel, from the Keene family vault."

He paled, noticeably, from the tips of his ears down his neck. "No, Sky. Absolutely not. You forget about this."

"If we planned carefully—"

"No, Sky."

I fixed my eyes on my brother Charles. He was the reasonable one, or claimed to be. If I could convince him . . . "Don't you see—"

Charles shook his head, not letting me even explain my very rational, very necessary, very satisfying idea. "Aren't you listening? It's too much of a risk."

"Liam?" I turned to him.

"Sorry, Sky." He wouldn't meet my eyes.

Tuck. "Please? Can't we even try?"

Tuck shook his head.

"Sky, I know how difficult this is. Believe me, it's hard on all of us," Dad said, his voice soothing, as if I were a tantrum-throwing toddler. "But we have to wait it out. Everyone understands this, except you, apparently—we stand precariously balanced on the edge of a cliff, and if we fall, then down will fall everything we've worked for, every-thing our ancestors ever achieved here on Earth. . . ." He kept talking, but the words didn't penetrate. I sank down on the piano bench. My own family, turning their backs on our future, refusing to even try. "I'm truly sorry, Sky," Dad said, "but the answer is no. Do you understand?"

I nodded.

"Say it out loud."

"I understand."

He beamed at me. "That's my girl."

I understood that they said no—and that I was saying yes. I was stealing that jewel, reclaiming our family honor, and finding Mom. And I was doing it without them.

CHAPTER FIVE

THERE'S AN ART TO sneaking out.

You choose first from a palette of lies: you're tired so must go to bed early, you have a headache so please don't disturb, you're going out to meet someone but not the someone you plan to meet. Next, you paint the scene: you put on your comfiest PJs, you groan and clutch your head (don't overdo it), or you conduct fake phone calls to discuss fake plans.

Or then there's my approach, which involves sappy music and a grappling hook.

After a silent and awkward dinner, I retreated to my room. All of us did, doors closing up and down the hall. Mumbling about reviewing the family finances, Dad locked himself in his office. My brothers didn't bother with excuses before shutting themselves in their rooms.

From Tuck's, I heard the whir of his new pottery wheel— he'd churned out three lopsided vases just today. If we had all still been speaking with each other, Liam and I would have made bets as to how soon before he tossed the wheel out the window. He'd lasted two weeks on his yoga kick and only one night on improv comedy. If we had still been speaking, Liam and I could have tried to convince Tuck to go back to cooking—he was an excellent chef. But Liam was already playing his video game, with the volume turned up so loud that it sounded like he was hosting car wrecks on his bed. He loved anything with explosions. As to Charles, no sound came from his room, but that was only because he owned headphones.

Searching my music, I picked my saddest, most bare-my-soul playlist, the kind of music you listen to with mascara running down your cheeks. It would keep my brothers out. But in case it failed, I also left a note on my desk: "Gone to Gabriela's," then climbed out the window, tossed a grappling hook up onto the gutter, and rappelled down the three stories into a flower bed.

I'm very fond of that grappling hook. It was a birthday present from Dad when I was twelve years old. I had all the usual mountain-climbing equipment already, clips and ropes and harnesses, but Dad thought I'd like a more old-fashioned challenge. Our distant ancestors used to live in caves in the mountains of Home, he said, and the children would all use ropes with hooks to visit one another until they were old enough to transform and fly.

He didn't talk much about Home, the world our ancestors came from, despite the fact that as a council member, he knew as much about it as any wyvern alive. It was a touchy subject, since said ancestors had supposedly been exiled here for being notoriously unrepentant criminals—

exile to Earth was supposedly a common punishment for a few hundred years, until the Door was lost. Since then, no more exiles.

To be clear, the source of shame wasn't that they were all thieves; it was that they'd been caught.

Like Mom must have been, I thought.

But how? And by who? And what had happened to her afterward?

Sneaking across the lawn into the garage, I shimmied over the front gate and unlocked my mountain bike, which I'd left chained beside it. Looking back once at the house, I wondered how much my father knew about what she'd done, or about what had happened to her afterward.

Don't think like that, I ordered myself. The answers lay with Ryan's family, not mine. Once I stole their precious jewel, they'd have to cough up their secrets if they wanted it back.

Jamming on my helmet, I mounted my bike and kicked off.

It took all my self-restraint not to let out a giant *Whoop!* You haven't lived until you've ridden a bike down a mountain without hitting the brakes. You breathe in wind—it races into your lungs, and it flattens your cheeks back. You watch the curves ahead, but you see the trees whip by out of the corners of your eyes, caught in your bike's headlight, so fast that they blur into a wall of brown and green. You can't think about anything else, and that's good, because I have been thinking too much lately. I don't want to think.

For ten glorious minutes, I am as close to flying as I've ever gotten.

And then the road flattens, and I'm sailing alongside cars in the narrow strip of the shoulder. If I veer right, ditch. If I veer left, smushed by a truck. It's a different kind of excitement, thanks to the variety of types of potential death.

Mom hates when I bike this fast.

Or hated.

Hates.

She's alive, I thought. Dad said so. And when I retrace her steps . . . Ugh, I was back to thinking again. Trying to focus on the road, I found my way to Gabriela's house.

Gabriela Marquez was more a classmate than a friend. Until the latest Reckoning, I'd hung out mostly with other wyverns. But I'd always liked Gabriela. She's the smartest person in our entire grade and embraces that. She's not afraid to be herself, and I admire that kind of fearlessness. It's very wyvern-ish.

I knew her address but had never been to her house before. Biking up to it, I slowed. It reminded me of her: small (she's very short) and somewhat disheveled. Wind chimes filled the porch—metal pipe wind chimes, seashell wind chimes, one made entirely of glass teddy bears—and sculptures decorated the lawn . . . or at least I thought they were sculptures. One was made from bicycle parts and a painted garden hose. Another was a birdhouse made of bottle caps. I remembered Gabriela saying once that her mother is an artist, specializing in "found objects."

I locked my bike up to the fence so her mother wouldn't "find" it.

Picking my way among the sculptures, I made it up to the front door. I ducked underneath a chime made of forks and spoons and rang the doorbell. From inside came a woman's voice, *"¡Vaya a ver quien es, Tito!"* and a minute later, a man in flannel and jeans opened the door.

"We aren't buying, we aren't donating, and we don't do surveys," he said. "Unless you're a Girl Scout, in which case, thin mints are always welcome."

This must be her father, I thought.

Maybe I should have called first.

"Thin mints are the best," I agreed, "but I'm here to see Gabriela. I'm a friend of hers from school. My name's Sky." I didn't say my last name; I didn't know how Gabriela's family felt about wyverns. Over the generations, wealthy wyverns have poured millions into public relations campaigns and politicians' pockets to sway human opinion away from "grab your sword and hunt the dangerous dragons," but there are still plenty of humans who aren't fans. "Can you tell her I'm here?"

Definitely should have called first. If she wasn't home, that shot my entire backup excuse.

"She's doing homework," he told me, but he called over his shoulder, "Gabriela! Friend for you!"

"Loser has no friends!" a boy's voice called back.

Ah, yes, she had a brother.

"Be nice to your sister, or you're doing her laundry!" A woman's accented voice, her mother?

"Noooo!" came the howl. "Her socks . . . they'll poison me! The stench, unbearable! Gahhh—I'm choking just thinking about it!"

"Don't mind him," Gabriela's father said to me. "He's at the age where he thinks insulting his sister is comic genius. He'll outgrow it. Come on in."

"Still waiting for my brothers to outgrow it," I said, entering the house. It was very hard not to stare. I'd never seen so much *stuff* stuffed into a living room before. Stacks of books were crammed up next to already-full bookshelves. Hockey sticks, baseball bats, and a variety of helmets overflowed one corner. The windowsill was packed with family photos. The coffee table was filled with snow globes and music boxes and vases of fake flowers.

"Go on up. Second door on the right. You can't miss it." He waved toward a narrow staircase that was cluttered with books and stacks of towels and folded laundry.

Picking my way carefully, I navigated between squished-together chairs and couches, stacks of books, and a pile of yarn. Somehow, I'd never expected a human home to be so full. It reminded me, in a way, of a dragon's treasure vault, except instead of gold and jewels, their house was full of books and photos and clothes and dishes and life.

Other wyverns called humans poor because the vast majority didn't have our gold. But Gabriela's house felt full all the same.

I wondered if it had been a mistake to come. After all, we didn't have that much in common, and I really didn't know her that well. She'd come with me to the movies, but I'd only asked her because all my wyvern "friends" had ditched me after the last Reckoning.

Still not forgiving them.

Might never forgive them. Emma had been the first to block my phone number, and Emily had very deliberately ripped off her friendship bracelet (the one she'd worn since third grade—though, seriously, it was time because that thing was ratty). Carlos hadn't bothered to do anything that dramatic, but he had been steadfastly refusing to make eye contact for weeks despite sitting next to me in English class. We used to like to mock our teacher (quietly, with eye rolls) for her insistence that all books are about death.

Anyway, just because I liked Gabriela didn't mean she liked me, especially since I'd then ditched her at the movies. Maybe I should have picked another human to bother. Plenty of them had been friendly enough, at least before our family lost half our fortune.

Upstairs, the second door on the right was covered in clippings from newspapers and magazines: a deep-space photo of galaxies, a bumper sticker with a Gryffindor logo, and a poster of Wyverns Through the Ages.

It was the poster that gave me hope. I had that same poster, but mine had a heart drawn over Sir Francis Drake, because I'd had a crush on him when I was younger and unclear on the concept of "lived centuries ago."

She opened the door. "Sky?"

Gabriela's hair was knotted up on top of her head and secured with pencils. She wore plaid PJ bottoms and a T-shirt that said "Protect the Ellcrys," whatever that meant, and she had headphones around her neck.

"Sorry for not calling first."

"Come in." She waved me inside.

Stepping between strewn clothes and piles of papers, I entered her room. On her bed, an orange cat fluffed its fur and hissed at me.

"Ginger, stop that," she scolded. "Sorry. He usually likes people."

I'm not people. I wondered if she'd ever had a wyvern in

her room before. So far as I knew, she didn't have any other wyvern friends. Or, really, many friends at all, as her brother had pointed out. "I wanted to apologize for running out on you at the movies." As soon as I said it, I realized I did feel bad about it. I'd used her, and here I was, planning on using her again.

Guilt is such a useless *human* emotion. I'm fairly certain that our ancestors didn't feel guilt over how they treated anyone. But then, they didn't have to live in a majority-human world. It was understandable that we'd picked up a few bad habits.

"Not necessary," Gabriela said. "You're going through a rough time. Frankly, I was surprised you asked me to come in the first place. You usually only call about homework."

And more guilt. I hadn't even realized I only called about school before now. Funny how a little social ostracism causes one to reevaluate all relationships. "Speaking of homework . . . we don't have any. It's April break, at least until tomorrow."

"Oh." She blushed. It lit up her cheekbones. But still, she raised her chin and looked at me as if daring me to laugh at her. "I like to give myself research projects."

See? Fearless. She had to know how that sounded. "I like to climb things," I offered.

"I know. You climbed to the roof of the school in third grade."

I was surprised she remembered that. Granted, it was one of my finer moments. I'd been sent to the principal's office, and Mom had been so proud. She liked to climb too.

"I made a list of the bones you were likely to break and

gave it to the teacher so she'd know what to tell the ambulance. Except I didn't know how to spell half the bones, and she thought it was gibberish. She was an idiot."

"She was," I agreed. "She never noticed when the gym teacher flirted with her. And it was obvious to even oblivious little third graders. Just whined about how she'd die an old maid, like her great-aunt Agnes—"

"—who had nine cats and was found dead with all of them sleeping on her," Gabriela finished. She grinned, and I grinned back. "You know, I don't think Great-Aunt Agnes even existed. Just a family story. Looked for her obituary once and couldn't find it."

"You researched her obituary?"

"I research *everything*. It's kind of my thing."

That was . . . interesting? Quirky? Alarming. "Have you researched me?"

"You're very easy to Google."

Now it was my turn to blush. Heat rose up my neck and stained my cheeks. "And you're still speaking to me?" I knew what the tabloids said about me, and I knew they weren't entirely wrong either. I *am* selfish and shallow—or at least I try to be. Makes life hurt less.

"I know you wouldn't be here if you hadn't broken up with Ryan," she said matter-of-factly. "You're usually sandwiched between the other wyverns and don't notice humans exist."

Ouch. Just because I hung out with only wyverns didn't mean I had no human friends. Well, actually, yes, it did. "That's . . ."

"Fair? True?" Gabriela shrugged. Crossing to her desk,

she straightened a few papers, tucked some into folders, and neatened her notebooks. I didn't know what to say. I certainly hadn't come here to argue. "Sorry, that was harsh," she said. "I just wish that when you'd left the movie theater, you'd told me. I had a hundred scenarios playing out in my head: You'd slipped in the bathroom, hit your head, and were lying there unconscious. You'd been kidnapped and held for a ransom. You'd been dragged into an alley and murdered. You'd been drugged and taken, and I'd have to explain to the police and your kind of scary father—"

"You have an overactive imagination," I cut her off. "I was just upset. Ryan . . ." I sank down on her bed. Hissing, the cat bolted out the door. Cats really don't like wyverns. "Well, you probably heard at least some version of what happened, and the details don't really matter." He'd led the official shunning. When the council voted to lower our rank at the last Reckoning, he was the one who had turned his back on us—on me—which forced all the other wyverns to do the same or be shunned too. It didn't matter that his parents had told him to do it. What mattered was he'd done it. I'd never thought he'd choose them over me. And once he had . . . everyone else had followed suit. Emma, Emily, Carlos, Topher . . . all the wyverns who'd eaten lunch with me, complained about homework with me, danced in a clump at school dances with me . . . None of them had even hesitated, because Ryan had done it first.

"He'd seemed nice. Are we supposed to hate him now?" She sat down next to me, knocking off a few books and a couple of stuffed animals that had been cuddled so much their ears were frayed. "You'll have to tell me what to do.

As my brother so nicely pointed out, I don't have that many friends."

"Guess we have that in common now."

She laughed.

Glancing at her clock—which had math symbols instead of numbers on its face—I saw it was 9:45. Fifteen minutes until it was time to meet Ryan. "I have another favor to ask, and it does involve ditching you again. But not publicly, and you won't have to worry about my dying."

Our secret meeting place was on the Top 100 Best Ice Cream Shops in America list in *USA Today* and had been featured on Food Network twice. So, not very secret. We used to meet here, though, and tell our parents we were studying together at the library—his family had zero interest in human-run establishments, so they never caught on. I really love blackberry ice cream. He likes red-hots mixed into vanilla. He was asking the girl at the counter to add more red-hots when I walked inside. Seeing him, I stopped and was tempted to turn around and run back to Gabriela's.

It felt like seeing the empty chair at our kitchen table.

He was my missing chair.

But then he saw me in the reflection in the glass over the ice cream. I saw my name on his lips, though he didn't say it out loud. Joining him at the counter, I ordered a cup of blackberry, two scoops. Extra sprinkles.

We took our ice cream to a booth in the corner, all without looking at or speaking to each other—the two of us radiating so much awkwardness, I was surprised it didn't drive everyone else out of the store. Their ice cream must have tasted too good to leave. We slid in across from each other, and Ryan handed me a napkin—a simple gesture, but it made me think, *He still cares*. I took the napkin.

"So . . . are we going to talk or sit in silence?" I asked.

"We could eat," he suggested.

I liked that plan. Digging in, I ate my first spoonful. Just as creamy as always. It tasted like someone had mashed up summer and chilled it. It reminded me of swimming at the lake, hiking up in the mountains, and climbing up a new rock face. It reminded me of the Fourth of July, lying on a picnic blanket and looking up at the fireworks. It reminded me of the smell of sunscreen on my face and the feel of Ryan's hand in mine as we leaped together into the water. "You broke my heart, you know."

"I know."

All the cold from the ice cream felt as if it had pierced right through me.

"I had to, Sky. My family . . ." He swallowed, and I saw his throat bob. His eyes flickered left and right, as if he were checking to see if anyone was listening. I'd already checked—no one was close enough to hear us. The nearest occupied table was three away, and it featured a screaming, out-too-late toddler who had somehow smeared ice cream on her eyebrows and in her ear.

"Did they threaten you? Say you'd be grounded? Say you'd be disinherited? Say they'd sell your car, burn your clothes, trash your computer? What did they threaten you with that was worth doing what you did?"

He shook his head. "It was my father, not both of them, and he didn't threaten me, Sky. He threatened *you*. Your house. The rest of your family's gold. Sky, he said he'd take everything from you. He'd make the council . . . Anyway, he was very, very mad."

That . . . I hadn't expected. I blinked at him. "So, you broke my heart to *protect* me?"

"Yes!"

"That's stupid. My family can protect ourselves." Of course, we hadn't protected ourselves against losing half our wealth or from losing our rank. We hadn't protected Mom, or Dad's seat on the council. "And anyway . . . you could have told me before now!"

"Dad ordered me not to even talk to you." He glanced around again, looking as furtive as it was possible to look. He'd make a lousy spy. He might as well have a neon sign that said "Suspicious." He was lucky that only humans were here, though that wasn't a surprise. We'd picked this place because most wyverns don't like cold foods—we could be alone here. "Only reason I can be here tonight is he's in Paris for a business meeting. He'll be back tomorrow."

His ice cream was dripping down the side of his cup. I sneaked my spoon over and caught a drip before it splattered on the table. "If your parents were so mad at my mom for trying to steal this jewel, why do you think it's a good idea for me to try?"

"Because you'll succeed! And then you'll have all the leverage you need to convince the council to restore your wealth, your rank, your everything." He reached across the table as if to take my hand and then stopped. He glanced again in all directions, as if expecting ninjas to burst out and attack. "And if my father can't threaten you anymore . . .

then we can get back together. If you want to. If you can forgive me."

The cold in my heart melted. But he didn't deserve instant forgiveness—he could have told me this sooner, spared me from feeling like my entire past, present, and future were shattering. "That's a lot of ifs."

"I know it will work. You'll have what your mother didn't have."

My mom was brilliant, beautiful, and amazing. I'd always been her lesser shadow, soaking up her sunlight. How could I do what she couldn't? "And what's that?"

"Me." He smiled, his little lopsided smile that made my heart lurch. "I'll be on the inside. I know our security systems. I can get you past the cameras. . . . Well, we'll have to figure out the rest, but we can work it out, you and me, together. Your skill. My knowledge. I know we can do this, Sky."

Yes, we could. Slowly, I smiled.

He smiled back, and I fell in love all over again.

CHAPTER SIX

CLIMBING BACK IN THROUGH my window, I landed lightly on the carpet. Music still crooned through the room. The sound of video games still permeated the wall. Only change was that my brother Charles sat on my bed, waiting for me.

"Hi," I said.

"Hi, Sky."

"You're in my room," I said. "In the dark. Listening to love songs."

"Yes. And you were . . . ?"

I pointed to my desk. "At Gabriela's. I left a note."

"I called Gabriela's, and her brother said you weren't there anymore."

"Her brother is annoying. Also he was in his room the whole time. He doesn't know when I came and left." If Gabriela was going to cover for me, we'd have to figure out how to handle her little brother. A bribe? Blackmail? You could plan for the behavior of people you knew, those you could predict. I hadn't planned for her brother. Next time I would.

"He said you climbed out the window. Why don't you ever use the door, Sky? That's why we have doors. For going into and out of buildings. Windows are for light and air. You should try doors sometimes."

"What do you want, Charles?"

He folded his arms, presumably so he'd look more foreboding big-brother-ish. "I want to know where you went. We can't afford to be sneaking out and going behind each other's backs. Not now, when things are so precarious. You heard Dad."

"Seriously? *You* are yelling at *me* for going behind your back? Hypocritical much? Besides, I just wanted ice cream. No crime there." When in doubt, stick to the truth. Or a little bit of the truth.

"We have ice cream in the kitchen. Again, let me introduce you to doors. You walk out yours. You open the freezer door."

"I wanted blackberry ice cream, from Baybridge's. It's a break-up thing. The popcorn and movie didn't work, so I thought I'd try the old cliché, a pint of ice cream. Next time, I'll bring you some of their hot chocolate mix—theirs is the best." Bribery could work on big brothers too.

He stood up, and the mattress creaked behind him. "Ice cream, huh?" He studied me, and I kept my face innocent— a look I'd practiced in the mirror. You widen your eyes a bit, don't waver your gaze, keep your lips relaxed, and tilt your head slightly. "All right. I just wanted to be sure you weren't doing anything we'd all regret."

I watched him, trying to read in his eyes what he knew

and what he suspected. His chiseled face was annoyingly difficult to read. He must practice in the mirror too. "I never regret ice cream," I told him.

He nearly smiled. I saw it! A twitch of his lips. Like Dad. The old Charles was in there somewhere, buried under the events of the last month. Maybe if I completed Mom's mission, he'd come back again. Maybe he wouldn't be so worried all the time. He headed for the door.

"Charles?"

"Yes, Sky?"

"Is Dad okay? I mean, does he tell you more than he tells me?" I hated that we kept so many secrets from one another. Lately, there seemed to be more and more we didn't say.

"Don't worry. Everything will be fine."

"It won't be fine until we make it fine." Good things don't just happen. Gold doesn't fall into your lap. Lost mothers don't randomly reappear. You have to *do* something if you want something. And I wanted so much!

He frowned. "There's a bigger risk of making things worse. Dad said no. Let it go, Sky." Great—I'd made him suspicious. And he'd confirmed he still agreed with Dad, even when Dad wasn't anywhere nearby.

I raised my hands as if in surrender. "All I'm going to do is go to sleep."

Somewhat miraculously, he believed me, wished me good night, and left. Switching off the music, I changed into my PJs and then tucked my lock picks into my socks.

Each of us four kids owned our own set of lock picks. As kids we all had lessons. Mom used to dump a bunch of locks on the dining room table, and no dinner for us until we'd opened them. For extra fun, she'd turn off the lights, which is fine unless you're trying to pick locks with three older brothers who think it's *hilarious* to dump a bucket of freshly caught toads onto the table with the locks.

To this day, I have a mild fear of toads.

But locks are no problem.

To pick a lock:

1. Insert a torsion wrench and press down.
2. Insert a lock pick.
3. Twist the wrench, and shimmy the pick back and forth until it catches a pin.
4. Repeat until all the pins click.

Just remember to keep all movements very small, or you'll break your tools and have to pay for a new set by drying the dishes with your breath for three straight weeks.

The lock on Mom's office was a basic pin tumbler. Child's play, only meant as a reminder to us that her room was private, not as a serious deterrent. Leaning against the door, looking oh-so-casual, I stuck my tiny torque wrench into the bottom of the keyhole and a pick into the top. I wiggled it until I heard the first pin click, then I moved on to the second pin.

Listening for the pins, for my brothers, for Dad, I barely breathed. It takes me less than a minute to pick a pin-tumbler lock, but in that minute, anyone could wander into the hallway and say, "Sky, are you picking the lock on your mother's office?"

Dad.

I swear I have the nosiest family of all time. First Charles, now Dad. Couldn't anyone just mind their own business while I skulked around suspiciously? "Um, yes?"

He humphed. "You're slow. Your brothers would have had the pins to the shear line by now."

Behind my back, I twisted the torque wrench. The lock popped open. "Done."

"Practice that," he said, and then shuffled past me toward the stairs. He was still wearing a suit from the day but had put on fuzzy blue slippers. I watched him until he reached the end of the hall.

"You aren't going to ask me *why* I'm breaking into Mom's office?" I called after him.

"You said earlier you knew she'd broken into the Keene family vault—I don't know how you ferreted that out, but regardless, now you're hoping she left some clue behind as to why she decided to rob your boyfriend's family without proper backup, without a thought to the consequences," he said without turning around. "I can tell you that you won't find anything satisfying. I know. I've looked." He tromped down the stairs toward the kitchen.

Okay then.

Popping the door open, I slipped inside and shut it behind me. All the lights were out. Staring at the shadows, breathing in the stale air that still smelled like her perfume, I felt smothered in the feeling that Mom was here, or nearby, or about to return home and ask what I was doing in her office and why hadn't I brushed my hair better. It felt like her chair should still be warm and there should be a cup of coffee next to her keyboard, but her monitor was dark and her desk lamp had dust on the lightbulb. No one had even come in here to clean.

Shaking myself, I flipped on the light. Usually her office was neat and tidy, but she'd left it a mess. It was completely overrun with books—like a cave with stacks of books instead of stalagmites. It was worse than Gabriela's house. I tiptoed between the stacks. Titles jumped out at me, some fiction and some not: *The Encyclopedia of Wyverns in Literature, The Oxford Book of Wyverns, Classic Fairy Tales, Saint George and the Dragon* . . . Hmm, I sensed a theme.

At last I reached her desk. She had lots of papers spread out, as if she were midproject. She'd meant to return. I was sure of that. Whatever had happened, it hadn't gone according to plan. She hadn't wanted to leave us.

Flipping through her papers, I skimmed over her precise handwriting. She'd been taking notes on the history of dragons in literature, clearly gleaned from all the stacks around the office, and as thorough as if she planned to write a book. But if she'd been working on a book, she'd never mentioned it.

Okay, that was odd but not alarming.

One by one, I searched through the drawers. Lots of the files in her drawers were financial, which made sense. Mom had majored in finance in college and worked at a hedge fund for several years before taking over management of our funds exclusively. Thanks to her, we hadn't had to steal a major hoard in a long time. All three of my brothers had been allowed to keep the gold from their first heists as their personal starter hoards, and Mom had coached them on how to best invest their wealth.

I wondered if that was part of why Father had said no to my heist idea. He was out of practice. I tried to remember the last time he'd been involved in a heist and came up empty. My brothers had all had their coming-of-age jobs, but he hadn't been involved in them. I thought of the family stories I knew. None of them were recent, but that was the nature of family stories. They had to be far enough in the past that they took on a mythic quality.

Opening the next drawer, I rifled through. Boring, boring, boring.

Sometimes I wondered if being a grown-up was all about paperwork.

I felt the back and bottom of the drawer, searching for hidden compartments. Nope. Crawling under the desk, I looked for any secret drawers. Nothing. "Seriously, Mom? I know you are not this dull."

Popping back up, I looked again at her handwritten notes. As I'd seen, all of them were about wyverns throughout history, with an emphasis on probably false stories and straight-up myths. She seemed to like particularly obscure references. I flipped through her papers. There was nothing here about any heist whatsoever.

Sighing, I opened a box of chocolates, her Valentine's present from Tuck, who had shoplifted it from a CVS. Mom had made him go back and pay for it, because we don't steal from humans—unless they have something we really, really want and it's made of solid gold and they have enough security to make it a challenge.

Lying in the chocolate box was an amulet shaped like a dragon's talon.

"Well, hello," I said to the amulet as I lifted it up.

Like my talon necklace, it was made of solid gold. Unlike my necklace, it was larger than my hand, and it was covered in markings that looked like runes or hieroglyphs or something. Running my fingers over it, I could tell the amulet was

18-karat, decent strength and decent purity. But there was something unusual about it. Lifting it to my nose, I sniffed it—it didn't smell like metal. It smelled like . . . a riverbank, that kind of mossy-wet-earth smell. *Weird*, I thought.

Mom's door opened, and I shoved the talon-shaped amulet into my back pocket—a mistake, since talons are pointy. Yes, I poked my butt. Sucking in a yelp, I plastered a smile on my face as Dad walked into the office. He was carrying two mugs of hot chocolate.

Handing me one, he said, "Find anything interesting?"

Taking the mug, I hoped I wasn't bleeding. There was no way to subtly check. Glancing at the hot chocolate, I saw he'd frothed the milk. Dad was obsessed with a frother he'd bought online. He was constantly making us hot chocolate with frothed milk. I didn't object. Froth on, Dad. "Thanks." Waving at the papers on Mom's desk, I said, "She seems to have an interest in dragons."

Blandly, he said, "Yes, that's a surprise."

"But why study so many human fiction books?" My eyes fell on a stack of paperbacks with garish covers: scantily clad warriors and drooping wild-eyed dragons. Oh, Mom.

He sipped his hot chocolate. Wyverns like chocolate, a lot. "Your mother always felt bad that she never did a baby book for you."

Dad was usually a lot subtler about changing the subject, but I went with it. "I'm baby number four. I'm lucky to even have a baby picture."

"You were her princess." He smiled into his mug. A sad smile.

"It's because I was born with a crown, isn't it? Admit it:

I came out with ten fingers, ten toes, a crown, and a host of angels trumpeting my arrival. On second thought, no crown. That would hurt." Like my rear end hurt. Stupid talon.

"She was interested in genealogy. She wanted to present you with a family tree, a history that you could be proud of. That's why all the research." He nodded at the papers and the books.

Ahh, so he hadn't changed the subject. It just . . . wasn't the answer I'd expected. I didn't care about who our family had been; I cared about who we are—or rather, what we're supposed to be: that is, together. "Our ancestors were exiled criminals."

"She wanted to go further back than that."

Glancing at her notes, I did see the repetition of certain themes. She'd pulled out every reference to the origin of dragons, as well as every mention of the word "home," no matter how irrelevant. "But humans don't know about Home. And why all the fiction books? What does"—I read a random title—"*The Dragonriders of Pern* have to do with our great-great-whatevers?"

"You'd be surprised at what humans know and what secrets they've hidden in their fiction. Plenty of wyverns have confided in humans over the years. There are even a number of human scientists with theories on parallel dimensions—what our legends call the Door, their theories call a wormhole into a pocket universe." He nodded at a stack of science books tucked in one corner. "These days, we have more in common with humans than not. We've made *this* our home."

Trying to drag the conversation back to what I really wanted to know, I waved at all the books and her copious notes. "So why did Mom try to rob Ryan's family vault?

Boredom?" It was the only explanation that made sense. She'd strangled her own brain with pointless research, and she'd craved the adrenaline rush. And the treasure, of course. "Didn't she talk to you about it at all?"

"Of course she did. And I said no. It was a fool's errand, and I wasn't going to help her. I thought she'd dropped the idea. Apparently she hadn't." His eyes were fixed on the stacks of books, but I didn't think he was really seeing them. He was caught in a memory.

I pushed harder. "Why did—"

He cut me off. "You were such a sweet baby. Slept through the night right away. Learned to gurgle very early."

Off topic again. "I've always been an excellent gurgler. But why did Mom—"

"She loved you. We all did. We all do. Your brothers used to fight over who'd play with you. I think they regarded you as a toy your mother and I had bought them." He fixed his eyes on me. "Wherever your mother is, I know she must miss you very much."

I felt a lump in my throat. *Don't cry*, I ordered myself. She wasn't dead, which meant she could come back. "But you don't know where that is?"

"I know it's not in here," Dad said. "Sky, leave her room. Leave her memories. Leave her past in your past." Opening her door, he gestured to the hallway. "Go to sleep. You have school tomorrow."

I hesitated for a moment, then walked past him, stepping sideways so he wouldn't see what stuck out of my back pocket. I kept walking backward down the hallway to my room, watching as he closed the door and, with his fire breath, melted the lock shut.

CHAPTER SEVEN

～

EVEN WERE-DRAGONS HAVE TO go to school, thanks to long-ago lawmakers who wanted to make sure we fit in. Sadly, not to dragon school, which would be awesome, but to P. Murphy High School, Home of the Fighting Badgers.

Liam dropped me off. He and my other brothers were all taking time off from college, to help Dad with our recent financial disaster in the wake of Mom's disappearance, but I wasn't allowed to skip even a day of high school. Unfair. "Have fun."

"Shut up," I told him as I stepped out of his car. All the other students were flowing out of their cars and the buses. Shouldering my backpack, I trudged in with them.

School is fine, in general. I have zero objections to learning things, though I wasn't quite as committed to it as Gabriela. Science makes sense—it's good to know how the world works. Math is fine—I like that it never lies. History is fascinating—humans are stupendously bloodthirsty, and wyverns have influenced human history both overtly and covertly for centuries. Other languages, sure. Computers. P.E. All fine. English class . . . nope, don't get it. I refuse to believe all books are about death when it's obvious that all books are about kissing. Or, in some cases, not kissing. Still, at forty-two minutes a day, I can tolerate it.

But the one part of school that is decidedly *not* fine is lunch.

I used to like lunch.

I also used to have a whole flock of wyvern friends, plus one best friend, whom I used to kiss before, after, and during lunch. Ryan still sat with them, flanked by Emily and Rosario, at what used to be *our* table.

Sliding into line, I picked up a tray and waited for my allotment of shepherd's pie and chocolate pudding. The chatter flowed around me like water, curving and swirling in circles as if I were a rock that couldn't hear. So I didn't listen. Without making eye contact with anyone, I walked through the cafeteria toward my new refuge, an empty table in the back.

Setting my tray down, I sat in the middle, thereby ensuring that no one else would use the table at all. No one ever joined me in social exile here. Given that the tabloids had all tarred and feathered my family, no one dared risk—

A tray plopped down across from me. "Hi!" Gabriela said.

"You know I was in the middle of feeling sorry for myself," I said.

"Noticed. You do it very dramatically." She seated

herself and began to organize her lunch, placing every food item in a line. First her milk carton, then her fruit, then her sandwich and mixed veggie side, and last her pudding.

"I should warn you you're risking social annihilation if you hang out with me in public," I told her. "I'm a pariah, if you hadn't noticed."

"You aren't a pariah. To be a pariah, you have to be despised and rejected by everyone, and I guarantee you most people in this cafeteria are entirely too self-absorbed to worry about anyone else. You're exiling yourself." She speared a mushy carrot and ate it. "You don't bring lunch either?" With her fork, she pointed at my shepherd's pie.

"Requires waking up early to pack a lunch," I said.

"Or you could do it the night before."

I shrugged. "Maybe I like cafeteria food. Mushy food is comforting. Why do you buy?"

She shot looks to the right and left, as if checking for eavesdroppers, then lowered her voice. "Because otherwise I'd have to bring homemade food, and I hate my mom's tortillas."

I laughed and then stopped. "You're serious?"

"Dead serious."

"But no one hates tortillas. They're not hateable. Sourdough bread, yes. You can hate that. But tortillas? They're like the mozzarella of the bread world."

Gabriela leaned forward, as if she were sharing a deep, dark secret. Tendrils of her hair fell across her eyes. "Her flour tortillas taste like Elmer's glue, and her corn tortillas taste like overcooked microwave popcorn. Please don't tell my family I said that. My mother would be mortified."

"What about other people's tortillas? Fresh tortillas? Fried up with cinnamon sugar?"

She made a face.

I scooped up a bite of my shepherd's pie and ate it. "How do you feel about wraps? Bagels? Donuts? I don't know if we can be friends if you don't like donuts."

She sighed heavily. "I guess our friendship is doomed. I could never base a relationship on carbs."

"That's a shame, because I really need a ride after school." I matched her sigh. "Can I at least hope you like ice cream?"

"Of course."

I beamed at her. "Excellent. That's something to build a friendship on."

She grinned back.

Food is a universal relationship builder. It doesn't matter if you're wyvern or human, you can always talk about food and find common ground.

Except that, technically, no one was supposed to be talking to me since I was shunned.

Certainly no wyverns would have risked talking to me, about food or anything else—they wouldn't want to face the same fate. Being shunned, losing your status in wyvern society . . . no one wants that. Cut off from Home, wyverns on Earth had had to forge their own society. Losing your status in it meant losing your definition of yourself.

Gabriela, though, being human, wasn't risking as much by being friendly. Really, she was just sacrificing ever being buddy-buddy with Emma, Emily, and the rest. And since she hadn't been friends with them to begin with . . . Over

Gabriela's shoulder, I watched my old wyvern friends laughing together at our old table. Carlos joke punched Jake's arm. He must have said something funny. I wondered what they were talking about, and whether they ever talked about me.

"You're going to see him again?" Gabriela asked. She didn't have to name "him." I knew exactly who she meant.

"We're not back together." It was a nice dodge, I thought. She wasn't fooled.

Twisting in her seat, Gabriela looked across the cafeteria at my old table and at Ryan. He was sitting between Emily and Rosario, who were talking with animated hand gestures per usual, but he wasn't paying attention to either of them. He was looking across the cafeteria at me, and for an instant I couldn't think or breathe. It felt as if the rest of the world had blurred. The voices blended into a buzz. His eyes felt as if they were boring into my soul.

"You're still in love with him?" Gabriela asked.

The shepherd's pie dripped off my fork as I stared at him, unable to look away. "He still loves me." And I knew as I said it that it was true.

~

Gabriela drove me to the warehouse after school. "So you love him and he loves you, but your families won't let you be together. Is this a Romeo and Juliet kind of situation? Because that ended badly."

"Don't worry," I said. "We won't do anything stupid."

She snorted. "Famous last words." But she parked the car and unlocked the doors. I hopped out, and she rolled down the window. "I'll pick you up in two hours. . . . Are you sure about this?"

"Gabriela . . ." I leaned on the open car window. "I think you're a great person. I really do. You're smart. You're quirky. You have weird taste in food. You know what it's like to have an annoying brother. But I need you to quit with the worrying about me and leave so that I can have a clandestine meeting with my ex-boyfriend that will almost certainly result in my getting my heart broken a second time."

She smiled. "You know what I like best about you? You're honest."

"You obviously don't know me well at all, but we'll have to fix that another time."

Laughing, she drove away, and I checked my watch. Two hours. A lot could happen in two hours. Fancy dinners. Love affairs. Bank robberies. Naps.

I scanned the area: vacant parking lot with more weeds than pavement, a shell of an abandoned ski lodge, and several large warehouses that used to house snow-grooming equipment. Hunter Creek Lodge had suffered a series of financial setbacks and then finally a fire. It had been on the market ever since but hadn't sold. I only knew about it because of the fire. We always paid attention every time anything burned down in a hundred-mile radius, if just so we could be sure to have an alibi.

Silent buildings surrounded me, and the remnants of the chairlift looked like the skeleton of some long-extinct creature. It lay on the hill, a forgotten carcass. A snow groomer was sitting in the corner of the parking lot, casting clawlike shadows on the ground. I shivered. Bits of trash and old leaves blew across the parking lot. I don't normally have much imagination, but this place fit the definition of "creepy" even in daylight.

I really hoped I was in the right place.

Ryan had slipped a note into my locker after lunch with the name and a time. He hadn't signed his name, but he'd drawn a tiny picture of a dragon so I'd know it was from him—he used to draw me little doodles, his version of a love note. He was an art geek. It was adorable.

Outside the closest warehouse, I halted. "Ryan?"

The door opened, and my usually inactive imagination provided me with a flurry of horror-movie villains, beginning and ending with a chainsaw-wielding clown, before my brain caught up with my eyes. "Ryan," I exhaled.

Putting one finger to his lips, he shot furtive glances around and then pulled me inside the pitch-black warehouse. My arm tingled where he touched it, and my breath felt faster. "Please tell me you weren't just waiting for me in the dark," I said, trying to keep my voice level, "because that's just asking to be murdered by a serial killer. Or asking to turn into a serial killer. Either way, not healthy."

"I turned the lights off when I heard the car. Left them off to open the door so we wouldn't be seen by anyone on the road." He flicked the lights on. They buzzed yellow, warming up, and then emitted a sickly orange glow. He looked at me. "I . . . wasn't sure you'd come."

I stared back.

Great, we were back at the awkward-staring stage again.

He swallowed. "Who did you get to drive you?"

"Gabriela Marquez."

"You're friends with her?"

"I can't tell if you're insulting her or me."

"Neither. Sorry." He scooted across the warehouse to an array of laptops. Opening them up, he began pushing buttons. Screens blinked to life.

Okay, straight to work. I could do that. Craning my neck, I looked around at the empty warehouse. Cobwebs coated the rust-pocked ceiling. "Cozy," I commented.

"My family owns it, through a couple of shell companies. There were plans to turn it into a water park, but Mom was afraid she'd have to pose for photos in a bathing suit. She had an anxiety attack, and that was that." He flipped a few switches, and red laser beams snapped on, displaying dots on the far wall. "You're going to want to throw some dust to see the beams, but I think I've created an accurate representation of the motion-sensing lasers in our vault."

Staring at the laser-beam dots, I whispered, "I love you."

Ryan's head shot up.

Walking forward, I dipped down to scoop some dust in my hand. I bounced it a few times to loosen the particles. "I was talking to the lasers." I tossed the dust into the air. It fell, but the dust lingered. Red lines glowed, crisscrossing.

"Oh, right . . . yeah. They're great."

He'd always been bad at saying the words "I love you." He didn't have much practice—his parents hadn't raised him with a lot of warm words. Especially his dad. I thought of the moment in the alley and wondered if I'd imagined what I'd heard. I wondered what he'd say if I said the words to him. "Tell me about the job." Eyes still on the beams, I kicked off my shoes and stretched my legs by lunging from side to side. "So there are the lasers, and . . . ?"

He nodded. "The jewel is in our family vault, which is beneath our house, buried in the mountain itself. Twelve feet of granite on all sides. You can't blast through or burn through. You can only go in through the door. The door itself is five feet of reinforced steel."

"So we have to open it. Okay."

"Ahh, but first we have to get to it. You can't just drive up the driveway."

"Easy. I'll climb the cliff by the lake—you know I can do it." I'd done it before, plenty of times. It was an excellent cliff for learning to rock climb—well, *I* thought it was. Ryan's family had "Dangerous—Do Not Climb" signs posted all over it. "You'll need to disable the security cameras on the garden, though, if I'm going to get close to the house."

"I can take care of the cameras. Inside the house, you'll need to go through the basement door in the kitchen. It has a simple tumbler lock—you can pick that."

I nodded. "With my eyes closed."

"Once you step on the basement stairs, it activates two spells: the first is a wall of fire in the stairwell, to keep out human thieves. It's magically maintained at 1,000 degrees. . . ."

"Not a problem," I said. "Yay for fire resistance."

He smiled, and our eyes met. His smile faltered, he looked down at his laptop, and he cleared his throat. I wished I could see what he was thinking. Did he regret helping me? He was taking a risk, defying his father, plotting against his family. He continued, "The second is in the hallway: a wyvern detection spell, to keep out wyvern thieves. . . ."

"Okay, that one could be a problem."

"After *that*, the entire hallway is also filled with motion sensors, aka the lasers that I've replicated here"—he proudly pointed to the array of lasers—"and monitored by more security cameras. Assuming we can figure out a way to disable or trick the wyvern detection spell, you'll have to acrobat your way between the lasers while I hack those cameras. That will get us to the vault door."

"Locks on the door?" I guessed.

He tapped a few keys on his computer and brought up an image of a vault door. "It's a combination lock, which I know you can crack, but to open the access panel to reach it, you have to breathe dragon fire."

Oh. This was *not* going to be easy.

"And once you get the door open—"

Seriously? "There's more? I thought *my* family was paranoid."

He took a deep breath, as if he were about to tell me he'd eaten the last slice of pizza. "The inside of the vault is guarded by a fire beast."

"*What?!*" Fire beasts are very dangerous. Very, very dangerous. Also expensive. Fire beasts aren't actual animals—they're created by magic, with a rather complex spell. And maintaining the spell that generates them requires a steady stream of gold. (Spells, at least as far as I understand them, are fueled by gold sort of like cars are fueled by gas. No gold, no magic.) I'd never heard of anyone using a fire beast spell to protect their vault on a permanent basis.

Fire beasts are also extremely hot, well above 2,000° F, which is past the limit of wyvern fire resistance. They generate a white fire that can burn us. We used to whisper horror stories about fire beasts to scare each other late at night next to the lake, while our parents drank wine by a bonfire.

"Yeah, it's wizard made. Costs an entire gold bar a month to maintain the spell. But my father swears it's worth it.

When he first told us he'd put one in the vault, I had night-mares for weeks."

I had no idea what we were going to do about a fire beast. *Mom must have found a way to defeat it*, I thought. Ryan had said he'd seen her *inside* the vault in the security footage. Inside and not fried by a fire beast. If she could do it, then so could I. Maybe there was a trick to defeating the beast, or a way to deactivate the spell.

"So what do you think?" He looked anxious. Looking at the array of motion sensors, he ran his fingers through his hair. "It won't be easy."

"But it will be fun." I cartwheeled over the first laser, ducked under the second, and rolled under the third. Popping up in the middle, I surveyed the area of remaining lasers.

It would take some experimentation to figure out the best way through. It wasn't impossible, though, not for someone whose mother enrolled her in constant gymnastics classes from age two through twelve. I'd wanted to take ballet, but my family didn't consider it practical. "So, how did my mother do it?"

He tapped a few keys. "Here. Security feed." It began to play on one of the laptop screens. He leaned back so I could have a clear view.

Empty corridor. Gray walls. Vault door. Dust clouded the view, and I saw a figure in black cartwheel and flip across the screen between the laser beams. *Mom.*

Barely breathing, I watched as she, agile and powerful as an Olympic gymnast, flipped her way down the corridor. Reaching the end of the lasers, she shot a grappling hook up to the top of the vault door, and she then affixed the line and zoomed across it without touching the floor.

"Pressure-sensitive floors," Ryan said. "Forgot to mention those. So you'll have to crack the lock without touching the ground. Both the motion-sensing lasers and the pressure floors deactivate after you enter the combination lock code."

Hanging upside down, she breathed on a steel panel. Fire blazed out between her lips, showing up as a dull amber on the grainy recording. The panel slid open to reveal a circular dial. Mom removed a glove, so she could feel the dial directly, and began cracking the lock.

Walking straight through the remaining laser beams (which caused the computers to beep anxiously), I joined Ryan. "Is this why she was caught? Because she was on camera? She should have disabled the cameras before she started." Leaning forward, I studied the lock. A few seconds later, I realized I was only inches from Ryan. I felt his breath on my cheek.

"Um, she, uh, hacked the live feed. . . ."

I tilted my head. Our lips were so close that I felt as if I were breathing in his exhale. It made me feel a little dizzy. "And the wyvern detection spell? How did she get past that?"

He licked his lips nervously, his eyes darting side to side, as if he expected his family to jump out of the shadows. "I don't know. Maybe there's a c-c-counterspell? She definitely used a spell to fight the fire beast, so maybe she had a second one?"

"Then we need spells too."

"Okay."

"I know a wizard." Maximus. It was hard to remember his name when I was so close to Ryan. I'd missed his smell. It reminded me of winter nights by the fireplace, hot chocolate stirred with a cinnamon stick, and the sweet scent of pure gold. . . . I remembered the gold talon amulet I'd found in Mom's office. "I know how to pay him." He wouldn't be able to resist that much gold.

Ryan was staring at my lips. "Good. That's good."

Leaning forward, I kissed him. Just a light brush of my lips across his, like tasting a piece of chocolate but not biting into it.

"Sky, I hate being apart from you. I hate what my father made me do. I want—"

But I didn't let him finish. I didn't need any more apologies or explanations. This—the sneaking around behind his parents' back, the lasers he'd set up, all the work he'd done—said more than any words. We kissed, and I felt something I hadn't felt in weeks: hope.

CHAPTER EIGHT

I ASKED GABRIELA FOR another favor after school the next day, because when you only have one friend, you become very needy and annoyingly dependent. Especially if said friend has a car. I promised myself I'd buy her a tub of ice cream from Baybridge's when this was all over.

As soon as the last school bell rang, we jumped into Gabriela's car, and she drove me to Maximus's and parked, neatly parallel parking her family's car between two SUVs with ski racks. Some people have parking skills; I do not. Another reason to admire Gabriela. Maybe I should buy her two tubs of ice cream.

"Exactly what do you need me to do?" she asked.

"Just stay near the window, look like you're browsing, and signal me if anyone is about to come into the store." Stepping out of the car, I checked in both directions. No Ryan. No nosy brothers.

"You mean like"—she flapped her elbows—"cock-a-doodle-doo!"

"Or you could choose something subtler." I headed for the front door. Odds were good that Maximus would assume I was here about Mom's jewelry. Either he'd try to sell it all back to me or he'd think I was there to rob him.

Gabriela locked the car door and caught up to me. "Why do you need me to keep watch while you're on your shopping spree? Are you not supposed to be here?"

I checked again up and down the street before pushing through the door. "Definitely not supposed to be here. Hello, Maximus."

Holding a magnifying glass, he was perched on a stool, examining a diamond underneath a light. "Already sold your mother's pieces. Fetched a nice price. You might want to tell your brother: if he has more, I'm willing to negotiate."

The words felt like a punch. I hadn't thought he'd sell them so fast. I'd planned to buy them back after my heist—ideally as a welcome-home present for Mom. Swallowing hard, I tried not to think about her jewels around the neck or on the hands of a stranger. "He shouldn't have sold them. *You* shouldn't have sold them."

He looked up. "You are aware this is a store? It's what we do."

I took a breath, tried to calm the way my pulse felt like fire. I wasn't here about my mother's baubles. Dredging up a smile, I said, "Yes, and I'm here to purchase from the special collection."

"Ooh, that sounds cool," Gabriela said in a low voice. She was standing close enough that her lips felt like feathers against my ear. "Is he going to push a button that causes the jewelry cases to flip up and display an array of weaponry?"

She hadn't whispered softly enough.

Maximus laughed. He had a laugh that made your stomach feel warm, the kind that pulled you in and enveloped you. "Your friend watches too many movies." He set down the magnifying glass and stepped off the stool. "Still, I doubt you could afford anything from the special collection."

Gabriela snorted. "She's still richer than—"

"I have this." I pulled out the gold talon amulet.

For a moment, the shop was silent. The strange smell of rivers and forests seemed to roll through the store, making me dizzy for a moment. The talon itself seemed to glow, though I knew it was only reflecting the many lights that lit the jewelry cases.

"And now we are doing business." Crossing the store, Maximus flipped the sign to "Closed," locked the door, pulled the shades shut, and spun around to smile at me. Prickles walked up my spine. "Congratulations. You two have caught my attention."

"She's not part of the transaction," I said quickly.

"She is now. She's seen *this*." Holding out his hand, he asked, "May I?" Noting the gleam in his eyes, I suddenly wished I'd left the amulet in Mom's office and taken something else, anything else, though I didn't know where to find such a large chunk of solid gold outside our vault.

"What is that?" Gabriela asked me.

"Proof," Maximus murmured. He turned it over in his hands. Lifting his magnifying glass again, he examined it thoroughly. "Your mother was right. It's not from here." He stroked it gently.

Leaning close to my ear again, Gabriela whispered, "Any second, he's going to whisper 'My Precious' at it. Sky, we're not actually breaking any laws here, right? That is yours, isn't it? You didn't, um . . . I mean, of course you didn't, but is that solid gold?"

"I'll sell it to you," I told Maximus.

His eyes didn't leave the talon. "Any spell you want."

I winced. Wizards were *supposed* to be secret. You'd think he would know that better than anyone. "I told you, she's not part of this. She doesn't know—"

"You brought her," he said. "You either explain to her or kill her. Or you can explain *and* kill her. Just don't do it here. I'm not in the murder business."

Oh, fabulous. I'd planned to repay my new friend with Baybridge's, not with danger. "Ha-ha! He's joking," I told Gabriela. "How about you do what we said? Keep watch for anyone coming in?"

Gabriela was walking slowly backward toward the door. "Sure. Happy to. And then I'd like to leave, if it's all the same to you." Her voice squeaked higher.

"Squeamish," Maximus noted.

"You shouldn't joke about killing people," I told him, with an emphasis on the word "joke." I then lowered my voice, making sure Gabriela was across the store. "I need two spells. The first is for bypassing a wyvern detection spell, and the second is a spell to defeat or subdue a fire beast."

Maximus looked at me sharply, with narrowed eyes. "Your mother came to me with very similar requests." He was still fondling the talon. "But I am guessing that you already know that."

I nodded.

"And dare I guess you also know whose vault she tried to rob?"

Wincing at the word "rob," I nodded again. He'd spoken at a normal volume—Gabriela must have heard. I shot her a look, but she was peering out the window.

Clutching the amulet, he leaned forward. "Tell me whose it is."

Every instinct in me screamed at me to grab the amulet and run out of there without looking back. Maximus's eyes were giving off little sparks—literal sparks, like the kind when you bring two live wires too close together. "I'm here to trade gold for spells, not information." If Mom hadn't told him, then neither would I.

"Changed my mind. Gold's not enough."

That was a *lot* of gold. It had to be enough! "But—"

Stepping toward me, he closed the distance between us again. "I want in. To your crew. To the job you're planning."

"Uh, Sky? Cock-a-doodle-doo?" Gabriela nodded at the door as the handle rattled. She shifted the blinds and said, "I think it's your brothers."

Oh, fantastic. Every nerve in my body screamed, *Run!* Gabriela and I could both bolt for the back door, escape through the alley. But I needed those spells. . . .

Liam's voice called, "Sky, I know you're in there! You better not be doing what I think you're doing."

"What does he think you're doing?" Gabriela asked in a whisper that traveled across the store. "Are those lock picks? Sky, I think they're picking the lock. Never seen anyone do that. Cool."

Charles called through the door, "Sky, come out right now, or we're coming in!"

"He can pick a pin tumbler in less than a minute. You don't have a spell on your lock?" Talking fast, I said, "Here's the deal: the amulet for the counterspells."

He continued to stroke the talon, possibly unconsciously. "There is no counterspell for a wyvern detection spell. You'll need to find another way around it, or persuade a human to block it while you pass by. Your mother must have found a solution. As for the fire beast . . . I can take care of it. But I come with you, all the way to the vault. That's the only deal I'll make. And actually I will need the amulet too, to fuel the spell. It eats gold at a ferocious rate."

The lock turned.

Why would he want in? And why should I trust him? And what was I supposed to do about the detection spell? There wasn't time to ask any questions, or even to think. I plastered a smile on my face as all three of my brothers shoved one another to tumble first into the shop.

Maximus quickly pocketed the talon, then spread his arms in welcome. His smile matched mine, brilliant and fake. "Boys, always a delight to see you."

Charles strode toward me. "Sky, you can't steal from a wizard!"

I avoided looking at Gabriela. If she was smart, she'd sneak out the door before my brothers even noticed she was here. "I wasn't stealing—"

"Look, we know that you hate we sold Mom's jewelry," Liam said.

Tuck shot a look at Maximus that redefined the word

"hostile." If our eyes could shoot fire, the wizard would have been a lump of char. "Trust me, not the way to get your first hoard."

Gabriela slipped out the door. Smart girl. Now I just had to hope she was also smart enough not to talk to anyone until I had a chance to explain. And by "explain," I meant "lie to her."

Maximus placed a hand on my shoulder. "Gentlemen, she wasn't attempting to rob me. She came here to ask me for a job."

I did?

Right. Yes. Of course I did. "I . . . spent my allowance, and I didn't want to ask Dad for more, given, you know, current events. So I thought if I got a job after school . . ."

All three of them gaped at me.

"But Maximus said I don't have any experience, so he—"

"Hired her," Maximus interrupted. "How can she get experience if no one gives her a break? She'll work here after school for . . . two hours a day? Does that work? I'd hate to interfere with your homework."

"Two hours is fine."

"Great." He clapped my shoulder again, and I realized he'd given me an excellent alibi. I'd have at least a two-hour chunk every afternoon to work on preparing for the heist without worrying about my brothers breathing down my neck. All I had to do was go along with it. "Then you accept my proposal?"

Only flaw was that it was no longer just Ryan and me. Now it was me, my ex-boyfriend, and a wizard I barely knew with unspecified motives. I wasn't sure Maximus would be a welcome addition.

Still . . . this wasn't about being able to spend one-on-one time with Ryan. If this worked, we'd be able to be together permanently. And my brothers would be thanking me, instead of literally breaking in on my conversations. Our family would be able to heal. "I accept," I said.

CHAPTER NINE

AFTER MY BROTHERS FINISHED apologizing to me, I had them drop me off at Gabriela's house. Ducking under a wind chime, I knocked on her front door and tried to think of what lie would cover the words "wizard," "spell," "crew," and "rob." Also, "murder."

I hoped she'd at least let me tell her my lies. If I were her, I'd hide under my bed and wait for me to go away. *So much for making a new friend*, I thought.

The door banged open, and Gabriela grabbed my wrist and pulled me inside. "Come in." She dragged me through the living room, nimbly skipping over the piles of laundry, and up the stairs to her room. Then inside, and shut the door. "It was a magic amulet, wasn't it?" Without waiting for me to answer, she pulled me to her computer.

"What?" I saw her screen, covered with images of golden talons. "You researched it." She'd said she researched everything. "But . . . there's no such thing as magic." I winced—

that was a ridiculous sentence, coming from a wyvern. But there really was no such thing as a magic talon. It was like saying there was a magic fingernail.

"Look!" She tapped a picture. It brought up a sketch of a similar talon, zoomed in on the markings. "It's called a dragon amulet. Supposed to have all kinds of powers. First one was seen being worn as a necklace by a dragon during the Middle Ages." She switched to a print of a woodcarving that depicted a stylized dragon wearing a chain with the talon around its scaly neck. "It was stolen by Saint George as a trophy when he slew the dragon. Excuse me, wyvern."

"Huh." She was wrong, of course. Not about Saint George—he was a brutal exterminator who still haunted our legends—but about a magic dragon amulet with "all kinds of powers." She went back to the sketch of the talon and zoomed in again. The markings really did look very similar. "What kind of website is this?" I asked.

"Fan art." Sitting at her desk, she began rapidly bringing up more web pages. "Actually been researching your family for a while. Um, does that sound creepy? That sounds a little bit creepy. You're just so interesting! You know there are three hundred fifty-four fan sites devoted to your family, and of those, sixty-four think you're not actually wyverns and that there are no real wyverns. But they're the kind of conspiracy theorists who don't believe in science or fact. Probably don't believe in gravity either."

I shuddered a little. All those fan sites . . . It was unnerving to have so much human attention focused on us. Humans significantly outnumber wyverns on Earth. If there hadn't been so many rich wyverns willing to use their wealth over the years to convince people that wyverns are harmless and friendly . . . Let's just say we've never forgotten Saint George.

Peering over Gabriela's shoulder, I saw a photo of me from the night of the last Reckoning. My mascara was streaked down my cheeks and my hair had pulled out of its twist. But that was nothing compared to how my insides had felt, as if they'd been twisted by a mixer. I felt sick looking at it. "Not my best moment."

In fact, it had been the worst day of my life.

It was the day when Ryan had turned his back on me, the day when I'd first let myself believe that Mom might never come back, the day when all the wyverns in the West had decreed as one that our family was lesser, that our mother had tarnished and abandoned us, that we weren't worthy of all that our ancestors had achieved. That photo was taken just after the Reckoning, the formal gathering when all the wyverns come together to determine the ranking of everyone in our society—what wealth we have, what wealth we deserve, what wealth we lose if we break wyvern rules.

Humans were not allowed at the Reckoning itself, unless they were married to a wyvern. But we couldn't stop them from stalking us outside. Some jerk had snapped that shot and sold it to the tabloids. Our kind weren't as popular with the paparazzi as movie stars, but we were considered unusual enough and wealthy enough to be fascinating, as all those fan sites proved.

My family's drop in wealth, for instance.

Newsworthy.

My mom's disappearance.

Newsworthy.

Ryan and my breakup.

Newsworthy.

I reminded myself that I'd forgiven Ryan. Mostly. Partially. *Stop it*, I told myself. *He explained himself. And he's trying to make it up to me.* Just seeing one stupid picture shouldn't undo those lovely feelings of forgiveness.

This—the churn of ugly feelings—was exactly why my family and I stayed off-line. Except for checking the weather. And movie times. And shopping. And reading the occasional fashion blog.

"None of this means anything," I said. "The tabloids like drama, and my family has had a bunch of it lately. Can we not look at that photo? In fact, I may need to scrub my eyeballs."

Gabriela clicked onto another page. "I didn't begin to put two and two together until I started to research wyverns and treasure." Jumping off her chair, she scooted past me and knelt on the floor, pulling out binders and opening them. They were full of print-outs—articles, photos, blog posts.

I had a sick feeling in the base of my stomach. The fact that wyverns were rich was common knowledge, of course. The fact that wyverns were thieves . . . not so well known.

She then took the Wyverns Through the Ages poster off her door and spread it out on her bed. "So here's the first wyvern who ever revealed himself to humans: Atahualpa in 1533." She tapped her finger on his picture. "He was king of the Inca Empire when the Spanish conquistador Pizarro arrived with about a hundred soldiers. Under a banner of truce, Pizarro met with Atahualpa—"

"And then Pizarro betrayed the truce, ambushed and slaughtered five thousand Inca with his superior weaponry, and took Atahualpa captive." I'd heard this as a bedtime story. In retrospect, it made for a rather gory story to tell a toddler. Not sure what Mom was thinking.

"Oh, right. Guess you totally know this, it being your history and all."

Gabriela looked so embarrassed and uncomfortable that I took pity on her. "Go ahead," I said. "I know you have a point."

"Pizarro agreed to free the king if the Inca filled a room with gold. A lot of gold."

"A room twenty-two feet by seventeen feet, eight feet deep." Every wyvern knew the size of that room. To this day, we built our vaults to precisely that size, in honor of Atahualpa.

"From all over the Inca Empire, the people brought their treasures, filling the room . . . but Pizarro again betrayed the Inca and didn't free their king. After a mock trial, he found Atahualpa guilty of treason and sentenced him to die by burning at the stake. Legend says that as the fire began to burn, Pizarro threw open the door to the gold room to mock Atahualpa for what he'd lost . . . and that was when the king of the Inca transformed into a dragon."

Still wasn't sure where she was going with this.

She pointed to the next picture on the poster, Sir Francis Drake. "Atahualpa was able to save the Inca Empire in Peru, but thanks to all the smallpox and the slaughter by other conquistadors, the rest of South and Central America was lost and their gold looted, which brings us to Sir Francis Drake. He was a privateer for the British Empire."

"A pirate."

"A royally sanctioned pirate. He waylaid ships carrying gold from the New World to Spain, on behalf of the queen of England. And when a very angry Spain began to build an armada . . . he revealed himself as a wyvern too. He transformed into a dragon and burned the half-built Spanish Armada as it sat in the harbor of Cadiz on the coast of Spain in 1587. They called it the Singeing of the King's Beard."

Again, this was benign information. Anyone could have found that out. It was taught in elementary schools. "You *do* have a point, don't you?"

Gabriela pointed to more photos and articles. "The point is, every time a wyvern has revealed him- or herself in history, treasure has been involved."

"No wyvern has transformed into a dragon since Sir Francis Drake. We lost the ability." But I knew that wasn't what she meant by "revealed." She'd noticed the connection between us and treasure. So what, though? Others had noticed our fondness for wealth.

Her face was flushed, and she was flapping her hands with excitement. "You're treasure hunters! Generations of Indiana Jones types. But not just any treasure. . . ." She paused, and there might as well have been a drum roll. "You hunt mythological objects! Dragon talons! Unicorn horns! Werewolf teeth!"

I opened my mouth.

Shut it.

Opened it.

Shut it.

Swallowed.

She leaned back, triumphant, kind of panting a little.

"Don't try to deny it. Today proved it. That man . . . You were talking about spells! He provides magic for your quests, like Q giving gadgets to James Bond."

"Um. That's . . . well, everyone knows wyverns like gold." Honestly, she wasn't far from the truth, except that she put a shiny, happy spin on it that didn't include any illegal activities. Plus we didn't care about mythological objects. Just gold.

"Say you'll let me come with you on your next adventure! I want to see a unicorn or a yeti. . . . Are there yetis? What about the Loch Ness Monster, real or dead? Fairies, elves—are they more like Santa elves or Tolkien elves?"

I placed my hand on hers. "Gabriela . . ."

She had tears in her eyes, bright in the corners. "Please, Sky, I need this. There's nothing special in my life. I'm no one special."

"You're the smartest person in our grade! And you're"— glancing around her cluttered room, I tried to find the right word—"unique, exactly as you are!"

She sank onto her bed. "Sky . . . all my life, I've studied things. Research—that's my hobby. I love knowing everything about everything. But I don't want to just see it secondhand. I want to *be* there. I want to touch the impossible. I want to do things that no other human has ever done. I want *magic.*"

I knew what I had to do: Tell her no. Tell her that except for my wyvern DNA, I'm just a poor little rich girl whose mother left her and whose boyfriend dumped her, like the tabloids all say. No adventures, no treasure, no heists, nothing to see here.

Except I didn't want to be that poor little rich girl anymore.

I wanted Mom back. And Ryan. I wanted my father to smile again, my brothers to joke with me, everything to be the way it was.

And to get that . . . "What would you do if I said yes? Tell the tabloids? Go on TV? Become famous? 'Girl discovers secret to wyvern wealth'?"

"I don't care what everyone else thinks. I want it for me! Maybe that's selfish, but . . . Sky, please, don't shut me out of this! You're on some adventure, and it has to do with that jeweler, the wizard—I saw his eyes spark. At least I think I did."

I studied her and thought about Maximus. He didn't have a spell to bypass the wyvern detection spell. *Dad will be furious*, I thought. And then I thought, *He'll only be furious if I fail. I'm not going to fail.* "If I let you on my crew . . ."

"Yes!"

"Gabriela, stop. It will be dangerous."

She beamed at me. "Danger is my middle name."

"Right. Okay. Well, your theory has a few flaws. One major flaw, really." I took a deep breath and hoped I wasn't making the worst mistake of my life. "We're not treasure hunters. We're thieves. Very, very good thieves." And I explained: who I was, what I wanted, and what I needed her to do. I also told her the truth about Maximus, as well as a few key details about Mom's failed heist.

The entire time, she perched on the edge of her bed, staring at me with her eyes wide. She was trembling slightly, vibrating, and the unshed tears were still pooled in the corners of her eyes. They clung to her eyelashes.

When I finished, she was silent.

"So . . . what do you think?" I asked. "Are you in?"

"You're only stealing from someone who stole from you," Gabriela said.

"Technically, he took our gold after the council voted at the last Reckoning . . . but yes, you could say that." If she needed to justify the theft as honorable, that was fine with me. It was true that we had strict rules about who one could steal from and how much, especially on a first heist. The rules were a practical necessity, to keep us from destroying the economy of the world.

Also, humans weren't nearly as fun to steal from.

"And there's a fire beast, whatever that is," Gabriela said. "And that man, the jeweler, is a wyvern *and* a wizard. And you really want *me* to help you. You need me?"

"I swear by the flame and the ash, all that I've told you is true." Closing my eyes, I concentrated. *Heat. Burning bright.* I felt a warmth stir in my stomach. *Mom, I'll find you.* Opening my eyes and my mouth, I let the spark of fire flick off my tongue. The flame danced in the air and then fizzled. I looked at Gabriela.

The tears fell, rolling down her cheeks. She put her hands over her face, bent over, and sobbed into her lap.

I patted her back awkwardly. "Gabriela? Um, are you in?" Really hadn't expected this reaction to asking a friend to engage in illegal activities, even if magic was involved.

She said something muffled.

Leaning closer, I asked, "What was that? I couldn't quite make it out."

"Luisa," she said. "My middle name is Luisa. Not 'danger.' But I'm in."

And just like that, I had my crew.

CHAPTER TEN

AFTER SCHOOL THE NEXT day, Liam picked me up, blasted his music as he tore across Aspen, and dropped me off at Maximus's shop. "You're sure about this?" he asked as I got out of the car. Across the street, at a tapas restaurant, three of my old wyvern friends were hanging out around an outdoor table. I did my best to avoid eye contact, focusing instead on Liam. "Retail, Sky? You're descended from some of the best thieves ever to walk this Earth, and you want to *work*?"

"I want my own hoard, Liam. If I'm not allowed to steal one, then I'll earn one." That sounded plausible, didn't it? Mature? Even noble? Shutting the door, I leaned through the car window. "Pick me up in two hours?"

"You're going to hate it," he predicted. "You have to be nice."

"I *am* nice!" Or not precisely *nice*, but I wasn't mean. I'd never bullied anyone. Never kicked a puppy. Never torn wings off flies. Never tossed chewed-up gum on the side-walk.

"Just saying, if you call me in ten minutes, I'm not picking you up. I have better things to do than be your chauffeur."

"Right. Again, thanks for your overwhelming concern."

He peeled out of his parking spot. "Have fun!" he called out the window. I waved and watched as he drove away, tak-ing the left that led back to our house. For a brief second, I wished I'd jumped back in the car with him. Especially since Rosario had noticed me and was whispering swiftly to Emma.

Up until now, all I'd done was recruit a crew. After I briefed them today and introduced them to each other, we'd be committed, and I'd be deliberately defying my father's orders. This was my chance to back out, no harm done.

But my old "friends" were laughing—at me? Certainly without me.

Squaring my shoulders, I walked into Maximus's store.

He was at the counter with a college-age guy who was typing numbers into the cash register as if he expected it to bite. "Good," Maximus said, clapping his shoulder. "Just remember, if you mess up, I tell your girlfriend you're saving up to buy an engagement ring."

The kid paled. "I won't mess up!"

"Excellent." Smiling at me, Maximus crossed the shop. "Sky! Hired a new employee to work the store in the after-noons, while you help me with cataloging acquisitions off-site. Need your keen eye on a few new pieces." He was talking loudly, for the benefit of the kid at the register. He escorted me past his new hire into the back of the store. Today it smelled like pickles.

He'd cleaned. Possibly with pickle juice, but still—all the uneaten food had been swept into the trash, and the gym shorts stashed away. The surface of the table gleamed, and the safes had been dusted and polished. A vase of roses sat next to the picture of his late wife.

As soon as we were out of earshot of his new employee, Maximus said, "We'll have to find someplace off-site for our prep. I can't have any of this traced back to me—"

"Got it covered." I led the way to the back door to the alley.

"Oh, excellent," Maximus said, following me. "This is going to be so much fun!"

Heroically, I managed to not roll my eyes. "Before we do this, I have to know why. Why do you want in? Why not just sell me the fire beast spell? Motivation, please, and if you want to monologue with heartfelt emotion, I won't stop you."

He spread his hands as if to show he was innocent. No tricks up his sleeve. "It's simple, really. Whomever your mother targeted must be in possession of an impressive treasure hoard. I'd like to pick out a few trinkets for myself."

"A few?"

"Just a few select items with a high resale value."

That sounded . . . fine. Plausible. "Why come yourself? Why take the risk? You could just give me the spell and tell me to pay with 'trinkets.'"

He laughed, a warm chuckle like we'd been friends for years. "Oh my dear, no offense, but you couldn't possibly know which ones to choose."

"I know enough to tell you're selling substandard gold in the front case."

"For the tourists, my dear." He clucked his tongue, as if I was being especially foolish. "For special buyers, I need special trinkets. Now, have I passed your cross-examination? Are my motives wyvern enough to suit you?" He was smiling, so I couldn't tell if he was insulting me or not. "Frankly, it's my risk to take, and you need me. Why not indulge me and let me tag along?"

He had a point. I couldn't do this without him. Or at least not without his spells, and if bringing him was the cost . . . "All right. Fine."

We went outside.

From the end of the alley, Gabriela waved cheerfully. She was wearing all black, except for bright-pink lipstick and a pom-pom-like flower clip in her hair—I'd never seen her in black before. I wondered if she expected us to be skulking through shadows. Probably. I hadn't given her many details about the heist. Today was about details.

Details make the dragon, Mom used to say.

As we joined her, Gabriela hugged me, a quick squeeze that made me feel like a ketchup bottle, and I couldn't help noticing that she smelled like strawberries. Not a wyvern smell, but a pleasant one. Probably shampoo. Or she'd just come from frolicking through a field of strawberries while rainbows danced all around her—that would fit her personality. Gabriela was babbling, "Really thought the school day would never end, and we'd been sucked into this time vortex where history class would stretch to encompass everything from the Fall of Rome to the eighties." Rising up on her tiptoes, she peered over me into the alley. "We're not practicing *here,* are we?"

"Just outside of town," I told them both. "I'll give you

directions once we're on our way." With a skip in her step, Gabriela led the way to her car. The back seat was crowded with library books, candy wrappers, and Mountain Dew cans. She shoved them over to make room for Maximus. I took the front passenger seat.

"I'd drive," Maximus told us, "but my car is noticeable." He pointed across the street at a teal convertible with fire decals and a license plate that said *THE WIZ*.

"Seriously?" I asked him.

"I like musicals."

"You just ruined my image of you," I told him. "Besides, I thought the whole wizard thing was a secret."

"Hiding in plain sight, my dear."

"That's not hiding at all! That's literally proclaiming what you are."

"Ahh"—he laid his finger against his nose, as if that made him look deep and mysterious (spoiler alert: it didn't)—"but everyone knows wizards are fiction." Getting into the car, he sang "So You Wanted to Meet the Wizard." He may have shimmied in the back seat. I refused to look. As he worked his way through the soundtrack, I spent the drive going over in my head what I wanted to say, to make the four of us into a team.

I hoped Ryan wouldn't freak out.

He didn't like surprises. But there hadn't been a way to tell him earlier that I was bringing two more to our party. His father was back from Paris, and from here on in, we had to be extra careful.

He'll have to deal with it, I thought. And I latched on to a little bit of my old anger at him. *He owes me.* Another part of my brain chimed in: *But he was protecting you!* And I answered, *So he says.*

Then I shoved those thoughts away. We had work to do.

At my direction, Gabriela parked behind the old abandoned lodge, and Maximus jumped out of the car first. We followed him inside—the back door dangled by one hinge.

"I like what you've done to the place," he declared as we joined him. "It's very dystopian chic." He waved his hand at the partially collapsed lodge. Everything had been ruined by fire or rain and then abandoned. Couches were coated in caked-on old ash that had congealed into hardened sludge. Birds had nested in the rafters, and weeds had sprung up between the floorboards. All the windows were broken, and graffiti covered the walls and the bank of broken ski lockers. The ceiling was missing large chunks, and daylight streamed in, catching the dust that floated in the air. But for us, for what I wanted, it was fine. Perfect, in fact. We'd discuss plans here, and we'd practice in the warehouse.

Ryan had been sitting with his laptop on one of the ruined leather couches. He jumped to his feet as we came in. "What . . . Sky, what's going on? Why are they here?"

Maximus clucked his tongue. "Such a welcome."

I braced myself. This was the most precarious time, before anyone felt committed, when it was all just a shiny new idea. If I could make it through today, we'd be okay. But this was the pivotal moment when imagined became real. Or failed to.

Coming in past the blackened fireplace, I said, "Ryan, good news. I've completed our crew. Maximus and Gabriela have joined us." I kept my tone reasonable, as if this weren't a shock. I wished I'd been able to talk to him before now, to prep him for this.

Gabriela waved. "Hi, Ryan."

"Um, hi. Um, Sky?" He looked panicked, which was cute but not a good sign. He was risking a lot by helping me, and now I was asking him to trust two people he barely knew. "Sky . . . But . . . I don't think . . . Why would . . ." He plunged forward. "Maximus already has his own hoard. How do you know we can trust him?"

Maximus flashed a brilliant smile. "Sky and I have already had the motives conversation. She approved me, so that should be enough for you."

Ryan continued as if Maximus hadn't spoken. "And Gabriela—no offense meant, Gabriela; my mom's human, so it's not that I have anything against your species—but Gabriela is not one of us, by either marriage or birth. If the council found out—"

I raised my voice. "Ryan!"

He stopped. Blushed.

I fixed my eyes on him. "I have to do this." *And you owe me.*

"I know, but—"

"You said you'd help. Did you mean that?" It felt, for an instant, as if we were the only ones here. Him and me, staring at each other.

"Well, yes, but Sky—"

"My heist. My call," I said. "My crew." *Radiate self-confidence,* I told myself. Like Mom. I'd never seen her nervous in my life. She oozed self-confidence from every pore. When she walked into a room, she owned the room and all its oxygen.

But Ryan surprised me. He nodded. "You're crew leader. I trust you."

Those words meant more than if he'd said "love." He trusted me. This was my heist. And if they didn't leave after I told them what we were up against . . . then this was my crew.

Maybe everything would be okay.

Maybe *we* would be okay.

Ryan sat back down onto the couch. He was still tense, his hands clasped together and neck bunched up. Still with me. Gabriela beamed at me, as if she were expecting birthday presents. Taking a tissue out of his pocket, Maximus dusted a chair and then sat. A plume of dust billowed around him.

It seemed they were willing to listen. Good. "All of us have our own reasons for being here," I said, looking at each of them. "I want to steal back what was taken from me: my family's place, our pride, our honor." *My mother*, I thought. "But to do that, I need all of you."

Maximus raised his hand. "Before we start, are there snacks?"

Ryan clutched his laptop tighter, as if it were a shield and he was prepared for battle. "Sky, if he isn't going to take this seriously . . ."

"I don't take anything seriously," Maximus said. "Except gold and jewels. And since this little adventure has the potential to involve both . . ." Sparks began to dance around his eyes as he got to his feet. "Let me show you how serious I am."

"Ooh, magic fight," Gabriela breathed. She looked on the verge of breaking into wild applause. Her eyes were wide so she wouldn't miss a moment.

I strode between Maximus and Ryan. "Enough."

Maximus saluted. "Sorry, ma'am." He flopped back onto the burned chair and put his feet up on a broken coffee table. Bits of burned wood crumbled beneath his heels. "I assume you have a plan?"

"The plan is simple: Our target is protected by a series of security measures, and we will overcome them one by one. First, we have to get on the property. We can't use the road. There will be too many guests using it, and it will be watched. But there's a cliff I've climbed plenty of times before. Once I'm up, I'll lower a rope on a pulley for you two. Ryan will leave the pulley hidden nearby, so all I have to do is set it up. Second, there are security cameras all over the property. Ryan will figure out a way to override them. He'll also be providing us with earpieces and mics for communication. Once the cameras are down, we enter the house through the kitchen and head directly to the basement. In the stairwell to the basement, we'll have to pass through a wall of fire. Maximus, can you provide a fire resistance spell for Gabriela?"

"Delighted to," Maximus murmured. "It will be a snap." He snapped his fingers together, and flame spurted out of his fingertips. He twirled it into a fireball and then caught it.

Gabriela gasped.

He winked at her as he rolled the fireball back and forth over his knuckles, twisting it around and tossing it like a juggler. Mouth hanging open, Gabriela gawked at him. I knew she'd be thrilled about the idea of a spell. I hoped she didn't mind the taste—wyvern wizard spells weren't done with words and a magic wand. They were potions and powders and enchanted stones. The potions tended to taste like fish guts.

"Very similar to the powder I've provided Sky's family with for fireproofing their walls. Except this is a liquid you'll ingest," Maximus said to Gabriela. "Only trick is that you have to *believe* it will work. You have to achieve the right psychological mind-set to trigger the spell within your body. For humans, that takes practice."

"We'll schedule practice time," I promised. To Gabriela, I said, "After you're through the wall of fire, you need to block the wyvern detection spell."

"Easy as pie," Maximus said. "All she has to do is stand in front of the spell's 'eye'—it will be content 'looking' at her and won't see us. Real weakness in the spell, but most wyverns don't have a human on their crew. Ingenious move."

I continued, "While the spell is blocked, I'll pass through the sensor lasers, suspend myself above the pressure-sensitive floors, open the panel with my fire-breath, and crack the lock—that will turn off the lasers and the floor. Once the vault door is open, Maximus will use his spells against the fire beast that guards the interior."

"Fire beast," Gabriela breathed, awe in her voice.

Maximus grinned at her. "It's a magical construct designed to combat both wyverns and humans. It creates a white-hot fire that's hotter than any wyvern can withstand. Because the fire beast itself is magical, fire resistance spells are useless against it. But I have a few tricks up my sleeve." He then looked at me. "I should be able to destroy it temporarily, but be aware that it will regenerate after thirty minutes."

Thirty minutes was plenty of time. "If we can manage to avoid setting off any alarms, escaping should be easy—everything will be shut down, so we run, back the way we came. Flee in the car, minus Ryan, who will stay and erase any trace of his hacking from the security camera system. And that's it. That's why I need all of you. You each have very specialized talents that will help us get through very specialized security measures." I was looking at Ryan as I said it, hoping he saw what I saw: we needed a crew. The two of us couldn't complete this heist by staring longingly at each other.

Maximus cleared his throat. He was still toying with the fireball as if he didn't have a care in the world, but there was something about him that didn't look casual. Maybe his eyes were staring at me too intensely. Maybe his muscles were coiled too tightly. "And what, precisely, is the target?"

"I want a jewel in Ryan's family vault, the same one my mother tried to take," I said. "Maximus, you may 'shop' for a few trinkets as your payment. And Gabriela . . . they have a unicorn horn. It's yours if we succeed."

Gabriela's eyes went wide. "A unicorn horn? Really?" she squeaked.

"No one get greedy," I cautioned. "Steal a small number of items, and the wyverns will applaud my ingenuity. Steal more, and . . . well, don't do it." Turning in a slow circle, I fixed my eyes on each of them to make sure I had their attention. I did. In fact, I couldn't have had more of their attention if I were a dancing bear in a tutu. Mom would have been proud. *Now don't screw up,* I told myself. "This is going to be an official 'first heist,' which means your names will be kept out of it. I will be the only face on this. I will take the credit and any blame before the wyvern council at the next Reckoning. That's what will keep you safe."

"What will keep *you* safe?" Gabriela asked, her eyes

round and doll-like. She looked for an instant like an innocent little kid, excited to be at the fair but worried about dropping her ice cream on the sidewalk.

Glancing at Gabriela, I felt a stab of guilt. This would change her. Succeed or fail, she wouldn't be the same. That's why stealing your first hoard is so important in our culture. You leave childhood behind after you orchestrate your first major theft. I wondered if she knew that, and I told myself her emotional well-being wasn't my responsibility. She'd begged to be a part of this. "Us not failing will keep me safe," I said. It was the truth. The only thing that would protect them from wyvern wrath was if it was clear that I'd led the team, and the only thing that would protect me was success. "So . . . now that you've heard everything: Are you in?"

Ryan nodded.

Maximus grinned at me.

Gabriela looked scared, but she pressed her lips together and also nodded. And I felt something loosen around my rib cage, as if I'd been keeping my breath and my heart trapped inside. I could breathe again, fully in and fully out. I felt myself smile and hoped that I didn't look like a grinning idiot.

We can do this, I thought. *We WILL do this.*

CHAPTER ELEVEN

GABRIELA WAS LOOKING AROUND the abandoned warehouse with awe, as if it were a ballroom and she were Cinderella. "Is this where you plan all your quests?"

"Heists," I corrected. "And this is my first time planning one myself, so no." Scooping up dust, I tossed it in the air across the warehouse. It lingered, suddenly bringing to life the dozens of crisscrossing red beams.

She knelt next to one of the motion-sensing lasers and waved her hand in front of it. Ryan's computer beeped, and Gabriela stopped. "The unicorn horn in Ryan's family's vault . . . the unicorn wasn't killed, right? Natural death? Because to kill a unicorn—"

"Old age," I lied. I had no idea. I only knew it was there because Ryan's mom had mentioned it once—being a human, she didn't have the wyvern obsession with gold. Most of the treasures they'd collected were because of her, including the horn. I wondered if the jewel I was targeting was specifically hers and how badly she'd want it back. Hopefully badly enough to tell me what happened to Mom. "The horn itself is very old too." That much I knew—it had come from Home with one of the exiles. There were no unicorns on Earth.

"So after I block the detection spell, you . . . do what exactly about the lasers?"

"This." Stepping back, I began: flipping, cartwheeling, stepping, ducking, twisting, rolling, and contorting myself until at last I reached the other side. Everyone was watching me: Gabriela with her jaw dropped open, Maximus with a half smile on his face. And Ryan . . .

Now *that* was the look that I'd been wanting these past few weeks. Or close to it. He was looking at me like I was a cupcake he couldn't eat.

Straightening, I sauntered back to Gabriela. "I've got the easy part."

"Who has the hard part?"

I tried to look encouraging. "You."

She gulped.

"All I need to do is control my body; you have to control your mind. Maximus will help you. He's a wizard, remember?"

"I do detection spells and fire-related spells," Maximus said, his voice carrying across the warehouse. "Actual wizardry is a lot more limited than in Dungeons and Dragons. Still cool, of course, but with less variety. And you have to be ready to walk through fire."

She didn't look reassured. But I guided her across the

warehouse, with lots of you'll-do-fine, it-will-be-great platitudes. She was key to all of this. Everyone had a part to play. "You wanted magic," I reminded her.

Maximus started with a small fire, a candle, and then gave Gabriela a vial of glittery purple liquid. "Ooh, pretty!" she said.

"Brace yourself," I warned her.

She frowned and opened her mouth to ask a question.

"Drink it fast," Maximus said.

She drank it, and her whole face squinched up like she'd bitten into a lemon.

Maximus ignored her sputtering. "Willing participation is essential to any spell. Or rather, essential to any spell not hurting. Put your hand into the flame."

Still scraping her tongue against her teeth, she slid her fingers into the candle. "Ouch!" She snatched them back and stuck her fingers into her mouth.

He drew them out. "Not burned. See? It's in your head. Try again. Once you're able to control your mind's reaction to the flame, the spell will ensure the fire doesn't hurt you, at least until the spell wears off. You'll need to cross the wall of fire before that happens."

She kept trying. And the next day, she tried again, making the same face when she drank the purple potion. And the third day again.

Each day she wore a different unicorn-themed T-shirt.

—

On the third day of practice, while Gabriela was working herself up to sticking her whole hand into a small fire, I asked Ryan, "How are you keeping your parents from guessing where you are?"

He didn't look up from his computer code. "They know where I am."

I shot a look at the warehouse door, half expecting to see his father burst through. His father was the size of a pro wrestler and looked as though he crushed cars with his bare hands for a hobby. Combine that with his strict insistence on proper behavior . . . He wasn't someone I was anxious to see, especially since we were training to rob him.

"My parents know where I am; they just don't know who I'm with." He turned his laptop around to show me the screen. On it was a delicate black-and-white drawing of the ceiling of the warehouse. He'd captured the shadows and the strips of light that poked through the spots where rust had eaten away the roof. Cobwebs almost seemed to be swaying. "I told them I'm doing an independent study for art."

"Ryan, that's really good."

Squirming, he blushed. "Just experimenting."

I'd seen his art before, when he'd first started drawing with his computer and in little doodles, but he'd never done anything like this. "It looks"—I paused, trying to find the right word—"lonely."

"Yeah. Anyway, my parents think this is why I'm here."

"Because you're lonely?" I asked.

He looked up at me for the first time since I'd come over. His eyes seemed to capture me. "Not for much longer."

Maximus passed by us. "Oh, for goodness' sake, just make out already."

I glared at him. "Don't you have magic to do?"

He leveled a finger at me. "You are too young to be this stressed. Calm down. It will be fine. Your crew has all the skills needed. Or will."

I watched Gabriela for a moment. She was supposed to place her hand into a coffee can with a blaze of fire in it. She was circling around it as if it held venomous snakes.

"I do understand," Maximus said. "Your family was shamed. You want to restore your honor, reclaim your reputation, and all that jazz. But did it ever occur to you that none of that actually matters? It's all manufactured nonsense. We're just pretending, all of us exiles. None of us can ever be truly respectable so far from Home."

"Maybe I just really, really want that jewel. It would look nice on my dresser."

"His family will want it back."

I'm counting on that, I thought, and smiled (hopefully mysteriously) at him. I left him to his magic and Ryan to his computer. Once I had the jewel, I had every intention of giving it back to them—in exchange for information about Mom.

As for me, I practiced cracking a Swenson lock.

I'd never cracked one of those before.

The Swenson lock is a top-of-the-line, bank-quality mechanical combination lock. You can't use lock picks on these kinds of locks, obviously—no keyhole. The basic concept remains the same, though: you have to line up a series of grooves within the mechanism. You can do it by sound, with a stethoscope, or by touch, like Mom did. I chose touch.

Every afternoon, I sat cross-legged in front of a safe that Maximus had lent me. Cracking a safe like this by feel is a lot like trying to touch a breath in the wind. It requires focus. Cutting out the world so that the only thing that exists is the sensation in your fingertips. You have to get to know the particular feel of a particular lock better than the feel of your own heartbeat. Breathing in and out, I settled myself and focused.

This lock had a wheel with one hundred numbers and required a four-number combination, which works out to 100 million different possible combinations and only one right one. Only Ryan's father knew the combination, and he was extraordinarily careful to block the lock from the cameras every time he entered the vault—Ryan had combed through all the security feeds, and no luck—plus he probably changed it regularly anyway. No, it was old-fashioned safecracking for me, which somehow felt appropriate. Mom had taught me to do this. I was going to prove to her I'd learned it well.

It took me three afternoons to crack it the first time.

Next try, it took me one hour.

Then forty-five minutes.

Thirty.

Fifteen.

Five.

And then I brought suction cups, the large kind that window washers use to attach themselves to high-rise windows—these were Mom's, from the time she robbed the First National in St. Louis. Family heirlooms. Ryan helped me set up a bar at the same height as the ceiling outside the vault. Hanging upside down, I cracked the safe in two minutes.

Maximus starting bringing snacks to our practice. Chips with sea salt and cracked pepper, plus a variety of hummuses. (Red pepper hummus, yum! I love human snacks. Not snacks made of humans. Gross. Snacks made *by* humans.) When he started bringing Cheetos too, Ryan seemed to forgive him for their rocky start. I'd come out of my trance with the safe to hear the two of them boasting about how many Choco Tacos they could eat in a single sitting.

I sauntered over to them and helped myself to the chips. "How long until you think you'll be ready?"

"For the Choco Taco battle?" Maximus said. "I could take this boy at any time."

Ryan snorted. "This 'boy' can eat you under the table."

I suppressed a smile and stole another chip. "Why not just call him a 'young whippersnapper' and be done with it? You know you want to."

Maximus shook his fist and said in a creaky voice, "Get off my lawn, ye young whippersnapper, and leave the Choco Tacos!"

Gabriela joined us. "That's more pirate than old man."

"Ye scurvy scallywags," Maximus said, "stop stealing me chips." He wrapped his arms around the bag of chips. Ryan offered me the Cheetos instead. Maximus made a grab for that bag too, but Ryan tossed it over his head. I caught it, and Maximus lunged for me, so I tossed it to Gabriela, who tossed it back to Ryan.

At last Maximus snagged the Cheetos out of the air by unleashing a lasso of fire at the bag—and I took the chips. Munching on them, I said, "Seriously, Maximus, where are you with the fire beast spell? And Ryan, how's the code? Can we pick a date for the heist?"

"Can you breathe fire on demand yet?" Maximus countered. "You'll need to be the one to do that, in order to open the panel for the combination lock. I won't be able to join you at the vault until the lasers and the pressure plates are shut off."

I thought of the chopstick and how difficult it had been to produce enough flame under stress to set off the smoke detector in our foyer. Fire breathing wasn't my best skill. If Tuck were with us . . . But my brothers wouldn't help. *It has to be me.* "Not exactly. But I will."

"My parents' anniversary is Saturday," Ryan said. "My father has announced he's taking my mother to La Belle for dinner." La Belle was a fancy French restaurant in a lodge outside Aspen. You needed reservations months in advance, and I'd heard their béchamel sauce was delicious enough to make a restaurant critic weep in joy. Tuck used to talk about wanting to work there someday, back before he began his ever-changing stream of hobbies. Dinner there could take a solid three or four hours, depending on how many courses they ordered. If we struck then, we'd have plenty of time to be in and out before they'd finished their dessert.

"Saturday it is," I said. Five more days. My calendar was open. Might as well fill it.

From then on, I switched off between practicing with the safe and breathing fire. Or more accurately, spitting out sparks. Three days before the scheduled heist, I still hadn't mastered it.

Flopping back on the floor of the warehouse, I sighed loudly and said, "Can't I just bring a blowtorch?"

"It's not the same," Ryan said. "The plate is specifically spelled for dragon fire." He looked worried. His art, I'd noticed, had gotten steadily darker and more intricate, as if he was taking out his stress in brush strokes.

I wanted to comfort him. And I wanted him to comfort me. I wished we could go instantly back to the way we'd been, when we trusted each other completely.

"I know." Kneeling, I focused on the block of wood in front of me. My goal was to generate enough heat to char it. If I could manage that much heat, then I'd be able to access the lock.

I kept trying.

Gabriela came by to watch me. She'd graduated from a blaze in the coffee can to stepping into a campfire. "You know, no offense, but it makes me feel a lot better about myself to see you not good at something," she said.

I glared at her and tried again.

There! A little more than a spark!

"Ooh, insult me again!" I said.

"Um, you're hard to insult," Gabriela said. "You're pretty much perfect."

"I know," I said. "Make something up." Concentrating, I tried to feel that warmth in the base of my stomach. There it was, maybe, sort of. *Come on, Sky, think heat!*

"You're not modest, that's for sure," she said. "Some people might call you a stuck-up princess who thinks she's better than anyone else."

My next flame was a tiny bit tighter. "Good. Keep going."

"Some might say you're selfish. Self-centered. Or maybe the word is self-absorbed. But I think they're mostly jealous and kind of afraid of you, because you don't care what they think."

I glanced at her. "I *do* care. You're the one who doesn't."

"I care what *you* think," Gabriela said, and then she fidgeted as if she wished she hadn't said that. "I remember when I first met you, my first day in second grade. We'd moved here in the middle of the year, and I was this weird kid who was overexcited about being everyone's friend. I brought these Pokémon cards to school—I thought I'd make friends with them. But this boy in our class, he took them, and when I told the teacher, he lied and said they were his. And she believed him. But you didn't. You didn't confront the boy or anything. You didn't say a word to the teacher. Or even to me. When I went to lunch, though, the cards were in my lunch box. And that boy had a toad in his."

I grinned. I'd forgotten all about that. The boy seemed to hate toads as much as I did. He'd screamed so loudly that everyone stopped and stared. "Can't believe you remember that."

"I decided right then and there that I didn't care what the rest of the class thought, so long as someday I'd become friends with you. Took you a long time to notice I was there." She smiled shyly. She was blushing, I saw, and the pink spread across her cheekbones all the way to her ears.

"I'm pretty good at being self-absorbed," I said. "It's like a superpower. For what it's worth, I'm sorry for not noticing sooner. I always had my family and Ryan and, well, all the wyverns."

"Do you miss them? Your wyvern friends?"

"When we lost my mom, we lost the respect of the entire wyvern community, and that was very nearly unbearable." I thought about the shunning nearly every day. It fueled me. That day . . . every wyvern had turned their back to me and my family. My own friends, who'd sat in the cafeteria with me and shared notes in chemistry class. And family friends. Friends we'd had barbecues with, like the Longobardis, who liked to play volleyball with a fireball. Friends we'd gone skiing with, like the Ortizes, who only skied on black-diamond trails, and Mrs. Harmon, who used to heat homemade hot chocolate with her breath on the chairlift for me. Friends we'd danced with at weddings and cried with at funerals and laughed with at picnics. . . . All of them had declared us unworthy. And Ryan had led them. He'd turned first. He'd spoken the words *I shun you* formally in front of every wyvern at the Reckoning. He'd spread the word at school that we were over, that he didn't want to be near me ever again, that I wasn't worthy of him—

A flame burst out from between my lips and seared a quarter-size hole in the wood.

Gabriela jumped up and down. "You did it! Oh, Sky, that was awesome!"

I let the flame die and looked over at Ryan. Maybe I hadn't quite forgiven him yet. Maybe I never would. Or maybe . . . all I needed was this heist, to fix everything.

Ryan was deeply involved in his laptop and hadn't seen, but I noticed Maximus was watching me. He nodded solemnly, as if he were bowing. I saw a hint of respect in his eyes.

And so that's how we spent the afternoons:

Maximus working on his spell to fight the fire beast (whatever spell that was—wizard secret, he said) and more fire resistance potions for Gabriela. Ryan working on his computer to hack the security cameras. Gabriela conquering her natural human instinct to fear fire. And me crouched in front of a lock or a piece of wood, trying to be both angry and calm.

Each day, we improved. Better. Stronger. Smarter.

In a weird way, it was a wonderful time.

CHAPTER TWELVE

ON THE NIGHT OF the heist, I stole Liam's car keys, pretended to eat dinner (being so close to my chance to fix my family = no appetite at all), and then shut myself in my bedroom. *You can do this*, I told myself. *Focus on the details.* First, I had to get dressed.

Standing in my closet, I rifled through my clothes. All black was a must, of course. Gloves. Face mask. Can't do anything about the whites of my eyes—I had to see.

A knock shook my door. "Sky?" It was Charles.

"I'm doing homework!" I called.

Another knock. "We know you're not." Liam. "Come on, Sky, open up."

What exactly did he know? I'd been careful. "Can it wait until tomorrow? I'm not feeling great tonight." I contemplated making retching noises, but then they might send Dad to check on me. Better to just be mildly ill.

"Open the door, Sky." Tuck. All three of them were out

there. Fabulous. "Really don't want to explain to Dad why we bashed down your door. He still blames us for the chandelier."

I shoved the gloves and face mask back in the closet. Wiping my sweaty hands on my black jeans, I shot a look at the clock. Still had a half hour before I had to be out the door. Or window. Opening my bedroom door, I began, "Guys, I have a headache and—"

All three of them stood there, shoulder to shoulder, smiles on their faces, with Charles in the center holding a massive tub of popcorn. They pushed forward, jamming together in the door, and I retreated as they argued, mock punched, and shoved their way into my room.

My three brothers can fill a room, even my princess-size bedroom. Immediately, they took over as if it were their turf. Tuck plopped onto my bed, Charles claimed my desk chair, and Liam carried my comfy chair from its reading nook to the center of the room. "Where's your remote?" Tuck asked.

"Found it!" Liam fished it out from between my jewelry boxes and switched on the TV. "I vote for a classic human comfort movie. Like *Die Hard*. Or *Reservoir Dogs*. Or anything with zombies." He then relieved Charles of the popcorn bucket and dropped into the comfy chair.

Like dogs that had settled into their new doghouse, my brothers already looked like they'd been here for hours and would stay for hours. "Um, guys?"

Charles glanced at me, his expression serious. He tapped the calendar on my desk, and I immediately worried that I'd left incriminating papers out. But I hadn't. Everything was at the lodge. We planned to burn all the evidence before we started the heist. "Do you think we don't know what tonight is?" he asked.

Inside, I felt as if my stomach were curdling. How did they know? How could they? They couldn't. I fought to keep my face pleasantly confused. "Saturday night?"

Liam flicked a kernel of popcorn at me. "It's the anniversary of your and Ryan's first date. You had it marked on your calendar, then crossed it out enthusiastically. We saw."

"That's why we're here, with popcorn." Tuck pointed at the bucket of popcorn and mumbled, "We'll even let you pick out the buttery pieces, though you should just grab a handful and eat what you get. Basic popcorn etiquette. Don't steal the butter."

"We're all going to watch a movie," Charles said. "And you aren't going to mope or feel sorry for yourself or even think about that idiot who doesn't deserve you." Liam nodded so vigorously that he spilled popcorn off his lap.

This was the worst-timed and sweetest thing my brothers had ever done. Getting up, Liam patted the armrest of the comfy chair. "You sit." He plopped himself on the floor and leaned against the chair.

"You guys, I really, really appreciate this, but . . . ," I began.

Charles held up his hand. "No arguments. You aren't going to be alone tonight. Whether you admit it or not, we know this is hard for you. So here we are."

I felt tears prick my eyes. "Really, I'm fine."

"Of course you're fine," Charles said. "You're a Hawkins."

Liam tossed another popcorn kernel. "Hey, pick a movie. Only rule is no crying scenes. Unless it's right before a scene with massive explosions."

"Rain check?" I tried. Any other night, this would be great. My brothers actually wanted to hang out with me again. It was pretty much miraculous. After weeks of glowering at me, all three of them were here, ready to comfort me, or whatever.

"Give up," Tuck advised. "You know we'll wear you down."

So incredibly sweet. But I had a heist to execute, wrongs to right, and dragons to humiliate. Maybe I could watch with them for a little while, then think of an excuse to leave. . . . "Pass the popcorn." Sitting down in the chair, I curled my legs underneath me and dug for the butteriest pieces.

"Let's go with the best movie ever made." Liam wielded the remote like a light saber. *"Star Wars: Episode IV—A New Hope."* He added sound effects.

"One half hour," I repeated.

He queued it up and hit play.

"Mood lighting!" Tuck jumped for the light switch. Shadows shifted as he flicked off the light. But it wasn't shadowy enough for me to slip out unnoticed. Maybe they'd get sucked into the movie and I could slip out while they quoted Obi-Wan. Chords thundered through the room, and the opening words scrolled up the screen.

"Anyone think to bring sodas?" Liam asked.

"I'll get some," I offered.

"Sky, stay," Charles ordered. "Tuck, get the soda."

"Why me?" he whined.

"Because this is for Sky."

"Oh, right." He peeled himself off my bed and trotted out the door. There went that opportunity to escape.

On the screen, the stormtroopers blasted through a door, and Charles passed me more popcorn. "Do you want to have a conversation about feelings?" he asked.

"Not really," I said.

He exhaled in relief. "Good."

I smiled. "You would have done it, if I'd asked, would you?"

"We're here for you, Sky." He meant it.

"What if I wanted to talk about makeup?"

"I think mascara is creepy," Liam volunteered. "Like lots of spider legs on a girl's eye. Really freaky part is if she starts to cry, and the spider legs dissolve and walk down her cheeks."

I tossed a popcorn kernel at him. "Girls don't wear makeup for you."

"Sure they do," Liam said. "Every girl I've ever dated puts it on before a date. Even if it's just a barbecue."

"They don't do it for you," I reiterated. "Girls wear makeup to feel stronger. It's armor for your face. You guys are stuck with the faces you have, which, in your cases, is unfortunate."

Liam snagged a pillow off my bed and threw it at me as Tuck came through the door holding cans of soda. He tossed one to each of us. "You shook them, didn't you," Liam accused him.

"Anyone who spills soda in my room cleans it," I said.

Tuck halted in the middle of the room. "Silence, everyone. Leia's on-screen!"

"Mm, should have watched the gold bikini one," Tuck said.

"Amazing she can keep that dress so clean in the middle

of a battle." I dug my hand into the popcorn bucket. We hadn't done anything like this in forever. Just hung out. Just been nice to one another. Not since Mom had disappeared. I'd missed this.

"Spoiler alert: the hair buns are headsets," Liam said.

"That's *Spaceballs*, idiot." Tuck threw one of my old teddy bears at him.

"You guys are all idiots," I proclaimed, and wished, for the first time, that I wasn't doing the heist tonight. Except if I didn't . . . then this night would end, and at breakfast, there would still be a missing chair.

We watched a few minutes more.

"Guys, I hate to say it, but I have plans tonight," I said.

"Skip it," Tuck said.

"Can't. It's important."

Charles snorted. "Important?"

"It's important that I'm out tonight. I want to be seen publicly not caring about Ryan. Gabriela and I are going to eat steak then ice cream, then dance at Ski Bunnies until midnight." Ski Bunnies was the only nightspot in Aspen that catered to high schoolers.

Liam opened his soda, and the bubbles gushed to the top. He held it over my trash can as it overflowed onto his fingers. "How about you skip the 'publicly' part and just don't care about Ryan instead?"

It was decent advice. But it was much too late for that. "I've cared about him since I was three months old. I can't turn it off just because he can."

"I don't think he can either," Charles said. "But that doesn't change what happened."

That stopped me for a second. What if Charles was

right? What if it was impossible to fix things? Impossible to go back to the way things were? *Maybe it is impossible to go back*, I thought. *But maybe I can go forward. Maybe I can make things better.*

If I can get out of this room.

"Oh, no, are we having a 'feelings' conversation?" Tuck asked. "If so, I'm out." He turned the volume up on the TV. The soundtrack blared, the bass rumbling through the floor.

Louder, over the sound of blasters, I said, "I need you guys to cover for me. Please. I don't want Dad to mess this up. This is my closure, you guys. I need this."

All of them were looking at me.

I wasn't lying. I would have closure.

"If it's what you need . . . ," Charles said.

"It is." I was firm.

Liam switched off the TV.

"Please, stay and keep watching. It will confuse Dad."

He turned it back on and raised the volume even higher, which I appreciated. It would drown out our conversation.

"But you'll need a ride," Charles said.

"Taken care of." I darted into my closet, grabbing the gloves and face mask and shoving them into my pocket. "Thanks. I owe you all. You're the best brothers ever."

"You're just saying that to butter us up," Tuck mumbled.

"Pretty much. Is it working?"

Charles sighed heavily. "We know we haven't been very good brothers to you lately."

Now who wants a "feelings" talk? I glanced at the clock. Everyone would be waiting for me. "Nah, you guys are great. Totally understand. All is forgiven."

"But we haven't been there for you," Charles persisted.

"It's been just as hard on you as the rest of us. Maybe more, because of that idiot Ryan. He put you in the spotlight, and you didn't deserve that."

I took a deep breath. "Did you guys think any more about what I said, about stealing a hoard as a way to fix things?" If they were willing, the plan could be adapted. It would be helpful to have three experienced wyverns with me. They could have my back. . . .

Charles scowled. "No, Sky. We talked about this. It's too dangerous."

Liam nodded. "Right now, we've got equilibrium. The human press has mostly forgotten about us. Even wyvern society—it's mostly moved on to other scandals. So long as we lie low, we can keep doing whatever we want, keep living here, keep living our lives."

"It could be much worse," Tuck said.

Charles nodded. "I know it doesn't feel that way to you, that it felt like rock-bottom end-of-the-world when Ryan did what he did. But it's not. We don't need them, or anyone. We have everything we need right here."

Except Mom, I thought. And friends. And a father who smiles and laughs. "But don't you want more?" I pressed. "Don't you want what we're supposed to have? What's rightfully ours?"

Charles looked amused.

"Okay, maybe 'rightfully' isn't the perfect word," I admitted.

"We have enough," Tuck said.

I stared at him. That was a very unwyvern-like attitude. All our kind wanted to accumulate gold, expend the hoard, increase the family legacy. "What aren't you telling me?"

They exchanged glances. Suddenly, I was sure: they were hiding something.

"Spill. What's going on?"

"Nothing!" Liam said. And Tuck echoed him, "Nothing. Don't be so suspicious."

I glared at them, as if I could stare their secrets out of their heads. "If you're lying to me . . ."

"We aren't, not exactly," Charles said soothingly. "It's just . . . We know we can't do a heist right now. It's too dangerous. Too much at stake."

"Why?" I asked. "What's at stake? You're keeping something from me." I was furious, even though I was keeping a secret from them. "Dad told you . . . what? What did he tell you?"

All three of them looked at one another again. "No," Charles said. "He'll tell her when he thinks she's ready to understand."

"Dad never tells me anything. He thinks I need protection. But I don't. I need the truth." I was trying not to shout, even though the movie would have drowned me out.

To my surprise, it was Tuck who answered. "Dad said the council was one vote away from destroying us entirely. We would have been stripped of everything—worse than just shunned. We'd have been declared outcast."

I stared at him, then Liam, then Charles. All of them looked serious, and I thought of Ryan and his worry about his father ruining us. But he couldn't . . . The council wouldn't . . . No one had been declared "outcast" in . . . well, ever. That was a thing the wyverns did at Home, at least according to the stories. Our families had never done it. Shunned meant we were disgraced, the lowest of the low; outcast meant we were disowned. Treated as if we did not exist, and with no hope of redemption. It was, to put it mildly, an extreme reaction for a botched theft. "But . . . it was just a heist!"

"We don't know why their reaction was so extreme," Charles said. "Apparently, they decided to make an example of us."

"Mr. Keene, your ex's charming father, pushed hardest for it," Liam said. "He lobbied for us to be outcast. Has a lot of sway on the council."

"Hate that guy," Tuck muttered.

"She should know what kind of family she's pining after," Liam said. "No idea why Mr. Keene hates us so much, but I heard there were bribes and blackmail. Fun stuff."

Charles nodded. "Dad had to make all sorts of promises."

"Including that we'd all behave ourselves," Tuck mumbled.

"And that means you too," Charles said. "Abandon this crazy idea about stealing back what's 'ours,' and just be grateful that we're still allowed to live here, still allowed to be wyverns."

I shook my head, more because I didn't want it to be true than because I didn't believe them. It matched up too neatly with what Ryan had said about why he'd done what he'd done. (He really had been protecting me!) His father led the wyvern council—they wouldn't have considered shunning us if he hadn't led the way. But why? Why did he hate us so much? And what did he know about what had happened to our mother? "No one can keep us from being wyverns."

"You know what he means, Sky," Liam said. "We'd be

shut out of gatherings, closed off from everyone. You think no one speaks to us now? That's just playground stuff. You can come back from a shunning—given enough time and 'good behavior,' we can be declared forgiven. If we were outcast, we'd be dead to them for all time. At least this way . . ."

"If we lie low, they'll forget," Charles said. "All it needs is time, and it will get better. Maybe Dad won't ever be on the council again, but we'll still be a part of wyvern society. We can earn back our reputations, gradually and quietly. Promise you'll let go of whatever half-baked, harebrained daydream you've been nursing."

My mouth felt dry. And I had the terrible, tempting thought: *I don't have to go.* I could stay here with my brothers, eat popcorn, and watch a movie. Gabriela, Maximus, and Ryan . . . they'd wait for me for a while, and then eventually they'd give up and go home.

If my brothers were right . . . If the council had seriously considered . . . Maybe I was risking too much to find someone who might not want to be found. Mom had made her choices, Dad had said—did I really want to follow her bad choices with the same bad choices?

Except *why* was her choice so bad? Wyverns stole from other wyverns all the time. It was tradition. Granted, you weren't supposed to fail, hence the shunning, but to know they'd been contemplating an even more extreme reaction . . . it didn't make sense. And *Star Wars* wasn't going to give me any answers.

I squashed down the bit of guilt that squirmed in my stomach. I *had* to complete this heist. Lives don't just fix themselves. Lies don't unravel on their own. And thanks to my brothers, I now had an all-new reason to proceed:

Mr. Keene, Ryan's father, had pushed for the most severe punishment. And Mom had gone missing after a botched mission in his house. Coincidence? Ha! Clearly, there was more going on than any of us knew. *If I can just get my hands on that jewel, I can get answers.*

Or I can get closure. Or revenge.

Or maybe, if I'm quick enough, smart enough, and lucky enough . . . I can get everything back the way it was.

"Promise us, Sky, and we'll let you go out with Gabriela," Charles said. "We'll even cover for you with Dad."

"Of course," I lied.

He held out his hand. I shook it. He'd forgive my lie when I came back with the jewel, when the council reinstated us, when Mom came home, I told myself.

"Cover for me?" I asked them.

"We will," Charles said. Tuck and Liam nodded solemnly.

"Thank you. You're the best brothers I could ever have." Quickly, before they could change their minds, I tossed my bag of climbing gear out the window. Using my grappling hook, I climbed out, scrambled down the rope, and landed in the flower bed.

Up in the room, I heard one of them say, "Did she say how she's getting to Gabriela's? You don't think she'll try to drive herself?"

"Nah," another said. "She has more sense than that."

Scooping up my bag, I ran for the garage and stole Liam's car.

CHAPTER THIRTEEN

I DROVE WITHIN THE speed limit, barely. Really tacky to be late to your own heist. Overhead, the sky was thick with clouds, grays and blues and purples and blacks overlapping like a bruise. Between the mountains up ahead, the clouds were streaks, the rain visible as sheets of thin diagonal lines. The sun had already set. As soon as I hit the outskirts of downtown Aspen, I sped up—the Ferrari shot forward, feeling as if it were skimming the surface of the road. I felt as if I were flying. Droplets spattered on the windshield.

Ryan was waiting for me outside, by the warehouse. He swung the doors open so I could zoom straight inside, and then he shut the doors behind me. "Sorry, sorry," I repeated, parking diagonally and then jumping out. I beamed at all of them.

It was really happening! Tonight!

Gabriela rushed over to me. "Are you okay? What happened? Wow, nice car. When did you get your license?"

"Fine. Family. And I didn't." I wasn't about to explain the conversation with my brothers—if we succeeded tonight, it wouldn't matter. If we didn't . . . Well, I wasn't going to think about that. Briefly, I wondered if this was how Mom had felt, that the reward was worth the risks. I wondered if she knew how much she was risking.

I knew, and it was making me mildly nauseous.

My eyes swept over the warehouse. Ryan's computers were already back at his house, and all the laser beam equipment had been dismantled. Every trace of Maximus's work with potions and powders had been swept away.

"Maximus, you have both spells? Fire beast and fire protection?" He held up two vials—one sparkly purple and one that looked like liquid gold—to show me, then sealed them away in a pouch at his belt. "Gabriela, did you pack my climbing gear and suction cups? Rope? My music?" Gabriela nodded and pointed to a black duffel bag. Turning to Ryan, I asked, "Do you have the mics and earpieces?"

He held out one set on the palm of his hand. "Everyone else is already wearing theirs." The earpiece was a nub of plastic that looked like a clear popcorn kernel, and the mic was a tiny clip for inside my shirt—they would connect us.

"It itches," Gabriela warned. "Wish we could just use cell phones."

"We don't use cell phones," Ryan said.

"No offense meant," she said, "but that's weirder than breathing fire."

"Paranoia, my dear," Maximus said. "No wyvern wants to carry around a GPS recording his or her every illicit movement." He was wearing all black too, but his outfit included a trench coat that swirled around his ankles as he walked.

Very stylish. I grinned at him. I felt giddy, as if I could do twelve backflips in a row.

Crossing to Ryan, I clipped on the mic, then fit the kernel snugly into my ear. These were top-of-the-line, designed to be discreet. With my finger, I teased a curl over my ear, but short of anyone kissing my ear, no one would detect it.

Ryan lingered beside me, watching me, and I wished I hadn't thought about kissing. I didn't need any distractions tonight. If this worked, we'd be able to kiss anytime we wanted, wherever we wanted, except not in the middle of class, because rules. But other times. *Sky, you're distracted again*, I scolded myself.

"You're sure about this?" he asked.

"Of course." Tearing my eyes away from Ryan, I looked at my crew. Gabriela and Maximus were both wearing gloves and had black masks around their heads. They pulled them down over their faces. "Do you need a motivational speech? Because I'm not sure there's time for that."

"We're good," Maximus said.

Gabriela gulped, loudly. "I think I can do it."

I turned to look at Ryan. "Ready?"

"Be careful," he told me.

"This will work," I told him. We'd planned, prepared, and practiced. We couldn't fail. And then I wondered if Mom had felt this way too.

"I believe in you," Ryan said.

And then, as if to prove it, he kissed me. Cupping my face in his hands, he pressed his lips against mine. You'd think a kiss in such a moment would feel like fireworks. But instead . . . it felt like coming home. I felt as if I'd been wrapped in a soft robe, given a mug of hot chocolate, and told I'd be kept safe forever.

When he released me, though, he still looked worried.

He got into his own car. He'd drive home, like usual, and shut himself into his room to do homework, like usual. And then he'd contact us when his code was uploaded and ready to overwrite their security camera system, *not* like usual.

Getting into Liam's car, I sat in the passenger seat. Gabriela took the driver's seat. She was examining all the bells and whistles. "Really nice car," she said.

For an instant, I didn't want her to put it in drive. The past couple of weeks had been nice. Full of hope and possibilities. From here on in, the possibilities would narrow to only two: success or failure.

But I didn't stop her. Gabriela backed out of the warehouse and onto the chunked-up driveway.

"We should have blown up the warehouse," Maximus said regretfully. "Then we could have done the slow walk away from the ball of fire."

I rolled my eyes at him. "Drive," I told Gabriela.

Fat drops of rain plunked on the car as we drove away.

Higher up in the mountains, the pines and aspens blurred like a watercolor. The storm clouds deepened the green of the pines, and the aspens looked like white candles against them, lit with a smudge of paleness from their growing buds. Dusk wrapped everything in a layer of gray. I felt the wind picking up, shaking the car. Two turns before the winding private road that led to Ryan's house, we took a left and headed down toward the lake.

Ryan continued straight home. I watched his taillights

recede until he was out of sight. My heart gave a little lurch, as if I wasn't going to see him again, and we drove down between the trees toward picnic tables.

Rain disturbed the lake. The surface rippled like silk in the wind, distorting the reflection of the cliffs, which was good. On a calm day, anyone in the house could have looked down and seen the cliffs mirrored in the lake. I didn't think it had ever occurred to Ryan's parents that on a rainy evening, they had a serious blind spot. Probably because it had never occurred to them that anyone would try to climb the cliffs—an oversight in a state that encourages rock climbing. In Colorado, when you're born, instead of giving you a baby blanket, the hospital wraps you in a climbing harness. Or they might as well.

Gabriela parked Liam's car beside the lake, in the shadow of the trees, and we all got out. I unpacked my climbing gear and pulled it on, then shouldered a large coil of rope.

Looking up at the cliff, I felt that rush: the moment before you defy gravity.

"She's going to climb *that*?" I heard Maximus ask Gabriela. "I thought she said it was an easy climb."

"She likes to climb things," Gabriela told him. "In third grade, she climbed onto the roof of our school."

"This is a bit higher than that. And note the 'Dangerous— Do Not Climb' signs?"

"She can do it," Gabriela reassured him.

I appreciated the vote of confidence. And truthfully, this wasn't the part of the heist that made me nervous. In fact, I'd been looking forward to this.

Climbing, I felt the rain slick the rocks, and I had to dig

my fingers into the crevices. My shoes slipped as I scrambled to place them. I felt adrenaline course through me, as if I'd drunk six cans of soda in a row and eaten all the Halloween candy (which I did once and only once). I knew I was grinning, even though no one could see me. My smile pulled at my cheeks and made me feel like a wolf baring her teeth. Or a dragon.

It was exhilarating.

And oddly peaceful.

I didn't think about the heist. Or my mother. Or Ryan. All my focus was, and had to be, on the rocks. You forget about past and future when you climb. That's one thing I love about it, when you slip into this moment that is purely *now*. In *now*, there's no guilt or regret or worry or fear. There's only the doing.

I was a little sad when I reached the top.

Scrambling up into the alcove, I panted for a moment. My calves burned and my fingers ached. I could feel a dozen scrapes begin to sting, but I'd made it in one piece.

The alcove was a natural formation, a cavelike notch in the cliff with a view of the mountains. Ryan and I used to come here to play out of sight of his parents. We told each other secrets here, mocked our relatives here, kissed for hours here. This alcove dripped with memories. This was where Ryan told me about his mother's illness when he was nine, how she'd almost died and how his father had flown in doctors from around the world. She'd recovered, but he'd been so terrified. He hadn't shown his fear to anyone else. Showing emotion was, apparently, bad manners. Ryan had had etiquette training since he was a toddler, so he knew these things. By age nine, he also knew how to waltz, how to serve a proper tea, and how to greet anyone politely in up to twenty languages. Here in this alcove was the only place he felt free enough to demonstrate that he could also curse in twenty languages. I remembered him, age ten, whispering swear words to me, delicious foreign words that meant things I couldn't even visualize. Still wasn't entirely sure how some of them worked.

"I'm up," I whispered.

The earpiece was silent for a moment, and then I heard Ryan's voice in my ear, as close as if he were pressed against me, whispering to me. *"Glad to hear it."*

"Where's the pulley?" I asked.

"I hid it behind the rock."

I scanned the alcove. "Ryan, it's all rocks."

"The big one."

Climbing over a scattering of other rocks, I found the pulley nestled between a boulder and a bush. He'd already secured it to the ground. All it needed was the rope, so I ran that through and then tossed one end down the cliff. "Gabriela, come on up. I've got you."

Positioning myself on the other side of the pulley, I picked up the rope and braced myself. Leaning back, I pulled as Gabriela climbed.

The earpiece crackled. *"Keep it up,"* Maximus encouraged her from the ground. *"You're doing great."*

"You could help," Gabriela said.

"I am helping," he said. *"I'm encouraging you."*

Leaning back farther, I kept pulling. At last, Gabriela flopped over the edge and then scrambled up into the alcove. She lay panting while Maximus climbed, with my help. Reaching the top, Maximus shook himself like a dog, spraying rain.

"You know, if you could transform into a dragon, that would have been a lot easier," Gabriela said.

"My wife used to say that often. She dreamed of the freedom of flying." His face took on a wistful expression, as if he were about to launch into a litany of memories. While I didn't want to be insensitive, we were on a bit of a clock. "She blamed the council for keeping us from Home and from reclaiming our legacy—"

"That's nice," I said. "Sharing later. Stealth now. Ryan, are you ready?"

"*One sec . . .*"

Creeping forward, I waited behind a bush. The nice part about the alcove was that its opening was inconspicuous. Just a hole behind a lilac bush. I pulled on my face mask and gloves. Out of the corner of my eye, I saw Gabriela and Maximus do the same.

"*Now,*" Ryan whispered.

We ran.

At night, the sculpture garden behind Ryan's house looked more like the set of a horror movie than a place of quiet reflection. The statues of dragons, hydras, and serpents loomed larger than normal, and their shadows stretched as if they wanted to swallow us. All the flowers and bushes were tangles of gray in the darkness. Rain covered everything in a slick sheen. My shoes sank into the wet grass, and it felt as if the mud was sucking at my soles. It wanted to trip me, to slow me, to stop me, but I was unstoppable. I saw the security cameras, mounted on the tops of gargoyles, but I knew they couldn't see me, thanks to Ryan.

We bolted across the gardens to the back kitchen door. I jammed my lock picks into the keyhole, jimmied it open in thirty seconds, and then we were inside.

Borrowing a kitchen towel, I wiped my feet, then gave it to Gabriela and Maximus. They soaked up the water from their shoes, and then we all tiptoed through the kitchen, taking care to leave no trace and make no sound. They returned the towel to me, and I tucked it into my bag—the police report would have to list one kitchen towel stolen, in addition to treasures.

As I crept forward, I saw our reflections in the stainless steel refrigerator, oven, and stovetop, in the microwave, and in the copper pots that hung above the center island. We were darker shadows in the already dark kitchen. I picked the lock on the basement door—twenty seconds.

Stepping on the first step, I heard a *whoosh*. Flames roared up in front of me—the wall of fire, the first line of security. The walls of the stairwell must have been coated in fire-protected paint, because the fire was contained. It formed a wall of dancing red and orange in front of us. Rather pretty, actually.

"Anyone bring marshmallows?" Maximus asked.

"Just give her the spell," I ordered. Holding my hands out, I let the flames lick over them. It felt comfortably warm, like the sun in August. The fire beast, I knew, would burn much, much hotter. Steel-meltingly hot. This was just your run-of-the-mill immolate-humans kind of fire. We could walk through it fine, but not Gabriela—and we needed her on the other side in order to block the wyvern detection spell.

Maximus dusted the three of us with a fire protection

powder, like what was on the walls and stairs, to keep our clothes from bursting into flames. My nose tickled, and I held in a sneeze. Then Maximus handed Gabriela the purple vial. "Bottoms up," he told her.

"Right. I'm ready." She drank it, making her lemon-eating face. "Ugh, never gets better." She wiped her lips and handed the empty vial back to him.

"Let's go." He trotted down the steps, into the fire. I followed him.

The fire felt like a tickle, and for a moment, all I could see were the red and amber flames. We passed through it and then waited for Gabriela. And waited.

"She's not going to do it," Maximus said.

"She will. Just wait."

We waited.

"What happens if she doesn't believe it will work?" I whispered.

"Then we'll hear a lot of screaming."

Through the earpiece, Gabriela said, *"Not helpful. I just . . . need a minute."*

Plunging back up through the flames, I found Gabriela on the other side, huddled against the wall. I took her hand. "Hey, you can do this."

She shook her head. Tears were welling up in her eyes. "I thought I was ready for an adventure. I wanted this, the excitement, the magic—my life was so boring. I wanted special. I wanted to prove to you that I'm worthy of having impossible dreams. But now that we're here, and you're depending on me—"

"Quit it with the melodrama," I interrupted. Pulling her forward, I drew her hand into the flame. She resisted, but

I kept pulling her closer. Her feet began shuffling, like she wanted to bolt. I made more soothing noises, as if she were a horse I was trying to coax with an apple. "I'm right here. You can do this. It'll be okay."

She squeezed her eyes shut but stopped trying to yank her hand away.

Flames licked over her fingers and her wrist. But she didn't cry out—the spell was working fine. "You know the spell will work, right? You tested it. You trained with it. You believe in it, don't you?"

"Yes, but . . . Sky, it's me. I don't believe in *me*. I'm just ordinary, boring Gabriela."

"You are anything but ordinary and boring." I clasped her hands and stared at her until she reluctantly met my eyes. "Would an ordinary and boring person have wanted to join my crew? Would an ordinary and boring person have trained for two weeks to do things she thought her body could never do? Would she trust someone who made outrageous claims and promised impossible things?"

She had fresh tears in her eyes, but she was nodding a little, listening.

"Hold my hand, and we'll do it together, okay?"

Hand in hand, we walked through the flames.

On the other side, I heard her exhale in a whoosh that sounded like a gust of wind. Her smile was so bright that I was half surprised she wasn't glowing. Maximus knelt and extinguished a bit of flame that had nested on her sock. She bit back a shriek, letting it out as only a small *Meep!*

"We're down," I whispered to Ryan. "Are these cameras out?"

"*Hold,*" he whispered back.

We waited on the third-to-bottom step, jumbled together. I heard Gabriela breathing close to my left ear and felt the warmth of Maximus's arm pressed against my shoulder.

Again, I touched Gabriela's hand with mine and glanced at her. In the shadows of the stairwell, I couldn't see her face, but she squeezed my fingers.

"You did it," I told her.

"I'm sorry I hesitated. It was just . . . Fire. Spells. Suddenly, it hit me that this is all real. And I'm doing this." Gabriela was smiling. I was sure of it—I could hear it in her voice.

Maximus drawled, "Great. Congrats. Now could you do something about that wyvern detection spell, please?"

"Oh! Yes." She stepped forward and knelt in front of a camera that we knew was active with the spell—her job now was easy. Just block it from seeing us. Blind it with her humanity. Ryan had already taken care of the actual security feed. To neutralize the spell, she just had to be herself.

And now it was my turn.

I tossed flour into the corridor. It lingered on the laser beams, and I began to move, cartwheeling forward, holding, and then ducking and stepping. Another cartwheel. Lean back.

My foot nearly grazed a laser, and my breath caught in my throat. I froze and then continued, flipping and twisting and stepping and bending, until I reached the other side.

"You did it!" Gabriela whispered from the stairs. "That was fantastic!"

"Not quite done yet." I pulled out the suction cups, ready to climb above the pressure-sensitive floor and crack the lock.

The earpiece crackled. *"My parents are home!"* Ryan's whisper was harsh, the sudden burst of panic clear. I felt it jolt through me. *"They came back!"*

I pressed a hand to my ear to try to stop the crackle. "Stay calm. We planned for this. It shouldn't matter." My heart started thumping faster anyway, but I reminded myself we'd left no trace of our entrance. So long as his parents didn't randomly decide to visit the vault—which they shouldn't, because they never did—we should be fine. "You know what to do."

If they went into Ryan's room, he had his art program ready on his laptop—they wouldn't see or suspect a thing. I was glad we'd wiped up the drops of water in the kitchen.

Jumping up, I affixed suction cups to the ceiling.

"My father's coming into the house," Ryan reported, his voice tense. *"Mom's in the car. He must have forgotten something."*

"Relax," I told him. "There's no reason for him to come to the basement. We've planned this perfectly." I hoped that wasn't just bravado. If we were caught . . . I didn't want to think about that, or how my brothers would react knowing how quickly I'd broken my promise.

We're not going to fail, I told myself.

Each suction cup had a loop of climbing rope attached—I slid my feet through them, one at a time, to hang upside down by my knees. Climbing across the ceiling with the suction cups, I dangled over the steel plate that protected the lock.

Now we'd see how well I'd practiced. Taking a few deep breaths, I tried to concentrate on creating flames. It was harder than I'd imagined, knowing how limited the time was, knowing Ryan's father was in the house. . . .

Opening my mouth, I breathed . . . air. *Focus, Sky, you can do this!* I'd done it in the warehouse. I'd even done it in my own foyer, dangling from the chandelier, in a situation that was almost as high-pressure as this. *You can't fail now.*

"*He's coming upstairs,*" Ryan whispered. "*Going silent.*"

I heard the fear in his voice. Not for me. But fear of his father. No one should have to be afraid of their own parents. It wasn't right. But that was a worry for another day. I can only fix one family at a time.

Opening my mouth, I let a stream of fire out. It was small, but it was enough. The flames heated the steel, and the plate slid open to reveal the combination lock.

"Yay, Sky!" Gabriela whispered.

Exactly as I'd practiced, I began to turn the wheel. *Focus,* I told myself. It didn't matter that Ryan's father was in the house. This was no different than any of the practices. All I had to do was focus on my fingertips.

My brain felt fragmented. I thought of my brothers, my father, Mom. I remembered the times I'd talked with Ryan's dad. He was an intimidating man, not just because of his size. You always had the sense that he was angry and that any minute, that anger was going to burst out of his skin. He and Ryan weren't close. Ryan called him "sir" to his face, not "Dad," and they never did any of the clichéd father-son activities. No baseball in the backyard. No barbecues. Mr. Keene was old-fashioned. Always wore a suit. Always insisted on respect and obedience. He ruled his family.

Ryan's mom rarely spoke. She wasn't meek, precisely.

Just distant. She always seemed pleased to see me, offered me milk and cookies when I was little, but then she'd drift away back to her private library. She was a mathematician who worked on esoteric problems and published them in academic journals, but she rarely left the house. Tonight was the exception: they always celebrated their anniversary at some fancy restaurant. A year ago, I'd snuck out with Ryan to our secret alcove while they were at dinner. We'd kissed. Though we hadn't officially started dating then, that was the date I marked on my calendar—the date that my brothers had seen crossed out. This was a very different way to spend the night.

"Music time," I said to myself. Inserting an earbud into the ear without the earpiece, I hit play. Focusing on the beat, I was able to drive the memories back.

Turning the dial slowly, I felt a tiny hitch—first number. Second, third . . .

Closing my eyes, I ignored the blood that rushed into my head. I felt dizzy from hanging upside down. My calves ached. But none of that mattered. *Almost there* . . . Last number.

I told Maximus and Gabriela, "Almost got it."

The lock clicked. I dropped down on bent knees to soften the landing, and no alarms blared. Gabriela tossed another handful of flour. It fell in an empty hall—cracking the lock had turned off both the lasers and the plates, as Ryan had said it would. Gabriela and Maximus hurried to join me.

Together we swung open the vault door.

And inside the vault, the fire beast roared.

CHAPTER FOURTEEN

THE FIRE BEAST BURNED so bright that I felt as if I were staring into the sun. On the security video, it had looked like a blur of light that whipped and writhed, but in person, I saw its shape. Its body was like a bear made of molten lava, its head was a wolf made of flame, and its many arms of white-hot lightning were like the tentacles of an octopus.

All in all, it was very impressive and very terrifying.

Every nerve in my body was screaming, *Run!*

Beside me, Gabriela was screaming in a loud, high-pitched shriek. Quickly, I clapped my hand over her mouth. She whimpered against my palm.

The fire beast, I noticed, did not cross the threshold of the vault. Maximus noticed that too. "The spell that created it also confines it," he said. "Stay here."

Not going to argue with that.

I let my hand fall from Gabriela's mouth. She clung to my arm, and I clung right back as Maximus stepped across the threshold at the same time that he drank from the second vial, the enspelled potion he'd said would require gold to make. He'd never explained what his spell did, and I'd pushed him on it. All he would say is that it was a spell to fight the fire beast, and that was enough information.

I should have asked more questions.

Shedding his trench coat, Maximus shuddered. His whole body seemed to suddenly writhe, and the fire beast lunged toward him. Suddenly, Maximus was engulfed in flames. And his body *became* flames.

He became a fire beast.

Glowing like a piece of the sun, Maximus wrestled the monster. Their flames merged into one another until I couldn't tell where one began and the other ended.

I watched, barely breathing. There was nothing I could do to help. I couldn't tell if Maximus was winning or dying. I saw the monster's head, its fiery teeth. I saw Maximus tear at the beast's chest, as if clawing at its heart. And then the flames whirled and spun like a tornado, faster and faster. White-hot light flared out.

Flinching, I covered my eyes.

And then there was darkness.

"Is it over?" Gabriela whispered.

I lowered my hands. My eyes fought to adjust, to see shapes in the darkness. Fumbling, I switched on a flashlight. I swept it over the vault—and the beam landed on Maximus, bent over and panting but alive.

"It's over," he panted.

"You did it!" Gabriela kept her voice hushed, but her joy was clear.

"Remember: it will reset in thirty minutes," Maximus

warned. Hurrying inside, I helped him straighten. He leaned on me. He didn't seem to be injured. Just drained. "We need to move quickly. The fire beast will regenerate soon."

I tapped my earpiece. "Ryan, are you there?"

"Yeah, I'm back," he said, his voice strained. *"Father left. Not sure where he is right now. That's the problem with taking down the cameras. Going to try to locate him."*

Looking around the vault, I saw gold.

Lots of gold.

So much gold.

Bars in stacks. Coins in glass jars. Goblets on shelves, with piles of plates. And then there was the jewelry, displayed on black velvet as if in a jewelry store: necklace after necklace, as elaborate as anything an Egyptian mummy would wear. Bracelets, rings, earrings, cuff links. All the gold filled my eyes until I felt as if I were swimming in it. I breathed in and tasted the sweet metallic flavor on the back of my throat.

"Steady," Maximus said.

Shaking my head, I tried to knock the sense of SO MUCH GOLD out of it. I wasn't here for the beautiful, shiny, sweet . . . *No, Sky, focus. Find the jewel.* It should be—

I saw it.

In the back corner of the vault. The jewel itself looked like a large moonstone or marble, milky white with swirls of shadowy gray. It lay on a pedestal, on top of a knot of wires.

"Sky, where's the unicorn horn?" Gabriela whispered.

"Ryan?" I asked.

"To the right, third shelf, behind a goblet with rubies on it," Ryan answered. *"Did you find the jewel? Can you see what kind of security is on it?"*

Mom was caught while she was in the vault, possibly by

this last alarm. "It's on what looks like . . . well, honestly, it looks like a bomb." I described it to him, which color wires and how they were connected. All the wires linked an enormous battery and a box wrapped in electrical tape.

Across the vault, I heard gold clink together, and a few coins rattled. "Got it," Gabriela whispered. "Oh wow, it's so beautiful. Sky, you have to see this." Beside her, Maximus was filling a bag with various statuettes and necklaces.

My eyes didn't leave the jewel. This was it! But . . . what was it? It wasn't gold. It wasn't even a diamond. There were other pieces here that had to be worth much more. Why would Mom try to steal this? "Tell me what to do, Ryan. Have you seen this kind of device before?"

"Sky. That is a bomb."

I walked in a circle around the stand. "Okay, so how do I defuse it? I'm not a bomb expert." Liam was, but my idiot brothers had refused to join my heist. Squatting, I tried to look under the jewel. "It looks like it's on a pressure plate."

"Most likely it's rigged so the bomb will blow if you try to move the jewel," Ryan said. *"You'll need to defuse the bomb before you try to take the jewel. This must be how your mother was caught—she must have set off an alarm when she tried to defuse it."*

At least she hadn't blown herself up.

But if Mom couldn't figure it out . . . I took a deep breath. I could do this. I'd come this far already. I had to do it. "Ryan, please tell me you know how to defuse it, preferably without either setting it off or triggering an alarm."

Before he could answer, Maximus stepped beside me. His eyes were sparking again. "Thank you for bringing me here, Sky, and I apologize if my actions bring you any difficulties. It's my sincere hope that your heist is able to be completed without a hitch."

That was an odd speech.

"Maximus . . ."

He handed me his bag of treasures, and I took it without thinking. Pulling off his glove, he placed his bare hand on the jewel. "Goodbye, Sky."

He vanished.

And alarms began to wail.

Ryan in my ear, *"What happened? Did you set it off? Sky, are you okay?"*

"Don't know. Maximus is gone." The jewel still sat there. There wasn't time to defuse the bomb. I didn't know if there would even be time to escape. "Gabriela, we have to get out of here." Hurrying toward her, I pulled her up to her feet. She shoved the horn into her pocket.

Together, we ran for the vault door.

"Sky, the camera feed—I lost it. It's blank. All of it, blank. I don't know what—" The earpiece shrieked, and I yanked it out. Doubled over next to me, Gabriela pulled hers out too.

I pulled her through the corridor. "Keep running." Ahead were the stairs. We ran toward them. If we could make it up the stairs, across the kitchen, across the garden, down the rope—it was too far, too impossible. As we reached the bottom of the stairs, the door at the top was flung open.

Ryan's father filled the doorway.

Mr. Keene, Ryan's father, wore a suit. Black pinstripe, with a blue-and-gold tie. His shoes were shined so they looked as bright as patent-leather tap shoes. He must have had the suit and shoes specially ordered for his size. He was as wide as a wrestler and filled the entire width of the doorway. The kitchen light filtered around him.

I saw all this while my brain helpfully went: *Aaaaaaaaaaaaaaaaaaaaaahhhhhhh!*

"What do we do?" Gabriela whispered.

Aaaaaaaaaaaaaaaaaaaaaaaaaaaaaaaaaaaaaaaaaaaaahhh!

I had a backup plan in mind, of course, as every good thief should, but given that the earpieces were dead, I couldn't tell Ryan we needed a distraction. Besides which, even a seventy-six-trombone marching band wouldn't distract Mr. Keene from the sight of Gabriela and me, decked out in all black with gloves and face masks, in his supposedly secure basement with his vault door open wide behind us.

I couldn't think of a single lie that would explain our presence. We couldn't have looked guiltier if there were neon lights over our heads blinking the word "THIEVES!" My only consolation was that since I had on the face mask, he didn't know who I was.

"Sky Hawkins." His voice was a rumble that reminded me of thunder. He shut the door behind him. As he thudded down the stairs, we retreated back toward the vault. "What a pity. Your father will be heartbroken." He stopped a few feet from us.

Okay then, my only consolation was . . . Eh, nope. Got nothing. "Then don't tell him." Taking off my face mask, I looked him straight in the eye. "He doesn't know I'm here."

Gabriela elbowed me. "Sky, do you think that's the best—"

I cut her off. "I did it all myself. I'm the one who's responsible, and I'm the one you'll bargain with if you want your jewel back." I lifted up Maximus's bag—the jewel wasn't in it, of course, but I was hoping Ryan's father wouldn't realize that before we were long gone. "It looks fragile. It would be a shame if it were to be smashed against the wall."

He flinched—I saw it. Just the briefest of reactions, mostly around his eyes. He did not want me to destroy this jewel. Or more accurately, the jewel I was pretending to have.

"Here are my demands: you tell me where my mother is, you convince the council to reinstate my father and restore my family's honor, and you acknowledge that I have completed my first heist and absolve my colleagues from all responsibility. And I will give it back to you."

He laughed, and I couldn't tell if he was faking it or not. He sounded downright jovial, as if I'd performed a hilarious trick. "Oh, Sky, I admire your gumption, but you didn't successfully complete your heist. You are in no position to bargain."

"I have your jewel."

"And I have you trapped." He sounded apologetic. Opening his mouth wider, he let flames roll out. Gabriela shrieked and scurried backward. He kept breathing flames. They grew, feeding on one another, and we backed up, closer to the vault.

Holding her sleeve to the mouth of her face mask, Gabriela was coughing. She dropped to her knees. Sweat was pouring off her. Maximus's spell must have worn off, or else the heat from his flames was higher than the spell could handle. Gabriela clutched my arm. "Sky!"

The flames weren't hot enough to hurt me, but they *would* hurt her. I put my arms around her, as if I could shield her from the smoke and heat. "Stop! She's human! You'll kill her! Please, you can have your jewel back. Just stop!"

He sucked in, and the fire flew back into his mouth—a stream of flames that looked like red, orange, and gold water as it poured in between his lips. He was drinking the fire, sucking it out of the room. The smoke dissipated until I couldn't even smell it anymore.

"Whoa, can you do that?" Gabriela whispered. Her voice sounded weak and rough, as if someone had rubbed sandpaper over her throat. I helped her to her feet.

"I didn't even know that was possible." There were many things council members were taught that ordinary wyverns weren't. I wondered if Dad could do that. He'd never mentioned it. What else could we do? Not that this was the time to explore that.

"How did you fool my security? Who else helped you?" He strode forward. We were both staring at him as if we were frightened rabbits and he was the hawk—if we held still enough, maybe he wouldn't see us. But he wasn't a hawk, and he saw us just fine. He plucked the earpiece out of my ear. Holding it up to the light, he examined it. "Who's on the other end, Sky?"

I didn't answer.

"Sky? Who's listening?"

"No one," I told him, and hoped he wouldn't fill the hall with smoke again. I didn't know how I could protect both Gabriela and Ryan.

He gave me a look that would have burned me to the ground, if our eyes could shoot fire. Sticking the earpiece into his own ear, he barked, "Identify yourself."

I held my breath and prayed that the earpiece was still broken, or that Ryan would have the sense to stay quiet.

Mr. Keene scowled. "Ryan, is that you? I know it's you."

I kept my face blank. *Don't give him away*, I told myself. "It's not Ryan."

He glared at me as if I were dirt smeared on his kitchen floor. "My son did always have an unreasonable soft spot for you. I told his mother that he'd try something like this. She maintained he was perfectly obedient, but I know my boy."

"It was my heist—my idea, my plan, my fault! Ryan didn't have anything to do with this. We haven't spoken since the Reckoning."

"See, now I know you're lying. While I admit I misconstrued the purpose of your meetings, I do know you met him two weeks ago at the ice cream store, and you have been meeting him every day at Hunter Creek Lodge."

I kept my mouth shut.

He tapped the earpiece again and raised his voice. If the mics were working, they would have picked up his words. "Ryan, can you hear me? I won't be angry with you. She *is* pretty. How about we plan a trip to Europe this summer? Two months. I'll arrange for you to meet more of our kind. There are many more youngsters there who might appeal to you."

I felt my heart squeeze. The thought of his meeting other wyvern girls didn't bother me. The certainty that his father wouldn't let us be together *did*. I had killed any chance of having a relationship with Ryan—the only question was what else I'd also ruined. I thought of Dad and my brothers and felt sick.

"Ryan, I have Sky Hawkins here with me. She is un-harmed, and I will allow her to remain so if you cooperate. Please, son. I know you care about her."

Gabriela clutched my arm even tighter. Her short nails dug into my skin, but I didn't dislodge her. It was the polite-ness that was chilling—if Mr. Keene were roaring in anger, it would be easier to roar back, but his tone was so very civil, as if we were talking about whether we'd stay for tea and crumpets.

He frowned harder. "Ryan, if you don't reply—"

"It's broken!" Gabriela chirped. She could have been right. Or Ryan could have been keeping silent to protect himself. Or to protect me. "The fire beast fried them."

It was plausible enough that I wondered if it was true.

"How very fortunate. It would break his mother's heart to lose him." Mr. Keene exhaled with true relief. He then plucked the earpiece out of his ear, and he crushed it be-neath his shiny leather shoe. "Yours as well, my dear."

Gabriela hesitated.

"Now." There was steel in his voice.

Reaching under her face mask, she dug out the earpiece and handed it to him.

It popped as he ground it into the floor.

Gabriela whimpered. "What are you going to do with us?"

He smiled, a little sadly. "I won't harm you. Have no fear of that. In fact, you will find you have a bright future ahead of you, if you cooperate."

I didn't trust him, primarily because of how ominous this whole conversation had been but also because of the way he was smiling, as if he pitied us. "Is this what you said to my mother, before you killed her?"

It was a shot in the dark, a hope that I'd surprise him into revealing something.

"Sky, I am shocked you'd think that of me. Our ancestors may have lacked morals, but we have a clear code we all follow. Wyverns do not kill wyverns."

Gabriela gulped. "You did not mention what you do with humans."

"We bribe them," I told her. As threatening as he looked and sounded, he wasn't going to hurt her, right? He'd offer her a large sum of money to never speak of this again, and as for me . . . more shunning? Stripping us of the rest of our fortune? Drop us to the lowest of the low? Take our house, our pride, our everything and declare us outcast? He was right: Dad was going to be heartbroken. I'd made things worse.

"Indeed we do, my dear. Sky, how very clever of you to use a human to evade the spell," Mr. Keene said. "Such great potential, wasted. But I do understand family loyalty. That is why I do all that I do: to protect my family. In a way, Sky, we have much in common."

This was beginning to sound like an evil-villain monologue.

I'm wrong, I thought. *He* is *going to kill us*. I hadn't expected it of Ryan's father. He'd always seemed intimidating but sane. I calculated the distance between us and the stairs. If I threw the "jewel" at him to distract him . . . It was too far. We'd never make it. Not both of us. "This is my first heist," I told him. "All I'm doing is following tradition."

Mr. Keene did not look as if he intended to let us go. Smoke was tendriling out of the corners of his mouth. "But you did not target gold. You took *that*." He pointed at my bag.

Now! I thought. "Then let me give it back!" Throwing the bag at him, I tackled him and screamed at Gabriela, "Run! Go!"

She ran.

I heard her pound up the stairs, and then Mr. Keene threw me backward into the vault. I skidded across the vault floor and crashed against a wall of shelves. Necklaces and coins fell around me like rain. On his feet, he advanced and then shut the vault door behind him. It sealed with a solid *whoosh.*

"Foolish," he said. "She's a danger to us all."

"She's not! She knows nothing."

"I very much hope that's true."

"I barely know anything." On my feet, I backed away. Gold goblets shook on a nearby shelf. One toppled over and landed on the floor with a clink. "I only targeted it because my mother wanted it. Why did she? What is it?"

"Oh, my poor foolish child. You don't even know . . . Well, you will understand soon enough. You have attempted to steal the Door." With a flourish, he opened the bag—and then frowned and peered into it. "Clever girl. I admire your gumption."

"A door?" I repeated. That made no sense. What did that mean? A door? To where? Also, it was round and smallish. Not door shaped.

I heard a voice, faint, through the vault door, and then a pounding on it. "Sky?" Ryan! He was here! "Sky, are you okay? Father, are you in there? Don't hurt her!"

Mr. Keene held his finger to his lips. "Say nothing, and I

will spare him. No punishment. No consequences. You can keep him safe."

"Sky!" Ryan called. "I know you're in there!"

Gabriela must have run straight to him. I hoped she'd fled after that. I didn't know how I was going to protect her if she saw and heard too much.

Ryan kept knocking on the vault door. He must have been pounding with both fists.

Mr. Keene looked at me. "If you call to him, I will have to send him too. If you don't, I can protect him. He will never know."

My heart was thudding in my throat, and my stomach had clenched into a hard knot. My eyes felt hot, but I wasn't going to let him see me cry. "He knows I'm here. He'll know you did something to me." Mr. Keene wouldn't dare kill me while Ryan knew I was here. He wouldn't want Ryan to think he was a murderer. I could call his bluff.

"He will think you ran, like your mother."

Mom. I looked at the jewel. It seemed so innocent and inert and non-door-like. I thought of how Maximus had vanished. "What did you do to my mother?" I asked.

"It's a simple choice, Sky. Stay here, and I will be forced to kill you to protect my family's secrets. Or touch the Door and be reunited with your mother. Alive and safe."

He wasn't bluffing.

"Don't hurt Ryan. Or my friend. Please! They're innocent. I coerced them. It was all my idea." The pounding was muffled. I knew Ryan couldn't hear our voices. I wondered if he'd believe that I ran—surely he knew me better than that. "If I do this, you have to leave them alone. You don't hurt Ryan or my friend or my family."

"Touch the Door, Sky, and all will be well."

Ryan hammered the door. *"Sky!"*

I looked at the vault door and understood, at last, why Ryan had shunned me, why he had refused to be with me, why he'd broken both our hearts. It had been to protect me from his father. And now it was my turn to protect the people I loved. Kneeling, I laid my hand on the jewel.

And the world vanished.

~

Shiny.

That was the one clear thought I had.

All around me, it looked like an oil slick in sunlight. It glimmered with rainbows, all streaked and smushed and twisted and—*oh no, I'm twisting!* I felt like a corkscrew, twisting, my arms wrapped around me, my legs pretzeled, my body . . .

And then I was stretched, like taffy, long and thin, but it didn't hurt. It just felt . . . stretchy, as if my skin was supple plastic that bent and twisted and stretched.

It was exactly as freaky as the intro to *Doctor Who*.

My mom used to watch that show when I was a kid, and I'd run out of the kitchen screaming, with my hands over my ears, when the theme song came on. I have a low threshold for scary TV. Forget horror movies. You'd find me wedged underneath my bed.

Mom.

Thinking about her calmed me. A little.

I couldn't feel my heart beating too fast.

I couldn't feel my feet or my hands or my face. Raising

my hands, I moved to touch my face—and saw my hands were streaked with the same rainbows. They burrowed through my skin, bursting out between my fingers. *Gabriela would have liked this*, I thought.

And then I started screaming.

Silently.

In my head.

Because I couldn't feel my body or my throat, and now the rainbows were darkening, as if the light were dimming slowly, slowly, slowly, in blackness, and I couldn't feel or see or hear or scream.

Thud.

Pain shot through my body. My body! I could feel it again! Groaning, I tried to open my eyes. My eyes stung as if needles had been jabbed into them. I squeezed them shut again.

"Amazing!" a voice cried. A young woman or a girl. A stranger. "On my watch! I never thought . . . Oh, this is incredible! Look at you! You're whole and alive!"

"Who are you?" I tried to say, but it came out as little grunts.

"Ooh, you're conscious! This is great! How do you feel? You must feel terrible. Don't try to speak. Just rest. You're safe. You're home."

CHAPTER FIFTEEN

AT LEAST WHEN I was inside the rainbow, it didn't hurt. Now it hurt. My body felt like a dozen kindergartners had been pummeling me with their small, vicious fists. I felt like my skin must be one giant bruise. Everywhere was sore. "Ow," I said. "Ow, ow, ow."

"You poor thing! Here, drink this," the same girl commanded.

A cup was pressed against my lips. It felt cold—metal. Gold? The liquid inside smelled like wet moss. I took a sip anyway, because being poisoned might feel like an improvement. It slid down my throat in a gob.

"Oh, this is so exciting!" the girl said. "On my watch! And so soon after the other one! Worm said it would never happen, but I told him you can't predict—"

"Other one?" I tried to ask, but a cough shook my body.

"Shh, you're all right. Breathe. In, out." She patted my shoulder. "You've had a frightening journey, but you're free of the darkness now and safe. Can you tell me your name?"

"Sky." My voice sounded rough. I coughed and tried again. "Sky Hawkins. My mother . . . she's supposed to be here. Anabeth Hawkins. Is she here?"

"Stay here. I'll send out word. Now, no more worries. Rest! You're in a place of peace." Footsteps retreated.

There was a cool breeze on my skin, and the air smelled odd. Like spring flowers and apples, except sharper. I should have asked questions: Where am I? Who are you? What happened? How do I get home? But all I wanted was to see my mom.

It occurred to me that she—whoever she was—hadn't actually said whether Mom was here, just that she'd "send out word."

A few minutes later, I realized that the pain had begun to fade. I only felt like I'd rolled down a hill covered in rocks and pointy sticks. Sitting up, I cracked open my eyes.

It was dark, except for the glow from the jewel. The milky orb sat on a pedestal of black stone that looked as if it had grown out of the floor. Pushing myself up to my feet, I toddled over to it, but I didn't touch it. How could it be here and also in Ryan's family's vault?

Stupid question.

It was a *door*. And I was on the other side of it.

And maybe Mom was too!

As my eyes adjusted to the dim light, I saw that the door and I were in a windowless room that dripped with wealth. The walls, as much as I could see of them, were covered in a mosaic of jewels—diamonds, sapphires, rubies. The floor and ceiling were sheathed in gold.

An archway led to a corridor. It was lit with sconces with candles inside, and the light bounced off the jeweled walls, making it look like the inside of a lava lamp, slowly writhing as a breeze breathed through the passage. I followed the source of the breeze.

Up ahead, I heard voices.

Friendly voices?

I couldn't tell. It didn't sound like anyone was cackling evilly, which meant that if I was at the mercy of murderers, then at least they weren't being clichéd about it.

My heart beat fast, and I wiped my sweaty hands on my jeans. *Don't be scared*, I told myself. No one had hurt me while I lay in pain. The unknown girl had been kind. Even oddly excited to see me. But I couldn't stop feeling as if my insides were churning.

The air tasted wrong.

Inching forward, I saw light ahead, actual sunlight, not the reflected candlelight that was dancing across the walls and making me feel seasick. Wherever I was, it was daytime. I went toward the sunlight.

Soon I heard more sounds. Birdcalls instead of voices, but not from any bird that I'd ever heard. Closer to the end of the corridor, the air tasted like flowers and frost and fire, charred trees and fresh soil and roses. It was sharper and cleaner than any air I'd ever breathed before. Emerging through a gold-encrusted archway, I stopped and stared.

I was on a cliff on the side of a mountain.

Spread before me was a valley, and it was filled with dragons: gold, emerald, and sapphire, winging freely in the sunlight, the sun glinting off their scales. Below in the lush green, a herd of unicorns—yes, actual unicorns with pointy, sparkly horns; Gabriela would have shrieked—raced next to a burbling brook. It looked like a tapestry come to life, or like the cover of a cheesy old paperback, but here, real, in brilliant colors that made my eyes water.

And I couldn't help the thought that went through my mind: *I'm dead.*

I'd walked through the Door and died, and this was heaven. I looked down. I was on a cliff. A few feet forward, the rocks ended in a plunge all the way down to the green valley and a snaking blue river.

The birdcalls echoed, and then I realized they weren't birds at all—they were the dragons, picking up the calls and amplifying them. Dragons, as plentiful as birds, swooped through the air, skimming the trees below and soaring up to the clouds. It felt like watching fireworks, but they didn't fizzle or fade. I'd never seen so many wyverns flying so freely and openly in daylight.

Honestly, I'd never seen even one wyvern in his or her dragon form. We'd lost the ability to transform over time—the skill was forgotten and the talent died.

But here were lots of dragons.

Not to mention unicorns.

I thought of Gabriela and the unicorn horn—truthfully, a part of me had thought it was fake. But maybe not. Maybe it was from here. From . . . Home?

"This is crazy," I breathed.

As they swooped and soared, their jeweled scales glinted. It looked as if someone had spilled rubies, emeralds, and sapphires into the clouds.

From between the clouds, a familiar voice called, "Sky!"

"Mom?"

It sounded like her, but . . .

A shimmering green dragon winged its way through the air to the cliff and then transformed to human in midair and dropped in a crouch. And then I was running toward her along the cliff, and she was running toward me.

She caught me in her arms, and we both fell to our knees. She was stroking my hair. "Oh, Sky, Sky, why are you here? Are you okay?" She pushed me to arm's length so she could look at me. "My beautiful, clever girl, what did you do?"

"Long story. You transformed! How did you transform? How could . . ." I didn't know what to ask or say first. "Oh, Mom, I didn't know where you were. I didn't imagine you were *here*. Is this heaven?"

"It's Home." Mom touched my cheek gently, as if she was afraid I'd disappear. I knew how she felt. I wanted to hug her again, like I hadn't hugged her since I was a little kid, and hold her tight so that I wouldn't lose her ever again.

"Home," I repeated. The place our kind had come from, the place where magic was born, the place we belonged. Over the valley, dragons—wyverns, like me—pirouetted in the sky. Sunlight glittered off their scales. "Wow."

She laughed. "Yes, 'wow.' Oh, Sky, I can't believe you're here! Where is your father? And your brothers?" Standing, she squinted to see into the jeweled tunnel, as if expecting Dad and my brothers to race out to greet us. "Were they caught as well?"

I scrambled to my feet. "They're going to be so worried!" They wouldn't know what happened to me. They didn't know my target or any of my plans. All they thought was I'd gone out with Gabriela. . . . They'd question her, if Ryan's father didn't get to her first. They'd blame her. And what about Ryan? His father knew he was involved. "I have to get back!"

Mom patted my hand. "Sky, calm down."

"I can't calm down! There's no time to waste—"

"Take a deep breath." She held both my hands and looked me in the eye. "Breathe with me. In and out." I inhaled and exhaled, deep and slow.

Inside, I was shrieking, *Mom!* I don't think I'd fully allowed myself to believe she was alive until this moment. But she was! "Dad said you weren't dead but you couldn't come home. He wouldn't explain why. He was really angry with you. It's been hard, Mom. We missed you."

"And I missed you!" She kissed my forehead.

It felt like a dream. A weird mixed-up happy-anxious dream, where I didn't know what I was supposed to think, but I felt like I'd been held upside down and shaken a few times. "Did Maximus come through too? Is he here?"

She frowned. Even frowning, she was beautiful. The little crease between her eyebrows was a perfect divot. "What does that wizard have to do with you?"

Behind me, I heard, "You know our recent arrival!" I recognized the voice—it was the girl who had spoken to me when I came through—and turned around to see her for the first time. She looked about my age, maybe a year older. She was dressed in what looked like a kind of armor, made of hard green scales. "I knew there had to be a connection between the two of you. He came through just before my shift started. He is in the Hall of the Returned, reunited with his wife."

His *wife*? But she was dead! How—

"Sky, this is Novi," Mom said. "She's one of the honor

guards who watch the Door and welcome . . . well, us. They call us the Returned." Mom bowed to her. "Thank you for sending the call to find me. You have given me a joy I never thought to have."

Novi was beaming as if she'd just received a visit from Santa. Not that she'd necessarily even heard of Santa. Did they have Santa here? How about ice cream? I felt a hysterical giggle bubble up in my throat, and I pushed it back down. *I found Mom*, I told myself. *Everything will be okay.*

"Novi herself is from Home but was raised among the Returned—that's how she speaks English and knows our customs. She's a good person to know."

"Are any more coming through?" Novi asked.

I thought of Gabriela and Ryan. "I don't know. There were two more in my crew. . . ." Mr. Keene wouldn't want to send his son away, and he didn't know who Gabriela was. Yet. I wasn't sure what would happen to her once he figured it out. I hoped he'd merely bribe her for her silence, but I couldn't be certain. "You said Maximus's wife is here?"

"She was exiled a year ago," Mom said. "Lovely woman. You'll like her."

Novi bowed to both of us. "I must return to my post, in case the other two come through. This is the most exciting day I've ever had! I can't wait to tell Worm!" She then pivoted and ran back through the archway, into the mountain, before we could respond.

Mom looped her arm around mine and propelled me toward the mountainside. "Come with me. There are people I want you to meet. And there's so much to show you! You must be hungry too—coming through the portal made me ravenous." As we approached, the jewels in the wall began to pulse with a golden light and then rearrange themselves. Shifting, they separated to create a new archway. "Neat, isn't it? It's technology, not magic, I'm told. The wyverns of Home have developed and changed since the Dark Ages too. But don't worry—you won't meet any of the purebred wyverns. They don't associate with us."

"Huh," I said as we walked through. "Mom . . ."

She propelled me quickly through the hallway—or more accurately, tunnel, though it was fancier than any cave tunnel I'd ever seen—which led to a set of stone stairs. Below was a vast hall filled with both people and dragons.

Not people and dragons, I corrected.

It was filled with wyverns.

"Welcome to the Hall of the Returned," Mom said. "These caverns are set aside for those of us who came from Earth, as well as their families. While the rest of Home may be very different from what you're used to, you'll feel comfortable here."

Yeah, I doubted that.

A blue dragon was stretched in front of a fireplace. Another, a red dragon, was draped on a set of steps. A third sat upright with wings folded, a circle of wyverns in human form around him. He looked as if he was pontificating about something.

"My friends!" my mother called. "My daughter has joined us!"

Heads turned—both human and dragon—and then cheers and chatter filled the hall, rising up to the gold-sheathed ceiling. She shooed me down the stairs, and we were surrounded by both people and dragons. I was hugged, was kissed, had my hand shaken. Meanwhile, my mom was saying names: Joseph, Ivan, Sophia, Serene, Alfred, and other names that didn't sound familiar, like Kyandra, Winar, Lysinari, Gendon . . . I lost track of which name attached to which face. But I did see a familiar face, by the hearth, who hadn't come to greet me.

Moving through the crowd, I headed for Maximus. "You—" I began.

"You're welcome," he said.

That stopped me short.

"You wanted to find your mother," he pointed out.

"You got me *caught*," I said. "You lied to me."

"Technically, I didn't lie," he said. "I merely left out details."

"Details are everything! You didn't know what Mr. Keene was going to do to me. He could have hurt me. Or killed me. Gabriela and Ryan could both be in danger because of you." I poked him in the shoulder, one poke for each of them.

Mom was beside me, a formidable tower of motherliness. "You endangered my daughter?"

He spread his hands as if to ward her off. "Calculated risk. I was certain he'd send her through if he caught her. Exile is, after all, the customary way Thomas Keene deals with threats."

"You wanted to come here," I accused.

"Absolutely."

It was only then that I noticed the blue dragon who had her tail wrapped around Maximus. She was watching me with swirling gold eyes. Her tongue darted around her teeth. "Maximus, did you endanger a child in order to be with me?" the dragon asked, a puff of smoke rising from her nostrils.

He smiled up at her with a look that was so adoring that I could practically taste the syrupy sweetness. "I'd endanger the world to be with you."

"That's sweet. But I believe you owe this girl an apology."

His face fell. "Oh. Um, yes. Sky, please accept my apology. And please allow me to introduce my wife, Angela. I thought I'd lost her forever. She'd told me she was searching for the Door to Home—a fairy tale, I believed. I have never been so happy to be wrong."

"I'd heard hints that a portal still existed," the dragon said. Her voice was mellow and smooth and flowed around us as if it came from multiple stereo speakers. "I followed the clues, and they led me to Thomas Keene. Before I could warn anyone, he came for me. Told me that the truth would endanger his family, and he sent me here."

"I thought she was dead," Maximus said, still gazing at her. "But when your mother came to me, I began to hope. And then when you, Sky, showed me the gold talon amulet, I knew. Angela hadn't been chasing a fairy tale. The Door existed, and there was a chance that my love still lived on the other side."

"How did the amulet prove anything?" I asked.

"It came from Home," he said. "Surely you could sense that. It smelled of this place. A wyvern from Home must have brought it through the Door."

"He did," Mom confirmed. "I was told it was all that remained of him after the fire beast within the Keene vault killed him, and I have no reason to doubt that. My contact was very convincing. Once I'd seen the proof, I knew what had to be done."

"As did I," Maximus said to her. "You should have shown

it to me when you came for the spells. I would have believed you. I thought you were chasing dreams, like my Angela." He gazed up at the dragon again, and I'd never seen an expression so full of love and devoid of rational thought.

"How were you caught?" I asked Mom.

Mom made a face. "My contact didn't know about the explosive on the jewel itself. Liam could have defused it without triggering an alarm, but I clipped the blue wire, which alerted security. Sky, how did you even manage to reach it?"

"She led her first heist," Maximus said. "And thanks to her bravery, ingenuity, and persistence, I've been reunited with the love of my life. Sky, I owe you a debt of gratitude."

I raised my eyebrows. His words were over the top, but he seemed to mean them.

Mom's face lit up. "Oh, Sky, I'm so proud of you!" She hugged me again—she'd never hugged me this much. As I was squished against her, I had to tell myself not to cry. It was all well and good that Mom was proud of me, but I had been caught. "I'm amazed your father let you lead. Such a dangerous target. You must have won his trust."

Or lied to him and snuck out. "Not exactly."

My stomach chose that moment to rumble.

Smoke puffed from Angela's snout. "She needs food," Maximus's wife declared. "She's been through the portal. You may take from my share."

"She's newly arrived," a man at a nearby table said. "We'll all share."

"Speak for yourself." An older woman. "Some of us don't have the ranking for it."

Thanking Angela and the man profusely, Mom swept me away from Maximus and his wife and toward a long table. She waved toward a silver-coated wall, and a door slid open. A faceless man of silver metal rolled out carrying a tray with bowls balanced on top.

"Home has *robots*?" When I'd pictured a dragon homeland, I hadn't pictured, well, *Star Trek*. But I supposed, as Mom had said, time had passed here, just as it had back on Earth.

Whoa, that was a weird phrase: "back on Earth."

I watched the silver metal man deliver bowls to wyverns throughout the Hall—he seemed to be moving in a deliberate pattern, but I couldn't tell what determined it. It wasn't by table, like in a restaurant, nor was it based on who seemed the hungriest. A few looked as if they hadn't eaten in days. With haunted eyes, they tracked the server's every move. Then I shook my head. "Mom, we can't stay here. You belong with us. Everyone will be so worried. They're already worried about you. But now me . . . We can't do that to Dad. And Charles, I know he'll blame himself. And Liam isn't making jokes much anymore. Tuck has been through at least a dozen hobbies since you left. He doesn't talk about becoming a chef anymore. Dad thinks he's only going to drift from thing to thing until he's exhausted. And Dad won't let anyone go on heists. I think it's only going to get worse. Mr. Keene will punish them for my actions. He'll insist the council declare them outcast—"

"Oh, sweetie, our people don't do that anymore. Your father will appeal to the council. He has sway. You can't worry about him—"

"Not anymore. They stripped him of his rank. They blamed him for you."

Mom paled. "They shouldn't have done that." She sank onto a bench. "He wasn't involved. He'd made it very clear he didn't want to be involved—like Maximus, he thought the Door was a fairy tale. Or at best, a lost treasure that would never be found. So I was careful to ensure he wasn't involved. Thomas Keene knew that." Mom looked at me, her hands clasped tightly in front of her. "Tell me what happened, Sky. Everything."

But before I could reply, Novi, the young honor guard, jumped in. "There's no point in wallowing in the past! Your future has begun. You've escaped! You're Home now." She plopped down on the bench beside me and beamed at me.

"Earth is my home," I said.

"You're only saying that because you don't know any better," Novi said. "As many of the Returned often say, you've escaped hell and found your way to heaven. You don't know how lucky you are!"

The silver metal man delivered a golden bowl to Mom. I watched him pivot and then glide across the hall, whirring to deliver another bowl to another wyvern. "Heaven has robots? Seriously?" When I pictured heaven, I pictured angelic choirs. And when I pictured Home, I imagined a medieval Tolkien-esque world, with dragons in dark, dingy caves squatting over their hoards. Not this—a cathedral-like hall, with high-tech servants.

Novi turned to my mother. "Anabeth, she has to start training. The next Reckoning is in three days, and she'll need to be ready."

"They have Reckonings here?" I asked.

"Of course," Novi said, smug. "They're the heart of our civilization."

Mom nodded. "Our ancestors brought a few ideas from Home to Earth. The Reckonings were one of them, though over time the criteria for determining ranking diverged between the two worlds."

"What do you mean?" I asked, then I shook my head. "Never mind. Tell me all about it when we're home. I mean, *home* home. Not Home. You know what I mean."

"You can't!" Novi chirped, horror written across her face.

"What do you mean, I can't?" I didn't like the way the wyverns around us had quieted, or the way they looked at me with pity.

"Sky, honey . . . you know why," Mom said gently. "There's a fire beast on the other side of the Door. You must have seen it—its heat is more intense than any wyvern can withstand."

"Everyone who has ever gone through has been sent back, dead," Novi said. She shot a pointed look at the wyverns at nearby tables, and they pretended they hadn't been eavesdropping.

"By now, the fire beast will have regenerated," Mom said. "You can't return."

"But all we need is a spell!" I said. "Maximus will help us—he lied to me, so he owes me. He can cook up another spell to fight the fire beast—"

"There's no wizardry here," Novi interrupted.

Mom nodded. "When I first arrived, I tried to find another spell, but there are no wyvern wizards in all of Home. Wizardry doesn't work here—there's a lack of ley lines to interact with the wizard's will. I'm told that's essential. Even if Maximus wanted to help us, he can't. Here, he is an ordinary wyvern, only as powerful as his wings and fire."

I didn't like what I was hearing. Didn't want to believe it. Didn't want to listen to it. I was only a second away from clapping my hands over my ears and shouting la-la-la, but her words bored into me anyway. "But . . . there must be a way!"

"Don't worry," Novi said. "You're going to love it here."

"No! No, no, and no! We have to leave!"

"I'm sorry, Sky," Mom said, "but we can't."

CHAPTER SIXTEEN

I ATE AFTER THAT.

Yes, it was upsetting news, but I was also hungry, and the soup was incredible. Golden in color, it tasted like what I'd imagined molten gold would taste like, if you could eat metal. So rich and sweet, it made my tongue tingle, throat warm, and head buzz.

Novi pressed a cup into my hand. The drink was minty water, and I couldn't tell if mint had been added or if that was just the way water tasted around here. Everything felt a little . . . odd. Some of the people smiled and laughed and talked the way I was used to, but others greeted each other with formal bows and curtsies as if they were in a royal court.

Everyone wore clothes that were strange too, though I suppose it makes sense for fashion to be different in another dimension. The vast majority wore cloths wrapped around them like saris. Novi was an exception, though I noticed a few others dressed as she was—it must be a uniform. Mom was wearing a deep-purple wrap that was held with a ribbon at her neck. She also wore an amulet at her throat shaped like a talon with markings on it that looked very similar to the one I'd found in the chocolate box—exactly like it, in fact. Looking at her closely, I saw she had deep-purple scratches around the amulet, on her throat and shoulders. They looked like fresh scars.

"What happened?" I asked, pointing at them.

"Eat," she told me. "You'll have time to get used to the way things are here."

I put the spoon down. "Okay, that sounded ominous. What aren't you telling me?"

"You don't need to worry yet."

"Again, ominous. You're worrying me just by saying that. Mom, is it dangerous here? Are you in danger?" I should have insisted we go back through the Door right away. If we'd been quick enough, the fire beast would still have been vanquished, and together we could have fought our way past Mr. Keene. Except given how long I'd talked with Mr. Keene . . . It might have been too late already by the time I'd been reunited with Mom.

"Don't be ridiculous! Your mother is not in any danger at all," Novi said, digging into her own food. "She's already established her place. It's you. You'll need to be judged in the Reckoning." She flashed me a cheerful smile.

Mom sighed. "Our Reckoning on Earth is a pale imitation of the original. While our council examines behavior and compares hoards to determine our place in society, here it is based on wyvern skill. You earn your rank with your abilities."

Yep, this *did* sound ominous. "What kind of abilities?"

"Finish your meal," Mom said. "Novi will take you on a tour. You'll understand better once you see." She smiled at me, but the smile seemed overbright and only made me more nervous.

Novi jumped up. "Come on! The sooner you see, the sooner you can begin to prepare." She beckoned to another guard, an older woman in the same scalelike armor, and began conferring with her.

"This isn't exactly the reunion I pictured," I commented.

Mom squeezed my hand. "I didn't picture any reunion. I thought I'd lost you forever." She smiled at me again, but this smile was tinged with sadness. "I would give anything to undo what happened."

"What you did, you mean," I said, and then immediately wished I hadn't said it.

The same sad smile. "I wouldn't change what I did; I'd only change the fact that I failed." She looked across the hall, and I followed her gaze—to Maximus and his blue dragon wife. The dragon had lowered her massive head, and Maximus was caressing her scaly cheek. "Thomas Keene has used the Door to remove his enemies for far too long. He's kept its existence a secret from the rest of the wyverns on Earth, even the council. And that's wrong. The Door is supposed to connect our worlds, not divide them. It certainly isn't meant to split families against their will or knowledge."

I stared at her. My mother, the idealist? "You weren't stealing for our hoard?"

She stood. "I don't expect you to understand. You're a young wyvern. Still . . . Come and see what the council has been denying you, denying all of us. Come and see your birthright." Her voice was ringing, and she'd caught everyone's attention. Especially mine.

Getting up, I wiped my lips with a napkin—it was nice to see they had napkins. If this was a different world or pocket dimension or whatever, everything could be different, right down to hygiene habits.

Funny how the brain fixates on little details when the big details are too overwhelming.

I gawked at all the wyverns as we passed through the crowd. Several of them stared back at me. An older man half waved, and I paused. He looked familiar . . . like one of Ryan's uncles, the one who always burned the hamburgers at barbecues. But I thought he was dead! Yes, in fact, the longer I stared at him, the more certain I was. He'd tried to lead a heist. It had failed, and he'd never returned. "Hey, Mom, I know him."

"You may know many here, or know their relatives. Thomas has been sending his enemies through for some time," Mom said. "He acquired the Door by accident—the wyvern he stole it from didn't know its worth, but Thomas quickly figured out what it was. I believe in the beginning, he intended to share it with the council, but then he fell in love with the human woman who became his wife. There were many on the council who opposed his marriage. Those who objected to his marrying a human, who made threats against her—they disappeared. And came here, to join the exiles."

"All these wyverns are from Earth?" I waved at all the people and dragons.

"Not all. Some are friends and relatives, born here in

Home. Like Novi. Novi was born here, but her father was exiled from Earth by Ryan's father—he was one of the first to object to Ryan's mother. After he came here, he married Novi's mother, a wyvern from Home. All the exiles from Earth and their families tend to live together. We are more comfortable with one another than the general wyvern population. For one thing, there is the language barrier. Most native wyverns don't speak English. For another . . . the general wyvern population doesn't trust us."

"It's not that we don't trust you!" Novi said, returning to us. "We're thrilled to have you back! You escaped a hell world that we can't even imagine."

"Mmm," Mom said. "Among those older than Novi, there is a measure of distrust, due to the reputation of our ancestors. Apparently, our ancestors were not satisfied with the outcome of the Reckonings, and that didn't sit well with those who *were* satisfied, the ones in power."

Exiting the hall, we were in another corridor. "Well, I'm happy you're here," Novi said. "And soon you'll be happy about it too. You'll see."

Mom squeezed my hand. She was touching me more than she ever had, as if she was afraid I was a dream that would vanish if she didn't keep proving I was real. I felt the same way. Never expected us to become a family of huggers. I wondered what my brothers would think of this new hug-friendly Mom. "Novi's right—you'll like it here, once you're used to it," Mom said. "There's beauty here beyond your wildest imagination. Wait until you see the waterfalls! Greater than any on Earth. And the mountains—they'll make you cry, they're so beautiful. I want to show them to you. I want to watch a sunset with you. The colors aren't the same. Oh, and the stars! You're going to love the stars, Sky. They remind me of when I was younger, when your father and I were first married, and we used to lie on the roof and look up at the stars. You could see so many on clear nights. Here, you can see so many more!"

"Sounds pretty." Watching her, I tried to understand what she'd gone through, coming here all alone, unable to return home. *I'll find a way home*, I thought. There had to be a way to defeat the fire beast.

"You can show her all of that after the Reckoning," Novi promised.

"Why are you being so nice to us?" I asked Novi. "Who are you?" She reminded me of Gabriela, bubbly and perky and optimistic. I wished Gabriela had come through the Door with me. She would have liked to see all this.

"It's Novi's job to be nice to us," Mom said. "Novi did very well for herself at the last Reckoning and was given the honor guard post. You could do worse than to have her show you what's at stake." She stepped back, and Novi propelled me forward.

I twisted my head. "Wait—you aren't coming with us?" I'd just found her again! I didn't want to leave her.

"She's not allowed," Novi said, pointing to Mom's amulet, as if that explained everything. "Your mother isn't ranked high enough to access all you need to see."

"But I don't—"

Mom's smile was tight. I'd forgotten how much she could convey with just a curve of her mouth. Her lips could speak volumes without a single word passing them. "I'll be right here when you get back, and then we'll talk more. I'll braid your hair, if you like. You've let it get tangled."

I touched my hair. I'd shoved it into a ponytail for the heist, and clumps of it had tangled during all the excitement. It wasn't exactly my top priority.

"Go with Novi," Mom urged. "She's an honor guard, allowed to go anywhere, and you're unranked, so restrictions don't apply to you yet. I must stay here." I wanted to ask a hundred more questions, about what she meant by "unranked" and why we weren't talking about defeating the fire beast and why . . . But Novi tugged on my sleeve and propelled me forward.

I let her lead me while all the questions swirled tornado-like inside me. Soon we reached an archway and emerged from within the mountain. This ledge was narrow, and the cliff drop-off was immediate. Novi swung herself over the edge, holding on to a rope. "One moment, and I'll find an easier way for you."

Obviously, I didn't wait for her. Grabbing onto the rope, I followed her.

She looked back in surprise.

"I like climbing," I told her.

With me behind her, we went from rope to rope up the rocky slope. "Most wyvern fly," she called, over the wind. "But there are rudimentary alternatives all over the mountains, for the disadvantaged to use."

We were near the top of a mountain, and the wind whirled around us. Snow clung to a few rocks, but so did tiny yellow flowers. The air had a bite to it but wasn't unbearable, and the sky above was a brilliant blue. I saw dragons soaring through it, twisting their bodies as if they were dancing with the sun. "Beautiful. But what am I supposed to be looking at?"

She pointed behind me. "That."

I turned and gasped.

There was a golden city on the next mountain.

As a rich girl whose family has owned at one time a fleet of Aston Martins and given the gardener his own Tesla, I am rarely impressed by displays of wealth. Plus I'd just seen a palatial cathedral built into a mountain and drenched in jewels and gold.

But this . . . this was impressive.

Gold sheathed the top of the mountain, with skyscrapers rising even higher. Pillars held the city, raising the tip of the mountain higher toward the sun, while beneath it waterfalls of what looked like—"Are those diamonds? *In* the waterfall?"

"Yes."

I saw dragons flying in and out of the city, from multifaceted domes that looked as if they were made of yet more diamonds. The dragons themselves were also impressive: large, beautiful, and draped in gold collars and anklets and bracelets. As they landed, I saw them transform into equally gilded people who strolled through the palace.

"Those are the best of the best, and they receive the best of the best," Novi said.

Servers, gold coated instead of silver, whirred around the human-shaped wyverns—I couldn't see what they carried, but they whisked between the people and then formed two lines. The wyverns walked between them. It was all as choreographed as a ballet; every move seemed graceful and purposeful.

"What are they doing?"

"To be honest, I don't know—the elite have their own

way of life. Even as a guard of the Door, I'm not allowed into the city. The Reckoning exists to determine who is worthy for what level of society. Next I have to show you what you get if you *fail* in the Reckoning."

She led the way from one rope to another, as we descended into the valley. Lower, the air was warmer and smelled faintly of woodsmoke. Soon we were at the base.

We weren't in the green part of the valley. Here, it looked as if the land had been burned in a wildfire. Walking forward, Novi called, "Worm? Worm, it's Novi! Are you here?" She strode across charred earth that crumbled beneath her feet. I noticed she kept her hand on the hilt of one of her knives. I walked beside her. My tongue rolled in my mouth, wondering if someone had breathed on this piece of the valley, or if it was a natural fire. With this many wyverns, I highly doubted natural fire.

Up ahead, I heard a rustling. And then the face of a boy popped over a rock. He looked about our age, maybe a year or two younger. As he stood, I saw he was bare chested and very thin, so thin that his chest was concave, sucked against his ribs. "Novi?"

She rushed toward him and hugged him. "Worm, guess what! You'll never guess. It happened! One of the Returned came through on my watch! You were wrong!"

He extracted himself from her hug. "So I was wrong again. Couldn't wait to come tell me that. And this is her?" He turned to me. He had soot streaked on his legs and arms. His hair was long and matted.

"Uh, hi." I waved at him.

"Sky Hawkins, this is my brother, Worm."

I stared at him, then at her. "You, um, live here?" I didn't know how to ask—why did he look so hungry and filthy if he was her brother? She wasn't those things. Why would anyone choose to live here? And was his name really "Worm"?

Looking around, I saw others in the distance, scuttling over the charred earth. Most looked older than Worm, and all were skeleton thin, with ragged clothes hanging off their too-skinny bodies. A few watched us as we talked with Novi's brother.

Novi blushed, her neck and cheeks turning pink. "Worm is one of the best with fire, but he can't transform. According to our laws, it doesn't matter if you can tie flames into knots if you can't fly. If you can't become a dragon, you're ranked the lowest of the low, on the fringe of life. Only one step away from being outcast from all civilized society."

He spat a lick of white-hot flame. It sizzled the air. Whoa, that was hot. Even Tuck, who once made crème brûlée without a torch, couldn't make white flame. "You're using me as an object lesson. How special."

How could she let him live like this? Her own brother! "He's starving. And practically naked."

"I failed at my first Reckoning," Worm said. "Before this, I was living with our parents, but a few weeks ago, I came of age. . . . This is what happens when you can't perform like a proper wyvern. No cave. No food. No anything."

"And no one is allowed to change that," Novi said. "He has to do it for himself. But you will, Worm! I know you will!" She hugged him again. Soot stained her armor. "Just keep practicing. This time, it will be different. You won't have to be here much longer." She beckoned to me. "Come on—I'll take you back to your mother."

I followed her back toward the ropes, trying to understand why she'd showed me the palace and this awful place. Both Novi and her brother seemed to think there was nothing wrong with the disparity, though Worm obviously wasn't happy with his place in the hierarchy. "You have a class-oriented society, with very wealthy and very poor."

"Yes. But unlike where you come from, our society is a meritocracy. If you perform well at the Reckoning, then wealth is yours. Poorly, and that's your reward. Here, your fate is of your own making. Life here is fair."

"Oh, yes, very fair," Worm said behind us.

His sister ignored his bitterness.

To be honest, it wasn't so different from Earth's wyvern society: Once we were of age, we made our own rank. Until then, we lived off our parents' wealth, but after our first heist, we were supposed to make our own way. It wasn't entirely true, of course, since most parents didn't cut off their children, especially if they wanted to go to college . . . but maybe they did here? "So you're telling me Home is a dystopia?"

For the first time, her shell of cheeriness cracked, and she glared at me. "I'm telling you that you need to train for the Reckoning. Or you'll end up like my brother, and there's nothing that your mother or anyone can do to change that."

I looked back at her brother.

As if to emphasize her point, Worm breathed a white-hot stream of fire and seared the already-charred branch of a dead tree. The wood crumbled to ash.

CHAPTER SEVENTEEN

MOM DIDN'T WANT TO talk about the Reckoning or the Door or my heist or hers. She wanted to talk about Dad and my brothers and me—what had we been doing, how had we been feeling, what had we been eating . . . I told her, "Not much, not well, and lots of pizza." And then I launched into a detailed description of the new pad thai pizza from the pizza place in downtown Aspen, because it's much easier to talk about food than to talk about broken family relationships. I also told her about Gabriela and how she didn't like tortillas, and Mom confessed she'd secretly never liked pasta. "How can you not like pasta?" I asked.

"Feels like eating worms," she said with a shudder. "I've eaten worms, you know. Once, on a mission. We had to camp in the woods." She launched into a story about how she and Dad had chosen a heist in Georgia—the state, not the country—and had to backpack into an old plantation that had been taken over by a wyvern family. . . . While she talked, I couldn't help thinking of Worm, Novi's brother. That could be me, if I failed.

"Did you go through the Reckoning when you arrived?" I asked.

"Yes, I arrived shortly before the last one. That's why I have this"—she held up the amulet. "You're given an amulet at the end of the Reckoning. The markings denote your rank, which determines where you live, what you eat, who you may socialize with, everything. But please, Sky, I don't want to think about that tonight. I want to just be with you. Soak up the you-ness of you."

I rolled my eyes at her, though I didn't really mean it. It was nice that she'd missed me. I'd thought she'd left us voluntarily. I'd thought she hadn't cared at all.

She must have done okay in the Reckoning, since she wasn't living like Worm in the barren char, but not that great. Her home was a hole in the wall, not unlike a rabbit would have in a warren. It had only a cot and a chest made out of rough wood. It was nothing like our house back in Aspen. *No matter how great Novi says Home is*, I thought, *home is home.*

I started yawning after about an hour, and she found me a shirt that looked more like a sack with a hole cut out of the top. It was soft, though, so I changed into it. She insisted I take the cot, since I'd had a harder day than she had, and she curled up on the floor to sleep.

She blew out the candle. "Tomorrow, we'll train you for the Reckoning. You need to do well enough so you can stay with me. Wyvern of different ranks aren't allowed to be together."

"Like I'm going to be able to sleep after you said that,"

I told her. "What do I need to do? I don't have any wealth with me. I failed my heist." Back home, the council would have been unimpressed.

"None of that is necessary. The Reckoning itself is steeped in long tradition and focuses only on the two core wyvern skills that no other being possesses. One, you will need to fly."

Of course.

"And two, you must breathe fire in a controlled manner, from the air."

Great.

"Sleep, Sky. We'll worry about it in the morning."

I worried about it for hours until, eventually, I slept.

———

"I'm not the best person to train you," Mom said over breakfast, which was a slab of seasoned rabbit. Odd but okay. I craved a bagel. "I'm a novice myself. Luckily, the guard you met—Novi—has been appointed to help. The Door guards are responsible for easing new exiles into the culture."

"I really think we should be focusing on how to get home," I said.

"She'll be here soon," Mom said. I'd never seen her so nervous before. Usually she radiated confidence and competence. But she wasn't comfortable. *Because we don't belong here*, I thought.

"What about Maximus?" I nodded across the hall. He was with a beautiful woman in a stunning blue sari-like gown—his wife in her human form. She had her gold amulet necklace and wore strands of gold balls braided through her hair. He was whispering in her ear, and she was laughing. He looked happy. I thought of Ryan and couldn't help but glare at Maximus.

Catching my eye, he at least had the grace to look embarrassed.

If the heist had worked, I could have had Ryan back *and* Mom.

"He's found his own trainer," Mom said, nodding at the woman in the blue dress. "I had hoped to bring her back with me, as well as the others who were sent here against their will. Thomas Keene has no right to tear families apart. Like them. Like us."

"Why didn't you ever tell any of us any of this?" I asked.

"Because it was dangerous. We all could have been sent here." She waved her fork to gesture at the hall. Novi had said that everyone in Hall of the Returned was an exile, or related to one. Comparing their clothes to the splendor I'd seen at the mountain palace, I guessed not many exiles ranked very highly at the Reckoning. "Your father cautioned me against taking on Thomas. He'd used the Door both secretly and strategically to consolidate his power on the council, and that made him a dangerous adversary. Once I knew . . . I couldn't turn away."

You could have, I thought. *We needed you too.*

"Eat," she told me. "You'll need your strength."

I ate a few bites, not tasting them, and shortly, Novi arrived, bounding across the hall as energetically as if she'd pounded down six espressos. She was in the same green armor, her hair slicked into a braid and a knife strapped to her belt. "Good morning! Are you ready to embrace your destiny? I have an hour until my next guard shift, so we can start now."

Hurriedly, I shoved the rest of breakfast in my mouth and chewed as I followed her through the bejeweled tunnels out onto a ledge. This time, Mom came with us. She needed the practice too, she said—all wyverns competed in the Reckoning, to reconfirm their status. Given that I'd seen her sailing around the sky as a green dragon, I thought she needed a lot less practice in transforming into a dragon than I did.

Me, a dragon.

This was crazy.

Looking out over the valley, I saw other dragons filling the air. So graceful. So majestic. So—

"You have to think like a lizard," Novi said.

"Sorry?"

"Scaly. Pointy tongue." She stuck her human tongue in and out to demonstrate. "Itchy back from the wings. Lack of opposable thumbs. Bit of drool. Plus you're cold when it's cold and hot when it's hot. . . ."

"You don't like being a dragon?"

Novi grinned. "I'm kidding. It's fantastic. But you should have seen your face!"

I hadn't known Novi had a sense of humor. I grinned at her.

Mom was not amused. "The Reckoning is in three days. Every dragon out there has had many more than three days to practice. If you don't want to teach my daughter—"

Novi waved her hand. "Sorry. All right. The truth is it's all about attitude. You have to own the sky. You deserve the sky. You rival the sun with your greatness. Let that sunlight fill you and *own* it."

That was just as ridiculous as the first bit of advice. "You're telling me if I believe in myself hard enough and strong enough, I can be a dragon?" Then I thought of Gabriela and how she had to believe to activate Maximus's spell— maybe this *wasn't* so ridiculous.

"Yes. And then you leap off a cliff." Without pausing to explain any more, Novi ran forward toward the edge of the cliff. My heart flew into my throat as she, running, sailed off into nothingness with a *whoop*.

She then plummeted, like a cartoon coyote.

A second later, I heard a *thump, thump* . . . and a small orange dragon rose up above us. She still wore a talon amulet around her neck. She flapped so she swooshed toward us; then her wings collapsed on her back, and her body shrank into Novi, in her green scale armor. "See?"

"You're not naked." I also could have pointed out she'd just violated several natural laws, including conservation of matter.

"Your clothes transform as well," Mom told me. "We aren't like werewolves, changing involuntarily into beasts. Mentally and emotionally, we remain ourselves. We're more akin to shape-shifters. Like that blue X-Men comic book character. But in our case, our transformation magic is tied to our self-image—if your self-image includes clothes, then those change with you. If you were a casual nudist, I imagine the result would be quite different. One caveat: the amulet from the Reckoning will not transform, nor will any other gold."

I frowned, trying to absorb this ridiculous lesson. I was

okay with violating the basic laws of physics, I decided—after all, Novi had just done that—but telling me that it all hinged on my self-esteem seemed less plausible. "So I believe I'm a dragon and just leap? I feel like your instructions are missing a few key steps."

Novi shrugged. "That's it."

"Don't I need some pixie dust or something? Click my heels together three times and say, 'There's nothing like being a large mythological reptile'?"

She smiled, even though I couldn't imagine she got the reference. I hadn't seen any TVs here. "Only if it makes you feel better."

Mom laid her hand on my shoulder. "Honey, it's in your blood. It's your nature. All you have to do is love who you are."

I looked at her. Looked at Novi. Looked at Mom again. "If it's this easy, why hasn't anyone on Earth done it? Why were we all told the ability had been lost?"

"We were lied to by the council," Mom said, "I presume to keep our kind safe. In the Dark Ages, we were hunted. There are many on the council who fear a return to those days—even with our firepower, humans on Earth have us at a disadvantage. We are vastly outnumbered. And Sky, it's not easy. You have to believe fully and completely."

"Right," Novi chimed in. "If you don't believe, you will splat on the rocks, which incidentally is what happened to Worm. Splat, splat, thud." Novi demonstrated by flopping her hands over one another.

"And once you fail, it's a lot harder to believe," Mom said. "It is, sadly, a self-perpetuating cycle for those with difficulties accepting their destiny."

I peeked over the edge of the cliff. "You are both lousy teachers."

"You have to learn this," Novi said. "The Reckoning is coming! No wyvern can avoid it, at least no wyvern who wants to eat."

"It's about self-confidence," Mom said. "And self-knowledge."

"It's about believing you can do it," Novi said, earnest and serious. "And knowing who you are. So who are you? That's the key question. Are you a wyvern?"

Yes.

I am Sky Hawkins, and I am a were-dragon. I've been called stuck-up both in the tabloids and in the hallways of P. Murphy High, a poor little rich girl who surrounded herself with false friends and shallow dreams. Arrogant. Conceited. Egotistical. Haughty. Self-absorbed. All the synonyms, I'd heard them. But they were wrong.

It's not arrogant to know who you are.

It's powerful.

And I am powerful.

I ran past my mother and past Novi, and I flung myself off the cliff. Wind hit me, and I spread my arms as I felt myself plummet. My stomach leaped into my throat, and I wanted to scream, and when I did . . . it came out as a roar.

CHAPTER EIGHTEEN

I felt huge.

I felt amazing.

Scales ripped over my body as I swelled larger and larger. My legs thickened and bent, and I felt talons grow from my feet and hands. My back burst open, and wings extended on either side of me. My eyes widened until I felt I could see the whole world. Below me, the valley floor was rising fast— its glorious green so vivid to my new dragon eyes. I felt as if I could see every blade of grass as it bent in the wind. And the smells! I inhaled and breathed in a thousand scents of earth and water and trees and grass and the warm bodies of burrowing animals beneath the soil and the sea-tinged smell of birds that had flown far . . .

"Remember to fly!" Novi called, above me.

Startled, I spread my wings and flapped them.

Two dragons were waiting for me as I rose shakily higher: a small orange one and a beautiful green one. Novi and Mom. Wobbling in the air, I tried to steady myself in front of them.

"Ready for your flying lessons?" Mom asked. While she was in her dragon form, her voice sounded musical. It sang through the air. She flew on one side of me. Novi flew on the other. I wobbled.

"First, you must understand how wings work," Mom instructed. "The lift—"

Novi swooped in front of me, drew in her wings, and spiraled. "You feel it. Trust your instincts." Giggling, she zipped toward a cloud.

I followed her.

The wind felt like it was a part of me. My wings knew the wind like my feet knew the pavement. I felt it beneath me, and I turned so that it pushed me up. Extending my wings, I glided forward. Looking down, I felt my body tip with my head, and then I dove down.

"Good," Novi said, matching me. "Don't overthink it. That was always Worm's mistake. Now, watch for—" A burst of wind caught the tip of my wing, and I flipped sideways, careening through the air. I yelped. "—cross winds," she finished.

Steadying myself, I flapped my wings to catch up to her again.

Side by side, we flew up toward the clouds, bursting through them. I felt the misty droplets on my face. Opening my mouth, I tasted the mist, and it cooled my throat. We dove down, and my mother flew beside me.

I was so wrong, I thought—freewheeling down a mountain road on an earthbound bike was nothing like flying. This . . . this was amazing!

"You're a natural!" Mom trumpeted with joy. "Oh, my daughter! Let's fly!"

Circling above the river, we saw the unicorns running in a herd below us. Dipping down, I felt the tips of the trees brush my stomach, and then we were up again, circling the tips of mountains.

We flew until my wings ached and my eyes felt dry and my scales felt sandpapered from the wind, and then we landed in heaps on the cliff. And then suddenly I was laughing, and I didn't know why. Just from the sheer happiness of it all.

———

I practiced for two days straight. Sometimes with Mom, sometimes with Novi, sometimes on my own. Fire, however, continued to elude me. I could make a spurt of fire, the same as I'd managed when I unlocked the vault, but I couldn't sustain it.

"Um, that's . . . a good start," Novi said.

"It's pathetic," I replied.

"Maybe a little."

Mom tried to give me advice filled with lots of tricks and techniques, but in the end, I had to practice by myself—all the advice and comments were making my flame smaller and smaller. And that was when I encountered Worm again. I was focusing on fire so much that I lost control of my flying, right above the burned bit of valley where he lived.

Veering, I crashed into a tree. "Ow." Sideways, stuck in the branches, I looked down and saw Worm. He was sitting, half naked, on a rock, chewing on a green stick.

"You're that girl, right? The newbie? You make a very big dragon. Guess you won't be joining me here." He let out a bitter laugh. "It figures. You're here for a few days, and you're a better wyvern than I'll ever be. I'm here for a lifetime and can't get anything right." He kicked at a lump of char. "Congratulations. You'll fit right in."

Carefully, I tried to detangle my wings.

The branch broke, and I thumped onto the ground. I pictured myself in my human form, and soon I was shrinking. The world seemed to dull and flatten as my eyes resumed their normal shape. The tree seemed to grow. It was the weirdest sensation, as if my body had been replaced with Silly Putty. Swallowing a few times until my throat felt normal, I asked, "If you hate it so much, why don't you leave?"

"And go where? Beyond the valley? It's uninhabitable." He opened his mouth, and flame shot out at the tree. It bored straight through the trunk.

I stared at the hole. "Will you teach me how to do that?"

"You want *me* to teach you?"

"Never seen anyone do that."

He snorted. "I know, but I can't fly so it doesn't matter."

"Teach me, and—"

"And you'll teach me how to turn dragon? Nope. It won't work. Plenty have tried. Novi's here at least once a week, drilling me on lessons, hoping the next Reckoning will be different."

Good to hear that Novi cared. I'd wondered about that. "Actually, what I was going to say was: Teach me, and when I figure out a way to go home—my home, Earth—I'll take you with me."

It was his turn to stare at me. "You'd do that? Take me?"

I pointed to the hole in the tree. "Teach me, and we'll go together."

"Deal," he told me. "But you've got to get me some food too. Secretly. They'll punish you if they think you're giving me what I don't deserve."

"Is that why Novi doesn't help you? She's afraid she'll be punished?" She might be giving him lessons, but she clearly wasn't giving him extra food or clothes.

"A lot of wyverns are afraid," he said. "But they don't talk about it. This is supposed to be paradise, right? Until this last Reckoning, I was considered part of my parents' household. As such, my rank was the same as theirs. But now that I'm considered grown . . . my fate is my own, and isn't it such a glorious one?"

I wondered how many wyverns would take my deal, if I could figure out how to fulfill it without dying. Mr. Keene could be in for quite the surprise. I found that thought very comforting.

~

As a well-trained thief, I could have stolen the food.

If I knew where it was kept. And *if* I knew the kind of security systems the wyverns used. And *if* I was willing to risk angering the whole community that had been offering me part of their rations until I could earn my own at the Reckoning.

In the end, I decided that it wasn't worth the risk and that I couldn't ask Mom to give up more of her share than she already was. So I went to Novi.

She'd said she was on guard duty, which made her

easy to find. She was patrolling outside the chamber with the Door. Flying up in dragon form, I transformed back to human and waited for her on the cliff while I watched other wyverns practice their flying, dropping into spiral spins and then pulling up at the last second. One of them, I thought, was Maximus—a rust-colored dragon flying alongside his wife, a blue dragon.

"Oh, hi! I thought you were out practicing. What are you doing here?" Novi asked. "Can I help you with anything?"

"Yes, maybe. Just got back from visiting your brother." Holding up my hands, I stopped her objections. "I'm un-ranked, right? So it doesn't hurt my status to visit him." As I understood it, once I had an amulet, I'd be given my own place to live and share of the food, but I'd lose freedom of movement. I'd also qualify for tests and training in whatever jobs were available to someone of my rank, and then I'd truly belong. Yay.

She blinked. Opened her mouth. Shut it.

"I'd like to bring him some food."

"You pity him," she said. "He brought it on himself by not—"

I cut her off. "It's not pity. I need him. I'm having diffi-culty breathing fire, so I asked him to teach me, in exchange for food. He *is* great with fire. You have to admit that."

She nodded. "Of course! He's the best! It didn't help him, though, since he failed to transform. Completely failed. Hit the ground so hard, it's amazing he didn't die. Just let me find someone to take my post for a few minutes. . . ." Scurrying off, she returned quickly. Another green-clad guard marched out of the tunnel, assuming her post, and Novi led me to her own quarters.

Her quarters were much more lush than Mom's. Her walls were striped with gold and silver, and she had automated lights, drawers, and even a bed that folded itself out of her way as she strode past it. But even so, it wasn't a large room. I wondered where exactly she ranked in the hierarchy and how secure her position was.

She dug out some food that she kept squirreled away in a chest. It was buried under blankets, and I pretended to study the ceiling while she blocked the view of the chest with her body. I wondered if I'd become like this if I stayed, hoarding food, aware of my rank, afraid all the time that I'd lose both my rank and my food.

As she handed over the food, I thanked her.

"No, thank you! I've wanted to help him, but . . . the rules . . . the ranking . . ."

I hesitated for a moment, then asked, "Your parents . . . do they ever visit him?" She'd never mentioned parents any of the times we were together. Only her brother.

"Not all parents are as devoted as yours." Novi was smiling as she said it, but I heard the bitterness clearly in her voice, as sharp as a bite into a lemon. It was so different from her normal cheeriness that I stared at her. I wasn't so sure she was right—after all, Mom had left us to pursue some idealistic right-the-wrongs crusade. Some of my doubt must have shown on my face, because she continued. "You should have seen her when she first arrived. It took three guards to restrain her—she kept trying to return. I'm sure you saw the wounds on her neck and shoulders. We don't normally resort to anything as crass as physical violence, but we couldn't let her just kill herself. Certainly not before she had a chance to experience what Home has to offer."

Guards had done that? Also, who actually says "crass as physical violence"? I wondered what they'd do when I tried to return through the Door with Mom, because I wasn't giving up. I just had to figure out how we were going to bypass the fire beast, which I was going to do as soon as this nonsense with the Reckoning was finished, and then I was out of here. "She really tried?"

"Before the results of the Reckoning restricted her movements, your mother talked to every wyvern she could, trying to find a way to get the spells she needed. But you can't make magical potions here."

It was nice to hear that Mom had tried to return. More than nice. Hearing it filled some empty bit of my heart that had been aching.

"When your mother realized she couldn't return, she sank into despair. It was only the hope that her husband would find the clue she left for him that kept her from giving up completely—she told me about it. She left it in a box of food that she knew he would want to eat."

"He didn't touch it. I was the one who found the amulet. He preserved her office like it was some kind of tomb. Sealed the door shut."

"It must be nice to have a family who loves each other so much."

It was. And I missed my father and brothers so much that it hurt. Tucking the food into my pockets, I thanked her again and hurried back to Worm.

Unsure how to carry food as a dragon, I stayed human and used the climbing ropes to descend the cliff. When I got to the bottom, Worm was waiting. "What did Novi say?"

Glancing around to make sure we weren't being watched,

I gave him a hunk of cheese and a bit of meat from Novi. It wasn't a lot, but he shoved it into his mouth and ate it fast, as if he expected someone to snatch it away from him.

I waited, saying nothing.

I'd never met anyone with nothing before.

There are homeless on Earth, of course. The poor. And also the very poor. But I didn't see them, and what we don't see tends to not exist. Shallow and selfish, yes, but natural for both humans and wyverns. I wondered how many wyverns were aware there were half-naked, starving people living in soot below their lavish city—and that at least one of them was a boy barely old enough to drive. I said nothing when he finished. Just waited until he was ready.

He glanced at me. "No pity?"

"Would it help?"

"No. Did Novi tell you about my failure?"

"She mentioned it," I said cautiously.

"Did she tell you that she saved me? Jumped off the cliff herself, transformed, and caught me before I hit the rocks. That's why she's a guard. Proved herself amazing in the same instant that I proved myself pathetic." His feet crunched as he walked over the burned earth. I thought I saw new scorch marks on the grass beyond. "You want to know a secret? Sometimes I hate her for saving me."

"That's stupid. If she hadn't saved you, you'd be dead."

"Better dead than this." He looked up at the sky. "Always wanting what I can't have."

"You don't believe that," I told him. I remembered Novi's version of Worm's failure. She hadn't mentioned her own role in it. She'd said he'd hit the ground. Splatted. Maybe she'd been embarrassed. Or ashamed. Or even afraid.

He sighed deeply, and his eyes looked lost in a way that made me want to either tear up or shake him. "You don't know me."

"If you'd given up hope, you wouldn't be helping me."

"Maybe I just like burning stuff." He plopped down on the ground. Soot plumed around him. He beckoned me over. "Let's begin."

If turning into a dragon was about believing you're the best, then breathing fire was about believing the rest of the world was the worst and deserved to be crisped. Worm, it turned out, excelled at that.

He pointed to a tree. "So I simply picture my parents and—" Opening up his mouth, flame poured out as if he were a person-shaped blowtorch. The heart of his flame was blue near his tongue, and the orange flame shot toward the tree and singed a strip of the bark.

"Okay, I can try that." Certainly I had enough recent emotional angst to draw on. I thought of Ryan's dad, picturing his smarmy smile, his overly cultivated muscles, and his expensive suit. I opened my mouth, but instead of breathing fire, I spat out a puff of smoke.

"Good," Worm said.

"Really?"

"No, not really. That was bad. You've got to work yourself up to it. Who's your person?"

"My ex-boyfriend's father."

"So what makes him so contemptible?"

Grinding my teeth together, I thought about the whole

litany of evils he'd done. "He threatened my boyfriend with destroying my family. Forced him to break up with me and publicly shun me."

Worm nodded. "Sounds like excellent inspiration for fire-breathing. What else?"

"He's responsible for sending my mother here, for taking her away from my family. He's also the one who insisted the council kick off my father and take half our wealth. He broke my father's heart by taking away his life's work and his wife. He tore apart my family. My father and brothers haven't been the same since then." I felt a warmth in the pit of my stomach. My hands were clenched. Oh yeah, I was getting angry.

"Come on. Give me more."

"He ruins everyone he touches. Look at Ryan—his father claims to love him, but he punishes him a hundred different ways. Makes him feel less. Makes him feel unworthy. Makes him feel small and alone." I looked at Worm. "Who makes you feel that way?"

He shook his head. "This isn't about me. It's about you."

"But if you could—"

"Burn the tree, Sky," he said. "Think of your boyfriend's father. Think of what he's done to you and your family. Think of how that makes *him* lesser and unworthy, and *burn him.*"

Turning to the tree, I pictured Ryan's father. His suit. His shiny shoes. His superiority. His complete assurance that everything he did was right and true and for the good of his family, while he ruined lives. And I opened my mouth.

A flame shot out. A single flame, but it shot straight and true and burrowed into the bark of the tree. It bored through and then flared out the other side.

"Nice," Worm said, and he meant it this time. "Do it again."

And I did. Again and again, until my mouth felt so dry I couldn't speak and my head felt so dizzy that all I could do was smile.

I practiced nonstop. By the morning of the Reckoning, I was feeling pretty good about my chances . . . at least until I saw Maximus casually breathe a rush of flames into the fireplace. *Stop it,* I told myself. *You'll do fine.* I'd practiced the most that I could. I didn't think I was the worst wyvern in the valley. That's really all I had to do: not be the worst.

A little part of me, though, wanted to be the best.

All right, a very large part of me. I'd seen all the Home-born dragons flying in complex spirals and figures through the air and wanted to show them that an exile could be just as good. I wanted to prove I was just as much wyvern as they were, worthy of their city with its golden servants and diamond-filled waterfall. I'd had only three days to practice, though. If I were to have longer . . . *But I'm not going to stay,* I thought, *so it doesn't matter.*

"Ready?" Mom asked me.

"Are you?"

She squeezed my hand. She was hugging me so much more now than she ever had, as if she was afraid if she didn't touch me once a day, I'd vanish. It was nice. "Don't worry about me. Concentrate on your flying and your fire."

Looking around, I saw all the wyverns in the hall looked nervous. They were showing it in different ways: pacing, picking at their fingernails, talking incessantly, not talking at all, stuffing their faces, not eating, smiling too much, not smiling at all. Maximus met my eyes. Sauntering over, he said, "Good luck, Sky."

"I can't tell if you mean that or not."

"Go with yes, and then you can think better of me."

I studied him. "You're pretty sure of yourself. You think you're going to do well."

"I feel like I've waited for this my whole life."

"Then you don't want to go home?"

"I am home. And so are you. Better get used to it." He swept on, and I watched him go. It didn't matter whether he did well or not at the Reckoning. All that mattered was how I did. Just concentrate on me, I told myself.

From outside, horns sounded. Low, booming horns that shook the hall. The jewels in the walls rattled together, and the fire in the hearth trembled.

"It's time," Mom said. She took my hand, and we walked with all the other exiles out onto the cliff overlooking the valley. I felt the press of wyverns around me, and I stood on my tiptoes to try to see what everyone was looking at.

Seven dragons flew in V formation across the mountain-tops. They soared up and then looped in a full circle around the valley.

"Those are our leaders," Novi said behind me. Her voice was a whisper. "Watch. They'll show you what you need to do."

I watched as the leaders flew with precision a series of complex maneuvers, weaving in and out among one another, flipping upside down and spiraling, then diving low to the ground and pulling up to skim the river. Everyone gasped, oohed, and aahed.

"Novi, I can't do that!" I whispered.

She didn't answer as the fire portion of the test began. Flying again in perfect formation, the seven dragons breathed fire along the river and then up. They danced in the air, breathing fire around them, so close to the other dragons that I realized I'd forgotten to breathe.

It was beautiful.

It was impossible.

I'm going to fail, I thought.

CHAPTER NINETEEN

SEVEN AT A TIME, to match the leaders, the wyverns of Home leaped into the air, transformed, and flew. Sandwiched between Mom and Novi, I watched. I knew Worm was watching too from down at the base of the valley, and I wished he were allowed to be up here with us. It had to make it worse for him to be separated from the "successful" wyverns.

This was no more fair than the council passing judgment on my family.

I began to feel more than a little angry at the wyverns here, for making us go through this, for judging the exiles as if they had the same knowledge and experience as those who had been born and raised to do this. I began to feel angry on behalf of Worm; of Novi, who wasn't allowed to help her brother; and of my mother, who had to worry about me.

I watched some plummet as they tried to fly. I saw others soar. None were as beautifully smooth as the leaders, but a few came close. Soon it would be the exiles' turn.

Don't get nervous, I told myself. I tried to hold on to my anger and my self-righteous pride. Just because they couldn't fly or flame as well didn't mean they didn't deserve food and shelter. Maybe they were smart or funny. Or good at pottery or writing poems or interpretive dance. This was stupid.

I wanted to go home.

That's where I belonged. Not here.

I wasn't a wyvern from Home. I was Sky Hawkins from Aspen, Colorado, and screw this. "I'm not doing it," I muttered. And then I said it louder, "I'm not doing it. I'm going home. *My* home."

Novi grabbed my arm. "You go through the Door, and you'll be burned to a crisp! Please, Sky, this is your world now, and you have to adjust. Focus on the Reckoning."

Mom nodded. "I told you: there are no spells here to fight the beast." She lightly touched my neck. "You need to forget about the Door and focus on flying and fire."

Fire, I thought. "Maximus's spell is just fire, isn't it? He fights fire with fire."

"Beast with beast, yes," Mom said. "Sky, I can see where you're going with this, and I don't like it. Your fire is nowhere near strong enough or hot enough to fight a fire beast!"

An idea was forming, beautiful and simple, the best kind. I should have seen it sooner, but I'd gotten stuck thinking that the fire beast *had* to be defeated by someone using a spell, which wasn't true. It simply had to be defeated. "I can't do it. But Worm can."

Novi jolted, as if I'd poked her with a fork. "Worm? He can't leave! This is his home!"

"He already said he wants to come," I told her.

"He did?"

But I didn't get a chance to respond, because it was suddenly time. Novi, Mom, and I, as well as four other exiles whose names I didn't know, were pushed forward by a surge around us—prodded by one of the wyvern leaders. And then we were at the edge of the cliff.

"Any last advice?" I asked.

"Whatever you do," Novi said, "don't die!"

"That is not how you give a pep talk," I told her. But before I could finish the sentence, she leaped from the cliff and transformed. A small orange dragon soared away from the crowd, and the exiles around us cheered. Next, another wyvern. He changed into a silver dragon with a long tail. And another, and another.

"You can do this," Mom told me.

"I know," I said, and I ran off the cliff.

My head was swirling with thoughts and worries: Was I right about Worm? Could his fire defeat a magical fire beast? His fire blazed hotter than any I'd ever seen. If he could fight the beast, could we escape the vault and the house? And then I pulled all these thoughts up into a mental fist and thrust them away for later.

First, I had to fly.

Wind roared around me, and the ground was zooming closer. *I'm not going to fail*, I thought. *I have to go home. Dad is waiting for me. And my brothers. And Ryan. And Gabriela. I'm going to fly!*

Wings burst out of my back, and I soared upward. Joining the other dragons, I flew with them. I knew I couldn't execute the perfect maneuvers of the wyvern leaders, but I could do what I knew how to do.

I let the wind guide me.

Feeling it, I danced through the air, spiraling and diving and soaring. I saw the other dragons out of the corners of my eyes—Mom and Novi were beside me, and the three of us flew together, synchronized, the way we'd practiced. We skimmed the river, we flew above the trees, we circled the mountains.

And I forgot this was a test. I forgot about the Door. I forgot about anything but this moment, the wind, and the sight of the sky above me and the world below me as I flew between them both.

"Fire!" Novi called. She breathed flame.

And I unleashed my rage at the unfairness of both worlds, Earth and Home. At the unfairness of being judged by things that were only a small part of who we were.

I let out my anger at Ryan's father.

My anger at Ryan for not being able to stand up to him.

My anger at Maximus for lying to me.

My anger at my brothers and my father for not helping me, not trusting me, not believing in me.

My anger at my mother for trying to do her heist without us.

My anger at myself for being caught.

And the flame roared out of me.

It wasn't the largest flame or the brightest or the most controlled, but it was enough. I flew with it before me, spiraling and diving and spinning. And then it was over.

The horns sounded. The next seven wyverns began their test.

I sailed back to the cliff, landed, and transformed. Other wyverns clapped my back, congratulating me, and I pushed through them, toward Mom. Novi met up with me partway through the crowd. "Worm truly wants to go to Earth?"

"Ask him," I said. This was the best chance we were going to get—all the wyverns were distracted with the Reckoning. "And meet us with him by the Door in ten minutes."

As the next group of seven wyverns soared into the air, Mom and I threaded through the crowd. Gripping my elbow, Mom whispered in my ear, "How can you be sure this Worm is strong enough? He failed at the last Reckoning. *Failed*, Sky."

"He failed to fly. Not breathe fire. I saw him produce white-hot fire." The more I thought about it, the more certain I was that he could do it. White-hot fire measures approximately 2,500° F, a match for the fire beast. "There's no real reason the fire beast *has* to be defeated magically. If we have hot-enough fire, we can fight fire with fire." I kept my voice low, even though the crowd around us was busy cheering for the new set of competing wyverns.

She was shaking her head. "He'd be risking his life. And even if it did work, he'd be leaving his home, his family, everything he's ever known. We can't ask him to do that."

"He's treated like dirt, Mom. Like ashes. He doesn't even get enough food to eat! Or clothes to wear! I guarantee he wants to leave."

She opened her mouth, then shut it, considering what I'd said, and I felt a rush of relief—she wasn't treating me like the baby of the family. She was acting like we were in this together, which we were. Our own crew of two. "All right," Mom said at last. "But I'll be the one going through with him. You stay here, safe, until I've found a way to disable the bomb and take the Door to a secure location."

Now it was my turn to shake my head. Crews stuck together. *Families* stuck together—if anything, I felt that more strongly than I ever had. "We're both going through. I'm not staying here, and I'm not leaving you behind."

"Absolutely not," Mom whispered.

We reached the edge of the crowd. We scooted around it, our backs to the mountainside. Glancing between the watching wyverns, I saw another dragon plummet, and the crowd gasped.

Mom continued, "It's one thing to risk my life; it's another to risk yours."

"You can't stop me," I whispered back. "After you go through, you won't be here to keep me from coming right after you."

She glared at me. "I am your mother."

"Exactly," I said. "I'm not losing you twice."

We stopped directly below the ledge with the Door's cave. We couldn't go through the jeweled door. Far too noticeable. We'd climb up to the cave. We didn't even have to discuss it to know this was the plan.

Except there was still too much of a crowd. Someone would certainly see.

Someone like Maximus.

Peeling away from the crowd, the wizard wyvern sauntered over to us. "Let me guess," he said to me. "You've hatched a daring plan to return to Earth and reunite your family?"

"You've nothing to gain by stopping us, Maximus," Mom told him.

"Quite true," he said. "And I've everything to gain by helping you. My Angela has been . . . vocal in her disapproval of how I treated you. But she'll forgive me once I've repaid my debt to you." Glancing over his shoulder, he waved at her.

"You can't do spells here," I said. "How are you going to help us?"

"I might not be able to do spells," he said. "But I *am* still a wizard." And with that annoyingly cryptic statement, Maximus strode into the center of the crowd and transformed into a dragon.

People around him yelped and fell back as he expanded to several times his size. Maximus as a dragon wasn't small and unobtrusive—his dragon form was as showy as Maximus himself. He was orange-red, with a long, sleek neck, which he stretched out toward his wife, who rolled her eyes at him.

Then Maximus stretched out his wings, opened his mouth—

And he began to sing and dance.

From his dragon throat came the lyrics to "So You Wanted to Meet the Wizard," his song from *The Wiz*. He shimmied. He sashayed. He grooved.

"I can't believe I'm seeing this," Mom said.

"Neither can anyone else," I pointed out. "Let's climb."

And as Maximus continued to repay his debt in the oddest way possible, Mom and I climbed toward the cave. Glancing out at the valley, I saw another set of dragons take to the air.

A guard was on the cliff, at the edge, watching both the dragons in the air and the dancing dragon in the middle of the crowd below. He wore the same green scale armor that Novi wore, and his back was to us. We didn't have to create a distraction—between the Reckoning and Maximus, the guard was well occupied. Punching his fist in the air, he cheered as a maroon dragon executed a flip through a cloud.

Mom put one finger to her lips, and then she pointed up with the other. The jewel-encrusted rocks on the walls of the tunnel were chunky. Climbable. Monkey-like, Mom began climbing, reaching high until she was on the ceiling. She hooked her feet around a dazzlingly decorated stalactite and held out her hands, like a trapeze artist waiting for someone to jump to her.

My mom is very impressive.

I grabbed her hands, and she swung me up to the next jewel-encrusted stalactite. I clung to it. We stayed there, stuck on the ceiling like bats, while the guard marched inside. He completed a patrol round, through the tunnel and then out again.

We moved slowly across the ceiling, stalactite to stalactite, careful to not knock any stones or jewels loose. Inching across, we crawled inside. Once we were out of sight of the guard, we dropped down and hurried into the chamber with the Door.

The jewel shimmered in the candlelight, and I couldn't tell if it was reflecting the flames or giving off its own light. It looked like a miniature moon. Beautiful. Not as beautiful as gold, but still quite pretty.

Worm wasn't here yet.

I paced around the Door while Mom watched me.

I wondered if Novi would have any trouble reaching the cave. She was a guard. I was hoping that meant she wouldn't be questioned. With luck, everyone was still focused on Maximus and the Reckoning.

"Say this works," Mom said, her voice a whisper. "What happens to the Door? And the other exiles?" She was watching me intently, as if this was a test.

"We can't take the Door with us; we still don't know how to defuse the bomb. Escape first, and then we'll come back for it, with Liam. He'll be able to do it."

She grasped my hands. "Then you understand how important this is. We can't allow Thomas to have control over the Door. It's not right. I tried to explain to your father, but all he saw was risk without reward. . . . But it's not about reward. It's not about any hoard. It's not about rank. It's about family, being together, being home, wherever your home is."

I thought of Maximus and his wife. "Yeah, I get it."

Voices echoed from the mouth of the tunnel. Both Mom and I quickly scanned the chamber—there was no place to hide. Jeweled wall, jeweled ceiling, and the jeweled pedestal that held the Door. That was it.

"Pretend you're stopping me from going through the Door," I said quickly. She nodded immediate understanding. Positioning ourselves, we got ready to lie.

But we didn't have to. It was Novi with Worm.

He was hugging himself, as if to hide that he wore what amounted to not much more than a Tarzan loincloth. He knew he wasn't supposed to be here—that knowledge was written all over his face. Maybe he'd be able to be himself on Earth, or maybe it would be even worse for him. I couldn't promise him better. Just different.

"The Reckoning isn't even over," Novi was saying to

him. "They haven't released the results. You could have improved!"

He was staring at the Door as if it were food. *He wants to come*, I thought. I'd been right to ask him. "She's offering me a new life, Novi."

"But you could die!" She was fighting tears.

Worm refused to look at her. His lower lip was stuck out, his chin wrinkled, the exact same stubborn expression that I've seen on Charles's face when he's convinced he's in the right. I almost felt guilty for breaking them apart. He was her family, and hadn't I just been thinking that family should stick together? "I can fight a fire beast," he insisted. Turning to me, he asked, "What do you need me to do?"

"Fire. Lots of it, as hot as you can make it. When we go through, if it's anything like coming this direction, you'll be disoriented and in pain. You'll need to shoot fire anyway. Just aim up, so you don't hit us. Can you do that?"

"Yeah." And he smiled, looking happier than I'd ever seen him. Giddy, even. Beside him, Novi was staring at her brother as if she'd never seen him before. I could tell she wanted to say more. I could also tell that he wasn't going to listen. She seemed to have guessed that too.

"Once the fire beast is disabled, you'll need to burn out the security cameras," I said.

Mom chimed in. "Opening the vault door will automatically shut off the laser motion sensors and pressure plates, but we'll have to cope with the wyvern detection spell somehow. We don't have a human with us to block it—"

"Fine, but then what?" Novi interrupted, and now *she* reminded me of Charles, with that I'm-older-so-I-know-best tone of voice. "Say you defeat this fire beast. Say you find a way past . . . all that. Then what? You'll be in a strange world, without your family—"

"I'll be happy," he interrupted. "Do you care about that?"

"Of course I want you to be happy!" Novi cried.

Footsteps, coming toward the cave.

"And so do Mom and Dad."

Worm yelped. "Novi, what did you do?"

A man and a woman burst into the cave. "Benden, what are you doing?"

These were their parents? Also, his name was Benden? Not Worm? I wasn't sure what was worse: the idea that he'd been named Worm at birth, or the idea he'd been nick-named Worm and accepted it. I *was* sure that the arrival of his parents was *not* a good development.

Worm and Novi's parents were clearly high-level wyverns, higher ranked than anyone I'd seen up close. Both wore rich gowns embroidered with gold and tied around their waists with belts made of gold discs. Their mother's hair was slicked into a triple bun on the top of her head, and their father's beard was expertly trimmed. "Your sister tells us you plan to go through the Door. Everyone who has gone through in the last decade has been sent back dead," Worm's father said. "This is a foolish risk!"

I raised my hand as if I were in school. "I do have a plan."

"It's an excellent plan," Mom said supportively.

I shot her an appreciative look. It was nice of her to say, especially since I knew she didn't consider it so excellent.

"What sort of plan?" Worm's father demanded.

"Me," Worm said. He stepped out from behind Mom. "I

can fight the fire beast. I'm strong enough. You know that. I'm stronger than—"

Worm's mother gasped. "It's suicide! Haven't you brought enough shame to us? We cannot allow this to happen!"

Mom spoke. "We're going through, and then we're going to find a way to open up travel between Earth and Home. Families will be reunited. You'll be able to choose where your home is." She was walking slowly in a semicircle, and it was only when she stopped that I realized what she was doing—placing herself between the two wyverns and the jewel. It gave Worm and me direct access.

I calculated the distance: three steps.

Mom was still talking: "As soon as we have the Door safe in a new, secure location, we will come back, and anyone who chooses can cross."

"You're talking about taking our son to certain death," the father said.

Worm let out a barklike laugh. "You've always believed in me so much. It's humbling. Really, Dad, thank you. And Mother, I'm glad you're more worried about your own embarrassment than my life." If Mom could maneuver them just right, we should be able to touch the jewel. . . . I began to shift my weight, preparing. She'd spring forward, and they'd react—in that instant, we could make it, and Mom could follow. She was positioning herself for that as well. A few more feet . . .

"You don't understand what you're doing, son," Worm's father said.

"I understand completely," Worm said, and then he

lunged for the jewel. *Dammit, not yet!* Mom wasn't in position! I jumped toward the jewel as Mom sprang forward to block the wyvern guard. She wasn't going to be able to make it—Worm's father and the guard were piling on her, stopping her, holding her down so she couldn't follow. His mother ran for me.

"I'll come back for you!" I called to Mom.

"Go, Sky!" she shouted.

I slapped the jewel, and the rainbow seized me and tore me away.

CHAPTER TWENTY

Heat.

Pain.

I felt as though a hundred knives were being jabbed into my leg. Stifling a scream, I croaked, "Worm, use your fire!"

He was moaning next to me. Cracking open my eyes, I tried to focus on him, but he was a blur streaked with lightning bolt–like light. The beast—it attacked both of us, burning, like needles driven into my skin.

Rolling side to side, I tried to put out the fire, but the beast kept coming. "Worm," I gasped out, "think of the Reckoning! Think of how they made you feel!"

"Worthless," I heard him grunt. "Pathetic. Weak."

"Show them your worth, Worm! Show them you aren't weak. Blast your fire at them. Blast them away." Every word hurt to say. Heat poured down my throat, as if I were drinking molten lead. My eyes hurt to open, but I made myself try to look, trying to see where the beast was.

It was raging above us, a smear of milky white.

"Worthless," Worm whispered. And then flame roared out of him, white-hot. I rolled to the side, behind a shelf of jewels. Cowering, I curled into a ball as his flames raked across the ceiling and walls of the vault. "Weak," he said, and the fire burned hotter. "Pathetic!"—and the vault was dazzling white.

The white light writhed.

Still curled like a pill bug, I lay still, staring up with tears streaming out of my stinging eyes, as Worm's white-hot flame burned away the fire beast, until at last there was only the single bolt of light, pouring from his mouth, boring a hole through the wall, through the solid granite.

"Enough," I croaked. "You did it."

He didn't hear me. Didn't stop.

"Worm, you can stop now." Unrolling, I reached over to touch his shoulder. He felt hot, like he was made of fire, and I pulled my hand back. "Worm! It's done!"

He sucked in, and the white fire was drawn into him.

And then there was darkness.

We lay there, in the dark, side by side. My arm hurt, my leg above my knee, the side of my stomach—everywhere the fire beast had touched me.

Mom, I thought.

She could still be fighting the guards. Maybe they'd arrested her. Certainly they'd dragged her away from the Door by now. If enough time passed, she wouldn't come even if she were free—the fire beast would return in thirty minutes, and she wouldn't risk it.

I'd found her and lost her.

No. It was only that the heist wasn't finished yet. I had to complete the mission: steal the Door and save my mother.

"I did it," Worm said, wonder in his voice.

"Told you so."

"You did tell me." And now the wonder was directed at me. "No one has ever believed in me before. My parents . . . even my sister . . . No one saw any worth, but you . . ."

I closed my eyes. "No."

"No what?"

"You do *not* get a crush on me," I told him. "My life is complicated enough. You want to fall in love with someone, fall in love with yourself. *You* defeated the fire beast. *You* saved our lives. Not me. All I did was say, 'Hey, let's do something reckless that will probably get us both killed.'"

He chuckled, but it was a painful wheezing kind of laugh.

"You okay?" I asked. "Do you think you can move?"

"Sure. Yeah. Maybe."

"How about more fire? Are you up for that?" I asked.

He groaned. "I don't know."

We couldn't stay. We had to be safely out of the vault before the fire beast spell reactivated, especially if Worm was spent. Thirty minutes, Maximus had said. That should be enough time, if we could muster the strength to move. "Any chance you could burn a hole through the rock out of here?" I knew he'd drilled a few inches. I'd seen it before all the fire went out. But this was twelve feet of granite, which would be an impressive miracle . . .

"No chance. I'd pass out if I tried that much heat so soon."

Okay. Fine. That would have been a lot more awesome,

but we could do it the old-fashioned way. "There are security cameras. See the tiny red light? Once we move out of this corner of the vault, they'll see us. You'll have to fry them here and also in the hall. I'll open the vault door—that should shut off the motion-sensing lasers and the pressure plate alarms—then you burn out the cameras, and we run like hell for the stairs."

I wished I could see his face. His voice sounded anxious, but I couldn't tell if he was ordinary nervous or about-to-freak-out nervous. "Your mother said there was a 'wyvern detection spell'?" he asked. "And what are 'motion-sensing lasers' and 'pressure plates'?"

"Don't worry about what they are. Just do what I say, and run when I say run."

"So the guy who set the fire beast . . . he'll chase us as we try to escape?"

"We aren't going to be trying to escape. Not yet. Just stay close to me and nurture that anger you have for me over how cryptic I'm being. There are six cameras, and you'll have to shoot them all. We need to buy as much time as we can so we can make it up the stairs before anyone comes to stop us."

"Okay," he said. And then: "What's a 'camera'?"

"See that red dot? Burn it out," I ordered. He complied, and I heard a sizzle and spark as the cameras were fried. "Now, grab as much gold as you can. We want this to look like an ordinary heist, not like someone came through the Door." Feeling around in the dark, I shoved necklaces and bracelets and gold rings into my pockets. I heard the clink of gold bars.

From there, I moved to the door. Vaults were meant to

be inaccessible from the outside, so I had it open fast. "Cameras will be by the ceiling in the hall. Light them all up," I ordered Worm. "Don't worry about the walls—they're fire resistant."

He stepped into the doorway, wreathed in flame, and the fire shot out of him, crisping the electronics. In his fire, I saw the hall: empty. There was no way to avoid the wyvern detection spell. From here on in, we'd have to really move.

"Now, run!" I grabbed his hand, and we ran down the hallway and up the stairs. Ahead was the kitchen door. This was it, the place I'd been caught last time, the moment we could be stopped—

We burst out. I ran toward the door to the outside and kicked it open so it would look like we'd run that way. Worm followed me. "Not that way," I told him as he went for the door. Grabbing his arm, I pulled him back with me. We wanted Mr. Keene looking for us outside, not inside.

We ran through the house, into the foyer, past the grandfather clock, and through the dining room to the back stairs. Stopping on the stairs, I put my finger to my lips.

It was time to sneak.

"Step exactly where I step." I knew these stairs. I'd crept up them often enough with Ryan. Carefully, I laid my foot on the parts of the steps I knew didn't squeak.

At the top of the stairs, I poked my head out into the hallway.

Empty.

Ryan's room was three doors down.

Scooting forward, we hurried along the hallway. I pushed on the door and then pulled Worm inside just as one of the other doors slammed forward and Ryan's father thumped down the hallway shouting to Ryan's mother, "Gretchen, stay in your room! Ryan, you as well! An alarm's been tripped, and the basement cameras are out. I'll handle this!"

I put my finger to my lips, and Worm and I flattened against the door.

"Sky?" Ryan. "How—"

Holding up one hand to silence him, I listened. Ryan's father ran down the stairs. His footsteps retreated. And then I turned around.

Beside his desk, Ryan stood, staring at me, eyes wide, mouth open. An instant later, he crossed the room in four strides, and he was kissing me, and I was entwined in his arms. He kissed me as if he'd been starved. His hands were in my hair, down my back, on my shoulders, and his lips were on my mouth, cheeks, neck.

"Are you okay?" I asked between kisses. "Did he hurt you?"

"Sky, this is a miracle," Ryan breathed. He was staring at me like I was a goddess who had suddenly appeared to bless him. "You ran. He said you—he said you were scared, and he tried to stop you, but you ran when he chased you. Right off the cliff. He said you died. Your funeral was yesterday, Sky. You were buried. Your brothers said your eulogy. . . ." He kissed me again.

"Did they say nice things?" I asked.

Worm cleared his throat. "Um, Sky?"

"Oh! Sorry. Ryan, Worm. Worm, Ryan."

Ryan spared him a nod, but his eyes were only on me. I wanted to bask in that look forever, but I knew I couldn't. It wasn't safe here. And I had to rescue Mom. "Do you have clothes we can borrow? We're a bit conspicuous like this."

Without waiting for an answer, I went digging through his dresser. I found a T-shirt that I'd always thought was extra soft plus a pair of jeans for myself, and I tossed another shirt and pants to Worm. He caressed the material as if he'd never seen it before, which he probably hadn't.

"Sky, what happened?" Ryan asked.

"The jewel that Mom tried to steal . . . it's not a jewel. It's the Door. A portal to Home." There was no delicate way to put this, so I plunged in, even though I knew the words would hurt him. "Your father uses it to exile people he doesn't like. The council doesn't know." I wondered at what point my father had known. Had he figured it out when Mom disappeared? Or had he guessed earlier? Mom had said he'd refused to come. . . . Maybe he knew but didn't believe. "But my mother found out somehow and was trying to expose him. He sent her through against her will, and then he did the same to me."

Ryan looked as if I'd slapped him, and my heart ached. He'd never been close to his father, but to discover he was capable of this . . . As gently as I could, I said, "Your father lied. He's been lying to all the wyverns. And I'm going to stop him. But I have to get home and talk to my brothers. I'm so sorry, Ryan."

His expression softened, and he touched my cheek. "You have nothing to be sorry about. You're alive! Gabriela said—"

"Is she okay? Did he hurt her?" Dumping the gold from the vault onto Ryan's bed, I ripped off the sari-like wrap and pulled on the shirt and jeans. Now both Worm and Ryan were staring at me.

Ryan reached toward me again. "You're burned!"

Glancing down, I saw streaks and blotches on my arms and stomach, where the fire beast had seared my skin. With all the adrenaline coursing through me, I'd barely noticed, but now the burns were starting to sting. "I'll be fine." I borrowed one of Ryan's belts and cinched it around my waist, then rolled up the jeans. Quickly and awkwardly, Worm dressed too. He fumbled with the zipper and snap. "Gabriela?" I asked again.

Ryan was still staring at my burns, and I wondered how bad they were. I didn't think any were serious, but there were a lot of them. It had all happened so quickly. "Gabriela's okay," he said. "My father scared her, I think, but she's fine. Her family's mortgage has been paid off by a mysterious benefactor, and she and her brother have enough savings to pay for whatever college they want. I don't think she would have accepted the bribe except . . . well, you were dead. She blamed herself."

"And my father and brothers? Are they okay? Has there been another Reckoning? Did they lose everything?" I wanted to ask if they were outcast, but I wouldn't bring myself to say the word.

He shook his head again. "The next Reckoning is scheduled for tonight. I don't know what's planned for it, but I know your failed heist is going to come up. I think your father and brothers are preparing for the worst."

It wasn't too late! Yet. "Where's it being held?"

"Here."

Good. This could work. If I moved fast enough. I thought quickly—we'd need to orchestrate the heist immediately. I needed my brothers on board, and Gabriela. I hoped she wasn't too freaked out by what had happened. This wasn't going to work without her.

"Sky . . . what do you need me to do?"

I loved him for asking that. I kissed him again, then crossed to the window and opened it. Ryan's window overlooked the cliff. The lake was far, far below us.

"You can use my climbing gear . . . ," Ryan began.

I flashed him a smile. "I'm not planning to climb. Come on, Worm." He trotted over to me as I opened the window. "Get ready to jump."

Worm paled. "But you know I can't—"

"Onto me," I clarified. "Me first, you second. Got it?"

Ryan blocked the window. "Sky?" All his worry, all his fear for me, all his hope for us was laced into his voice—I heard it loud and clear.

"Trust me." I grinned.

He stared at me, then said, "Always."

Outside the door, there was a loud knock. "Ryan, who are you talking to in there?" His father! The knob began to turn, and Ryan strode across the room and threw himself against the door.

"Just talking to myself." Ryan called, pushing against the door. To us, he whispered, "I'll buy you time. Leave the gold." Adding to my pile, Worm deposited the gold bars on Ryan's bed.

"Open the door, Ryan," his father commanded.

I wanted to say more, to tell him to come with us, to tell him everything I felt, but there was no lock on the door. Ryan couldn't hold it for long.

"Go!" Ryan whispered.

I hoped he could read all that I wanted to say in my eyes. "Thank you." And then I turned and jumped out the window. Wings grew out of my back, and I transformed fast this time.

I felt a thump as Worm landed on top of me.

Through the open window, I heard the door bang open. His father was shouting, and I heard Ryan claim that he'd done the heist: he'd robbed their vault. See, there was the gold, on his bed. He'd completed his first heist and wanted to be presented to the council tonight, per wyvern tradition.

Clever boy, I thought. He was buying us time.

I didn't stay to hear more, but it was enough. Ryan was lying to his father, for me. He'd made a choice again, and this time he'd chosen me.

With Worm on my back, I flew away. Toward home.

CHAPTER TWENTY-ONE

THE AIR TASTED RIGHT. Like snow and spring and smoke. And the mountains looked right too: the Rockies, with the sun positioned between two peaks perfectly, like it was posing for a photo.

"It's beautiful!" Worm called.

It took a fair amount of self-restraint not to say my world was better than his, but I managed, because I'm heroic like that. "On our world, you don't have to stay in a single valley. Our world extends for thousands and thousands of miles, and you can go anywhere in it!"

"And will I be welcome here?"

"That all depends on who it is you want to do the welcoming. You'll have to enroll in high school, and that can either be the best time of your life or the worst." I marveled at myself for thinking about something as normal as school at a time like this. "I can't promise it will be better than Home, but it *will* be different. Unless we fail. In which case,

Ryan's father will either kill us or shove us back through the Door. Maybe we should worry about that first, and then worry about how well you'll fit in at P. Murphy High?"

"What's P. Murphy High?"

"Home of the Fighting Badgers." Up ahead, I saw my road. "Hang on." Tilting, I flew into the wind. From the air, my house looked kind of like a birthday cake. The white brick walls were frosting, the copper gutters were icing trim, and the chimneys were birthday candles. Yum. I hoped Dad had some decent food in the kitchen.

I know, I know, but I couldn't save my mother and unite two worlds on an empty stomach. I also had to pee. You have to remember these kinds of things when you're planning a heist, or any sort of activity that will change your life.

I flew toward the backyard. Spiraling down, I aimed for the wide space of grass. "You're coming in too fast!" Worm yelped. "You're going to hit—"

I crashed into the top of a pear tree. It bent under my weight, then snapped, and we thudded to the ground. Worm rolled off me. "No offense, but you need more practice."

I tested my wings. Unbroken. Legs, okay.

I heard shouting from the house.

Dad! Charles! And then Liam and Tuck came barreling out behind them. I began to lope forward, my tail swinging. And Dad roared, shooting flame out of his mouth.

Yikes! He didn't recognize me.

"Dad, stop!" Quickly, I changed, and the world around me expanded as everything shrank—or more accurately, as I shrank into my human form. Since I was midrun as I tried to change, I stumbled over my feet and skidded into the grass, chin and hands first.

Dad broke off the flame. "Sky?"

I jumped to my feet. "Hi! Not dead. Really long story. This is Worm. Do you have any pizza? I seriously need pizza. And we need to pull off a heist tonight, or we're never going to see Mom again." Could not resist sneaking that last bit in there like that. I hoped my voice didn't sound as hysterical as I felt. "This time, I'm not taking no for an answer. We're going—"

And then my father and brothers were hugging me, all of them at once, which made for a tangle of arms and torsos that nearly knocked me over again. I squeezed them back just as hard, wrapping my arms as much as I could around my brothers and burrowing my face into my father's chest. He smelled like familiar forests, the kind around Aspen.

Over my head, Dad said, "Welcome . . . Worm, is it?"

"Benden," Worm said. "My name's Benden."

Liam was the first to pull back. "Sky, you were a dragon! You transformed!"

"Seriously cool," Tuck said.

"The secret is surprisingly cheesy," I told them. My voice was only shaking a little. My eyes felt hot with un-shed tears—I was home! "You have to believe in yourself. And leap off a cliff without dying. I can do fire in dragon form too, sort of, though not as well as Wor—as Benden. He helped teach me, along with his sister, Novi, and Mom—I saw Mom. I was with her."

"Mom?" Charles could not have looked more shocked if I'd said I'd seen a dinosaur. My brothers also wore simi-lar expressions of stunned amazement. "Where? How? Sky, what happened? Where were you?"

His arms still wrapped around me, Dad shepherded all

of us inside. He beckoned for Worm to come too. "Are you being chased?" he asked me.

That depended on how well Ryan had covered for me. If his father believed him, then we were safe until tonight's Reckoning. At the Reckoning, Ryan would have to explain to the council how he executed his first heist—and then the truth would come out, because even if Ryan lied like a champion, he wouldn't be able to explain any of it without mentioning me. "I don't think so. But we don't have much time, and there's a lot to explain."

Dad shooed us all into the kitchen. "Get her food," he ordered. "Check the security feeds—make sure all our alarms are working." He kept looking at me as if he expected me to disappear. All of them did.

Liam sprang out of the room.

"I'll get the food," Tuck said, hurrying to the refrigerator. He pulled out a box of leftover pizza and began adding to it—strips of prosciutto, slices of olives, all the toppings that he knew I liked best. "What kind do you like?" he asked Benden.

"Ahhh . . . ," Benden answered.

"He's never had pizza. He's from Home."

Their eyes widened so much that I nearly laughed out loud.

"I think you'd better start at the beginning, young lady," Dad said. "You're alive. How . . . ?" There were tears filling his eyes. He didn't let them fall. "You've been Home? And you saw your mother?"

I told them everything.

As Liam returned from checking the security, I started talking, beginning with the day that Ryan came to me and told me about the jewel. I didn't leave anything out. Maximus. Gabriela. Mom. Novi. The wyvern Reckoning, and the realization that the underappreciated wyvern called Worm was the key to returning. All of them were, for the first time in their lives, listening to every word I said.

I stopped once to dart into the bathroom and then again when Tuck served us the pizza. Both Benden and I ate our slices, shoving the pizza into our mouths as if we'd never tasted anything like it, which for Benden was accurate. The cheese was perfectly melty, and the prosciutto was perfectly salty. I wished Mom were here to eat it with us.

Soon, I promised myself.

Talking as I ate, I continued, "So we need to break into the Keene family vault. Only twist is that we have to do it before Ryan testifies to the council at the gathering tonight, or Mr. Keene will know something's wrong, and he might move the Door to a location that we won't know. If he does that . . . I don't know how long it will be before we can save Mom." I swallowed hard and tried to keep my voice steady. "Besides, if we do it tonight, during the Reckoning, in front of everyone, we can expose him. Bring him down."

Dad stood up abruptly and moved to the window. "You want to endanger yourself again. After I . . . after we . . . You can't imagine what it was like, believing you'd died!"

Putting my pizza down, I looked at each of my brothers. All of them seemed to be in various stages of shock. "I didn't, though, and now we have to act quickly."

More quietly, Dad said, "You can't imagine what it was like believing you'd died doing what I should have done."

"You knew?" Of course he knew. I should have realized

it. He'd been hinting at it. All the cryptic statements, the way he was so sure she was alive . . .

"I guessed," he admitted. "She'd told me what she intended—invited me to join her, in fact—and I thought I'd convinced her it was too risky, especially since it was unlikely the Door still existed at all. . . . But I was wrong. By the time I realized she was going through with it anyway, I was too late: she'd been caught. And he'd banished her." His voice broke. "Exile or death—that was the choice he gave her. He told me everything when I confronted him, after I realized what she'd tried to do. I tried to challenge him, but . . . she was already gone. And I had to promise secrecy. He threatened to force the council to destroy your lives if I didn't. I thought, by making that promise and accepting our disgrace, it would keep you all safe."

I felt anger buzzing in my ears. But I forced it down and kept my voice soft, gentle. *He did what he thought was right*, I told myself. *He was trying to protect us.* But if he'd come to us, trusted us, told us . . . we could have worked together as a team, as a family. "So you just abandoned Mom?"

"I protected you!" Smoke curled around him as his voice rose, and then it dissipated and his shoulders slumped again. "But not well enough. Sky . . . I shouldn't have lied to you, to any of you. I should have told you all the truth."

My brothers looked troubled. Especially Charles. "You told us Mom had been banished by the council," Charles accused Dad. "You didn't tell us where. We assumed another continent. Or a desert island somewhere. You said we weren't allowed to know—that was part of the punishment. You didn't tell us *you* knew."

"Believe me, I thought it was for the best," Dad said. "It wasn't safe for you to know."

Oddly, that made me feel better. He hadn't told them everything. My brothers, though, did not look happier. If we made it through this, I had the feeling we were in for a *lot* of family discussions. But there wasn't time for that now.

Seeming to realize that, Charles turned to me. "Your heist tonight—do you have a plan?"

Gratefully, I smiled at him. "Yes. But it needs an explosives expert. Mom thinks Liam can do it." I looked at my brother, the joker, the one who caught the toads to scare me with when I was younger, the one whom Dad had once accused of being determined to go through life without a serious thought in his head, the one who broke the silence.

Charles and Tuck stared at him as well. Liam paled. "You want to put your safety and Mom's safety in *my* hands? But . . . I always fail. Charles, you know I always fail. Look at the piano heist. That was my fault." Wow, I didn't expect him to take responsibility for that.

"You're the best of all of us with explosives," Tuck mumbled.

He looked a bit wild-eyed. "What kind of bomb is it?"

"It's on the Door," I said, and I described it, detailing the wires. I'd stared at it for long enough to memorize it. "I can draw a picture for you. It needs to be defused before we can get the jewel out of the vault. Please, Liam, will you do it? Charles and Tuck—I'm going to need your help too. Last time the house was empty when we broke in. This time, the Keenes will be home, plus every wyvern in the Western United States, outside the California Stronghold, will be there for the Reckoning. Even worse, the gathering will be catered."

"Why is that worse?" Liam asked.

"The kitchen will be full of staff, and that's where the entrance to the basement is. Charles, do you think you could . . . I don't know . . . lock the chefs in the pantry?"

"I can secure the kitchen," Charles said.

"And Tuck . . . I'll need you to cook. We can't let anyone know what's going on until we're done. You'll have to keep the food flowing out of the kitchen so the servers don't suspect anything. You're lousy at pottery, but you're a really good cook. I know you can fool them. You just need to keep things going until Liam, Gabriela, Benden, and I get the Door."

Tuck mumbled, "You came back from death. Or Home. Lead on, Sis—we'll follow."

Liam thumped the table. "Let's do it!" he cried.

Charles was looking at Dad, waiting for him to turn around, waiting for him to react. We all looked at him too. Tentatively, I asked, "Dad, what do you think?"

He didn't answer.

Silence. Benden munched his third or fourth slice of pizza.

"Will you help me?" I asked.

"Us," Charles corrected.

Liam and Tuck nodded in agreement.

I looked at my brothers and felt my eyes heat up for the second time in less than an hour. I appealed to Dad again, "Will you help *us* bring Mom home? The Keenes will be home. We'll need someone to keep them out of the kitchen and away from the security monitors without raising their suspicions. You'd be perfect for that. You're supposed to be at the gathering, mingling. It would be natural for you to talk to them. Much more than for any of us."

He didn't answer for a long time. We all stared at his back, and I saw that as he looked out the window, he wasn't looking at anything outside—he was looking at our reflections.

He whispered so softly that I wouldn't have heard him except that I was watching his face, reflected in the window, "I can't lose you."

"Then help us," I pleaded.

He turned to face me, and I saw there were tears on his cheeks. "I lost you once."

"And I came back. We can do this." I stood. "Daddy, please."

He smiled as the tears rolled faster. "I'm proud of you."

I felt my own tears threaten to fall. Those words were more wonderful than ice cream. I could feel myself storing them inside me, making them part of my bones, my blood, my heart. I'd pull them out later, if I needed them. "Is that a yes?"

"Yes," he said.

He sat at the table, and Benden continued stuffing yet another slice of pizza in his mouth. "Tell us what to do," Charles said to me. "It's your heist. You lead; we'll follow."

I drew a deep breath. "Okay, let's plan."

CHAPTER TWENTY-TWO

TUCK WARMED UP A hundredth slice of pizza for Benden and a second for me. He heaped extra olives on mine. Charles disappeared for a moment and then returned with a white-board and a bunch of markers. He scrawled the word "Target" and the word "Crew."

Getting up, I wrote under "Target":

The Door

And under "Crew" I put:

Sky
Dad
Charles
Liam
Tuck

"Hey, why did you list Liam before me?" Tuck asked.

Benden

"Are you in?" I asked Benden.

"You've offered me a new life," he said. "Yeah, I'll burn stuff for you."

Gabriela?

"We need her to get through the wyvern detection spell," I said, "but I don't know if she'll do it again. I need to visit her and ask."

"No way," Charles said. "Can't risk you being seen. You're dead, remember? You need to stay out of sight. If Mr. Keene hears you're alive, he'll know you came through the Door."

"I'll go get her," Tuck said, standing.

"What are you going to tell her?" I asked.

"As little as possible," he said, and then he left the kitchen and jogged toward his car. I saw him out the window as he peeled out of the garage.

I added to the whiteboard:

Ryan?

Tapping his name, I said, "He'll help if he can, but we aren't going to be able to communicate with him ahead of time, so we can't plan on it." And then I wrote:

Mom

"Obviously she can't help until she's back," Charles pointed out.

Getting up, Benden added to my list:

Novi
Other exiles

"Good." It was a much larger crew than last time, so that had to help. Of course, it was a more complicated heist. We had to execute it while every wyvern in the West was there.

Charles started another list, this time with "Security" at the top.

I ran down the different security measures that led to the vault. "Benden fried all the security cameras, so that should be fine. There's a wall of fire on the stairs . . . Do we have any fire protection potion?"

"Yeah," Tuck said. "Got some leftover from when I took cooking lessons—the chef was human."

"Good." Gabriela would need it. Really, really hoped she'd agree to come with Tuck.

"It's possible the security cameras will be fixed before tonight," Dad said.

"Then we fry them again," Benden said with a shrug.

As I continued to describe our last heist attempt, Charles continued to write on the whiteboard, listing out every item with arrows that pointed to a solution. He put a big fat question mark next to security cameras.

I broke off talking. "Do you always whiteboard your heists?"

"It's important to be organized," Charles said.

"It feels like we're making a supermarket list."

"We *are* out of cereal," Liam said.

Dad shook his head. "How can you joke? Do you realize what is at stake here? If we fail, we will, at best, be exiled from this world, from our home, from everything we have ever known." He met each of our eyes, as if he wanted to impress us with the seriousness of this.

"At least we'll be together," I said.

"Unless this Mr. Keene decides to kill us all instead," Benden pointed out.

I shot him a look.

Shrugging, he ate another enormous bite of pizza.

Before anyone could say anything else, the front door slammed open. Charles quickly grabbed the eraser to destroy the record of our plan, but Dad put his hand on his wrist. "It's your brother and Sky's friend. Sky trusts her."

Footsteps came, running toward the kitchen, and then Gabriela burst inside, followed by Tuck. "You're alive!" She barreled across the room and hurled herself at me, hugging me so tightly that all the air whooshed out of me.

"Ryan's father is a lying liar who lies," I told her. "The jewel is a portal. It leads to the world that my kind originally came from. We call it Home. Our ancestors were exiled from there generations ago, but then the Door—the jewel—was lost, or supposedly lost. Turns out that Mr. Keene has had it in his vault and has been secretly exiling people there for years. Including my mother. And now, most recently, me."

She drew back to gawk at me. "Whoa, seriously? You were sent through a portal dimension?"

Charles shook his head. "Sky, you can't just spring that kind of thing on a human—"

"So cool!" Gabriela said.

Charles blinked. "Or maybe you can."

Out of the corner of my eye, I saw Liam gawking at Gabriela with nearly the same expression that she'd just worn. I smirked. *Nicely done*, I thought. Gabriela had impressed my brothers. Especially Liam.

"We're going to try to steal the jewel again," I told her. "It's going to be dangerous. More dangerous than the first heist. And I can't guarantee they'll just bribe you if we fail. They might decide you know too much."

Gabriela gripped my hands. "What's it like? Double suns? Unicorns? Is the gravity the same? Do they speak the same language? Are there parallel versions of all of us? Killer robots?"

Liam's expression turned even more admiring at the words "killer robots."

Oh, I was going to be teasing him about this later. *If there is a later*, I amended.

"There are a lot of dragons," I told her. "And unicorns. No double sun. There are a few robots. All the exiles spoke English, but I didn't meet any of the wyverns who weren't connected with the exiles—pretty sure they don't speak English. But the ones I met taught me how to turn into a dragon."

She blinked fast. "Oh, that is so awesome. I think I'm going to cry."

Dad loomed over us. "It's not a game. Sky, we trust you, but it's irresponsible to include a human—"

"We need her," I said. "Unless you have a counterspell to the wyvern detection spell? Maximus told me no such counterspell exists. We need a human. Specifically Gabriela. She's done it before, and I trust her."

Gabriela blushed.

Quickly, I summarized everything we needed to do, while Charles pointed to the relevant points on the whiteboard—I introduced Worm/Benden as the substitute for Maximus and explained that Liam was an expert on explosives.

Liam gave Gabriela a little wave with a goofy smile on his face.

She beamed back at him.

Rolling my eyes, I continued, "We need a plan for how we'll arrive and gain access. . . . You guys can arrive by car, as if everything is normal, but I can't be seen. As soon as Ryan's father knows I'm here, it's over."

"Then you should stay here," Dad said. "Let us handle this. You've done enough. Stay here, and stay safe, where I don't have to worry—"

"Dad, no! I can't!" Going up to the whiteboard, I thumped on the security measures. "Gabriela passes the wall of fire and blocks the wyvern detection spell. Then I cross the lasers and crack the lock—then Worm blasts the fire beast and Liam defuses the bomb. You need me for this to work! We need all of us!"

Studying the whiteboard, Charles said, "She's right."

I took a deep breath and added, "Besides, it's my heist." After I said it, I held my breath—Dad could shoot down the whole idea if he wanted to. Or he could take control of the heist. Or give leadership to Charles as the oldest.

"How are we going to get in?" Gabriela asked. "If there's a party going on . . . Last time we came across the gardens, but that won't work if there are people outside."

"You can't drive in with the rest of us, that's clear," Liam said. "You know human photographers like to lurk outside our gatherings. Reporters will have a field day with your miraculous return to life. Mr. Keene won't even have to see you for yourself—he can watch you on TV."

"Obviously, she has to fly in." Worm—Benden—helped himself to another slice of pizza. He stared at the microwave for a moment, shrugged, and ate the slice cold. "That's how we got out."

"I can fly in while everyone's arriving." I continued to watch Dad, who was scowling so hard that it looked like his face would crack. "No one will expect a thief to come in dragon form."

"Ooh, can I see your dragon form?" Gabriela clapped her hands.

Liam was gawking *again* at Gabriela. "Is she for real?"

"She's human," I explained. "They're excitable."

Gabriela looked faintly injured. "Well, it's exciting. Don't you think? A portal to another world? Dragon transformations? Not to mention the fact that Sky isn't dead. You have to agree that's worth a little excitement."

All of them looked at me again. "We do like that fact," Charles said.

I tried to imagine what it must have been like for them, speaking at my funeral. I also wondered how Dad was going to explain this to the school attendance office. And, like, everyone. We weren't going to be able to hide the fact that I'd been ruled dead. . . .

"We will wait until night," Dad declared. "Your brothers and I will arrive by car for the Reckoning. Benden will come as our guest, a distant cousin. And you will fly in with Gabriela." Everyone nodded. It was the most sensible plan. But it would make the timing tight.

Tuck looked out the window. "Still got a couple of hours until night."

Liam joined him to look outside. "Yep. What do we do until then?"

"We must wait," Dad said firmly.

⁓

Waiting is hard.

We discussed the plan some more.

We each practiced our roles.

We ate dinner, though no one was hungry and Benden declared he felt nauseous.

We each peed a few times. I changed my outfit twice. And then finally we went outside to be dragons for a little while. I wanted to practice transforming on the ground without needing to leap off an object—I'd need to do that when we flew to the Keenes' house—and I wanted to practice transforming back to human while in midflight (just a foot or two off the ground, of course). And Charles, Tuck, and Liam wanted to learn how to transform too.

Teaching my brothers how to turn into dragons by encouraging them to leap off the roof of our gazebo was not something I'd ever thought I'd be doing. Liam and Tuck grasped the concept quickly. Oddly, Charles didn't.

"It's self-doubt," Benden told me as we watched them practice. "Worse, it's a cycle. Once you fail, you expect to fail again. You're lucky it came easily to you."

The twins cavorted through the flower beds as a matched set of blue dragons with black wings and yellow tongues. Gabriela was staring at them as if she could memorize every second. I noticed she seemed to be watching Liam more than Tuck.

"Are you sure your dad will be able to distract your enemy?" Benden asked. He was eating again, an apple this time. He'd made himself sick with the pizza, but it hadn't slowed him down. He ate as if he was afraid he'd never have enough to eat again.

"Of course he can." All he had to do was attend the Reckoning and keep Ryan's father occupied, ideally outside with the rest of the guests, until we had the jewel.

"It's just that he doesn't seem so keen on this whole plan." He winced as Liam and Tuck head-butted each other. "Ooh, that had to hurt." The twins then turned on Charles, who was sitting cross-legged on the roof of the gazebo with his fists clenched and eyes squeezed shut.

"Dad's just worried about us." Understandable, given that the last heist hadn't worked out so well. But I had come back, and I'd found Mom. So in a way, it was a success. Sort of. "He'll do it. I know him."

Looking over at us, Liam winked his overly large dragon eye at Gabriela, and he and Tuck both hunkered down and crept up on Charles, one from each side of the gazebo. Gabriela giggled.

"I think Charles is going to—" Benden began.

As the twins leaped for Charles, he suddenly ballooned out. Scales broke out over his body, and he transformed into an enormous golden dragon, crushing the poor gazebo. Roaring, he swatted Liam with his tail and swiped at Tuck with his claws.

The three of them began chasing one another around the garden.

Gabriela scooted closer to us. "Aren't you going to trans-form?" she asked Benden. She'd already seen me do it, as I was explaining the process to my brothers.

"Can't do it," he said.

"Why not?"

"Self-esteem issues," I chimed in.

She frowned. "But you're a wyvern."

"So?" Benden scowled. "Still can't do it."

"Because you don't believe you can?"

"It's more complicated than that," Benden said.

"No, it's not," I said.

Gabriela brightened. "How about I believe for you? Will that work?"

He stared at her, and for a split second I was sure it would work and he'd solve all his emotional issues in the blinding light of Gabriela's faith and optimism. "Tell me about the Home of the Fighting Badgers," he said.

She blinked. "School? Um, okay . . . but why do you want to know about that? Compared to this"—she waved her hand at my dragon brothers—"it's boring."

"Not to me. Tell me about being human. Please." And *he* was looking at *her* with the same expression she had worn when I'd told her about wyverns.

So Gabriela started talking about the quirks of high school, while Benden listened with rapt attention. As she talked, she grew more and more animated—she'd been so busy thinking about other worlds that I don't know if she'd ever noticed all the great things in her own.

While she expounded on the glories of research papers, I thought about Dad. How it must have felt when he'd heard I'd died. How he must have blamed Mr. Keene. How he must feel now, knowing that Mr. Keene had lied, knowing that Mr. Keene had torn apart our family for a second time. Would Dad be able to talk civilly with him?

After my brothers had successfully transformed a few times, Benden worked with all of us on fire breathing. My brothers were far more advanced than I was—they already could control their fire with the precision of a blowtorch. So I ended up practicing with Benden, while Liam chatted with Gabriela.

Benden and I etched patterns with our breath in the grass. I'd just finished drawing on a tree with my thin stream of fire when Dad came outside.

And like that, playtime was over. The magnitude of what we were about to do crashed down on all of us, and every worry that we'd been suppressing surfaced again.

"Earpieces," he said, holding out his hand.

My brothers transformed into their human shapes, and we all trotted to gather around Dad. He'd prepared one earpiece and mic set for each of us. Sticking mine into my ear and attaching the mic inside my shirt, I tested it. "Lalala, can you hear me?"

"You're standing right next to me," Liam said. He then turned to Gabriela and helped her insert her earpiece. She smiled at him as he pushed her hair back from her neck. I made a mental note to tease her later too.

When we were certain all the earpieces were working, I took mine out and put it into my pocket—I'd wear it after I was done with the dragon flight part of the plan. "Okay. Gabriela will be with me. Dad, you have to keep Mr. and Mrs. Keene outside the house. Charles—"

"I keep an eye on the kitchen. Before you arrive, I clear out anyone who's there."

"Tuck?"

"I take over for the cooks," he said. "Keep the food flowing so the guests don't get suspicious. I'll tell the servers that the cooks are on break."

"Liam?"

"I'll meet you in the kitchen, ready to defuse."

"Benden, you'll be with Liam," I told Benden. Then I looked at each of them, making sure I had their attention. Good. Now, we needed an emergency backup plan. "If anything goes wrong—"

Dad interrupted. "If anything goes wrong, fly out of there."

"Nuh-uh, we're not going to do that," Liam said.

"You must," Dad barked. "I'll have your promise on this. Each of you. If we fail, you leave and don't look back. There are emergency funds—draw on them and melt into the world. Stay away from any enclaves of wyverns. No Colorado. No California. Hide among the humans far away from any of our kind."

"But we won't fail," I said.

My brothers echoed me.

And then I made the promise anyway, because Dad needed to hear it, because in his eyes I'd already died once, because I didn't want him to have to be afraid anymore. But it was a promise that I planned to break.

Either we came out of this together as a family, or we didn't come out of it at all.

CHAPTER TWENTY-THREE

WE PILED INTO CARS. Gabriela and I crouched in the back of Dad's, with Dad and Charles in the front, and Benden went with Liam and Tuck in Liam's car—to his credit, he didn't ask too many questions, though I knew he hadn't seen a car before. My brothers had lent him a tux. Gabriela and I wore all black.

By the turnoff to the lake, Dad slowed. "Be careful," he told me.

"Always," I promised.

He looked as if he didn't believe me.

"I'll try. Really. Aside from flying through my boyfriend's window and breaking into a high-security vault, I won't do anything crazy."

He nearly smiled.

Gabriela and I got out of the car and scurried into the underbrush. We watched Dad and Liam drive up toward the gate. "Are you ready?" I whispered to Gabriela.

"Can I rename myself Gabriela the Dragon Rider?"

Grinning at her, I transformed between the trees—every time I changed, it was easier, probably because I didn't doubt I could do it—and Gabriela the Dragon Rider climbed onto my back. "Hold on," I told her. "And do you have my grappling hook? Keep it ready. But still hold on."

"This is the coolest night ever," she announced.

I flew.

Higher.

Higher.

I reached the clouds. Mist closed around us. As we flew closer, I saw Ryan's house beneath us, blurred from the mist. Circling, I came at it from behind. I knew exactly which window was Ryan's. I hoped he didn't mind if we broke in through it.

He wouldn't be there, I knew. As the host's son, he would be in the courtyard, greeting guests with his father and mother.

"Ready?" I called to Gabriela.

"I think I'm going to be sick!" Gabriela called back.

Diving down, I hoped she could hold it together. We needed to time this right—otherwise we'd end up plummeting down the cliff. I couldn't go through the window as a dragon—I'd have to transform. "Ready with the hook?"

She had my grappling hook—the same one I used to climb out my bedroom window. As I swung past the roof, Gabriela tossed it, and it caught the edge of the gutter. She hung on to the rope as I kept flying, clinging to it as she slid off me.

Climbing down, she reached Ryan's window. She had a rock to break it, but she didn't need to use it. The window opened, and Ryan stuck his head out. "Gabriela? How did you—"

I dove toward the window.

With Ryan's help, Gabriela climbed inside. I saw her explaining to him, but the wind was too loud and I was too far away to hear her words. Hopefully she was saying something along the lines of *Get back from the window.*

I'd only practiced a midflight transformation in our backyard, a foot or two above the nice, soft, grassy lawn. But there wasn't time to consider whether this was a good idea or not.

Flattening my wings, I picked up speed. Closer, closer, closer . . . *Now!*

Transforming, I shot through the window in human form. Skidding across his carpet, I crashed into Ryan. He caught me, and the momentum propelled us both back against the side of his bed.

"Ow," he said.

"Hi," I said. "Good catch. Thanks."

"No." *Huff.* "Problem." He tried to catch his breath. Apparently I'd knocked it out of him. I couldn't help grinning as I looked at him.

"Earpiece, Sky," Gabriela reminded me.

I inserted it in time to hear Charles say, *"Are you in, Sky?"*

"Here," I told my brothers and Dad.

I heard the buzz of other voices—my brothers should be making their way to the kitchen. For a brief second, I worried about them. They'd have to herd the cooks into the pantry, but what if they resisted? What if they fought? My brothers would fight back, but it could cause noise, raise an alarm, draw attention. . . . There was a lot more that could go wrong this time around. I preferred sneaking into an empty house.

"What's your plan?" Ryan asked. "How can I help?"

My earpiece crackled. *"Everyone, we have a problem. Dad can't find Mr. Keene. He's not outside greeting the guests,"* Charles warned.

The wyvern gathering always occurred outside, under the stars. In this case, in Ryan's yard, between the manicured bushes. Waiters would be roving through the crowds, distributing drinks and hors d'oeuvres. All the reporters would be stopped at the gate, but the wyverns would be pausing for pictures before coming inside. Ryan's parents should both be there to greet them.

"Your dad," I asked. "Where is he? Why isn't he outside yet?"

"He's just in his office, preparing his speech. He's planning to present me to the council tonight—I told him I'd completed my first heist. Sky . . . once the wyverns start questioning me about your heist, the truth is going to come out. There's no way I could have executed it on my own. They'll know I'm lying. But I can buy you time."

"Thank you." To Dad, I said, "He's in his office."

"I'll take care of it," Dad said. *"Sit tight."*

"How?" I asked. "Dad, he's dangerous."

"I will tell him that I am requesting a reevaluation of my family's status. I'm challenging the council's ruling. I want to be reexamined. That will get him down here."

"Dad, are you sure you can do this?" Charles's voice whispered in the earpiece. *"He's responsible for Mom, for Sky's almost-death. If he figures out we're on to him—"*

"Trust me," Dad said. *"Like I am trusting you. I won't fail you all again."*

Okay, it was only a slight change in plans. We could deal with this. "Ryan, any changes to security on the vault? Are the cameras back online? Any new spells?"

"Cameras are still out, but the other security systems are operational. He hasn't added anything new—there hasn't been time, and with you gone . . . Well, he didn't expect you to come back."

"Good. Counting on that. Anything else we need to know?"

"You need to know I love you. I should have said that before. Long time before. I should have said it to the whole gathering, instead of listening to my father."

His words made me feel like a hundred balloons were attached to my arms. I felt dizzy but in a good way. I shook my head. "Your father is dangerous. I understand that now. You did what you had to do to protect yourself and me."

He crossed to me and took my hands. "I will never hurt you again, Sky. I love you. A million times over, I love you."

In my ear, Tuck mumbled, *"Dude, we can hear you."*

Tears were in my eyes. "I love you too." And then we were kissing again, and this time it did feel like fireworks, exploding inside me, with a fanfare so loud in my ears that the rest of the world was blotted out. When the kiss ended, I felt as if my head were spinning.

"Did not need to hear that," Charles said.

I was grinning at Ryan and couldn't stop.

"Um, Sky?" Benden said. *"Shouldn't we, you know, do the heist?"*

"Right." I was too happy to even blush. Ryan was *mine*.

He'd lied for me. He loved me. And we could continue this conversation (and the kissing) just as soon as we survived the next hour.

In the hall, outside his door, we heard footsteps on the stairs. A door opened. A door closed. I heard voices: my father's and his. I couldn't hear words, but I could hear tone. And then a door was thrown open. A door slammed. Footsteps. Two sets. They were in the hall, coming toward Ryan's room. "Have you been talking to my son behind my back?" Mr. Keene was asking Dad.

"I've got this," Ryan whispered to me. "Hide."

Gabriela ducked behind his bed, and I hid under his desk.

My father spoke. "We've had no contact, beyond a handshake at my daughter's funeral. I am surprised that you attended." He sounded civil, completely cordial. Nice emphasis on the word "daughter's." I was impressed.

"She was a child. It was a tragedy. I hope you know that you have my deepest sympathies. The loss of a child, no matter how misguided she was, no matter how poor her decisions, is the harshest pain. I know you must blame yourself greatly. The questions you must ask yourself: if only you'd watched her more carefully, if only you'd instilled a greater sense of caution, if only you'd erected firmer boundaries, would it be different?"

My father began to speak, but Mr. Keene cut him off.

"I am not criticizing your parenting style," Mr. Keene said. "Far from it. Your sons are everything a wyvern could hope for: ambitious yet obedient, independent yet respectful, talented and hardworking. You should be very proud." They were just outside Ryan's bedroom.

"I was proud of my daughter as well," Dad said stiffly. "She was strong in all the ways someone should be strong. She knew her own mind, and she pursued her goals. Her mother was proud of her too."

"Ahh, it is that blind spot that is the reason that I will not vote for your reinstatement," Mr. Keene said. He sounded truly regretful. "I am sorry, but your judgment is clouded."

"Loving one's family is not a weakness. It is a strength!"

I wondered if Mr. Keene was trying to bait Dad. It sounded like it, as if he wanted to force Dad to say something that would incriminate him, something that Mr. Keene could use against him at the Reckoning. Suddenly, I was sure: everything my family had said about Mr. Keene was true. He wanted my family to be cast out of wyvern society for good.

We had to take him down.

"Your 'strength' led to the loss of your wife and daughter," Mr. Keene said. "Do you really want to jeopardize your boys as well? Right now their fate is precarious, tainted by their association with failure. Keep them on the straight and narrow, and all will be well." The bedroom door opened. "Son, it's time," Ryan's father said.

"I'm ready," Ryan said. He blocked his father's view as he went out, and he shut the door behind him. It was smooth—Mr. Keene had no reason to suspect we were here. "Hello, Mr. Hawkins."

"I heard you completed your first heist, Ryan. Congratulations. That's a mighty achievement. Thomas, you must be very proud of him."

"Indeed I am," Mr. Keene said heartily.

I was proud of Dad—he'd kept his head with Mr. Keene.

And I was proud of Ryan. He'd given no hint to his father that anything at all unusual was happening.

All three of them headed for the stairs. I listened for their footsteps, counting them. Soon they reached the bottom. Beckoning to Gabriela to follow, I crept out of Ryan's room, through the hall in the opposite direction, and then down the back stairs to the kitchen.

My brothers and Benden were waiting for us. Tuck was busily adding stuffed cherry tomatoes to a tray and passing it out the window. Charles was standing guard in front of the pantry door, arms crossed, biceps bulging, like a bouncer in a club.

Without a word, Liam and Benden joined us as we crossed to the basement door. I picked the lock and we headed down.

The wall of fire was just where we'd left it, but Gabriela didn't hesitate. She downed the vial of the fire resistance spell and strode through the fire. Liam, Benden, and I followed. I stopped the boys at the base of the steps, while Gabriela knelt in front of the wyvern detection spell.

I then danced my way through the lasers. On the other side, I shut them off, and Liam, Benden, and Gabriela joined me. As before, I hooked onto the ceiling, hung upside down, and cracked the lock. It took me two minutes. Less. When the vault door opened, Benden blasted the fire beast. It withered, and we entered the vault, crossing directly to the Door.

"We're in," I said to the earpiece. Then I turned to my brother. "Liam, your turn."

He knelt by the jewel.

"Hurry," Dad said. *"The council is questioning Ryan*

about his supposed heist. He's lying for you well, but the cracks are showing. They're beginning to become suspicious."

Concentrating, Liam muttered to himself. "Blue wire . . . red wire . . . connect to black wire . . . and yes, come to papa, that's it, careful . . . careful. . . ."

We watched him, not daring to breathe, hoping he was as much of an expert as we all thought . . . hoping a childhood spent accidentally blowing things up was actually time well spent . . . hoping it was okay to trust someone else, to trust family. . . . A heist is all about trust. Each of us was trusting everyone else to do their job. And each of us had to trust ourselves to deliver in the clutch.

"You can do it," I whispered.

My other brothers echoed me, softly, and Dad. Gabriela whispered too, "Come on, you can do it. I believe in you."

He snipped a wire.

Nothing happened.

His shoulders relaxed. "Done."

The earpiece crackled. *"Sky, get your team out of there now!"* Dad ordered. *"Charles, Tuck, to me! Get ready!"* And then the earpiece squealed. I yanked it out.

Pulling on gloves, I picked the jewel up and shoved it into a bag. Slinging the bag over my shoulder, I hurried out of the vault. Gabriela, Benden, and Liam came with me. We ran through the hallway, up the stairs, and into the kitchen—it was empty.

Reaching the door first, Liam threw it open and then reeled back.

Outside on the lawn, blocking our way to the party tent, Dad, and freedom, was a very massive, very angry dragon with fire in his mouth.

CHAPTER TWENTY-FOUR

—

Mr. Keene—it had to be him—reared back, wings spread wide. Fire shot out of his mouth, and he slammed his front talons against the house. Gabriela, Benden, and Liam yanked me backward, and we stumbled away, back against the kitchen cabinets. The copper pots clanked against one another. A tray tipped off a counter and fell onto the floor.

Rearing again, Mr. Keene slammed into his house even harder.

I saw Dad rush forward, trying to reach us, as Mr. Keene bashed the house a third time.

The wall burst apart. Bricks rained down, and we ducked, huddled together. Yelping, my father was hit. A brick knocked against the side of his head, and he fell. The ground shook, and instead of a wall, there was now a gaping hole to the outside.

"Dad!" I cried.

Beyond him, I saw Charles and Tuck transform.

Straddling Dad, Ryan's father roared. He was a massive red dragon, twice the size of my brothers. Beside me, Gabriela was screaming. She clutched my arm. Liam was on my other side, squeezing my arm. Benden was somewhere behind me.

More wyverns were here, I knew, stuck in their human forms, but they were on the other side of Mr. Keene, beyond my brothers, in the gardens and under the party tent. I didn't know if they could even see me, and I knew they couldn't hear me, not over his roaring.

I'd planned to make a speech. Reveal the traitorous lies of Mr. Keene. Expose his secrets. But Mr. Keene was standing over my father, his talons resting on Dad's neck, and I knew if I spoke, he would rip those talons into Dad's soft, human skin. He'd broken the wall to his own house to reach me, to show me his power.

Around me, everyone was shouting. My dragon brothers. Liam. Gabriela. Dad. Benden rushed forward, his mouth open wide to spurt flame, but Charles, in dragon form, blocked him. I thought I heard Ryan and even Ryan's mother, her shriek shrill and frightened.

I grew quiet.

I was the one who was holding the Door.

"Give it to me," Mr. Keene said, "and he lives." His dragon voice echoed, like a stereo pumped up too loud. It reverberated inside my bones.

And I felt myself lose my temper. The world zeroed in on just me, the jewel, and Mr. Keene. *It's all about power,* I thought clinically.

Who had it. Who didn't. Who thought they had it.

Mr. Keene wasn't a massive dragon because he worked out at the gym as a human. He was large because that was how he saw himself: as more important than anyone else. There was no conservation of mass physics rule being followed here. It was shape-shifting. Magic.

Power.

I had the Door.

But he had Dad.

Shaking off Liam and Gabriela, I drew the Door out of the bag and held it in my gloved hands toward Mr. Keene. I felt very calm. As I walked toward him, I was making plans. All I had to do was take off a glove. If I touched the jewel, I could end this. I could go through and return with the exiles. That would be proof of what Mr. Keene had done. That would end his power. But I had to time it right. . . . I had to be far enough out of the house so the other wyverns could see me, see that I was alive, see me use the Door. . . .

Dad saw me first. Guessed what I was about to do.

"Sky, no!" Dad cried. "He'll destroy it and trap you there."

Ryan ran past his father and jumped over mine, vaulting into the kitchen. "He won't destroy it while I'm there." Before I could speak or even react, he placed his hand on the jewel.

Ryan vanished in a rainbow.

"No!" Mr. Keene howled.

His mother rushed toward us. "You swore you wouldn't! You promised me! Not our son!" But she wasn't talking to me. She was talking to Ryan's father.

Stunned, he was silent. She'd never raised her voice to

him before, at least not that I'd heard. She was always quiet, always in the background, with a meek smile. She'd served us muffins and milk when we were little, and she'd have her husband's dinner ready when he was home from work. I'd never expected her to be the one to step forward. Clearly, he hadn't either.

I seized my chance. I held the jewel over my head. "This is the Door to Home!" I shouted, loud enough for all the other wyverns to hear me. "Thomas Keene has been using it to rid himself of his personal enemies. For power. This is how he became the head of the council. This is how he became the wealthiest wyvern. It wasn't because he followed our rules better than other wyverns. It was because he broke them!"

"Give it to me," Mr. Keene roared.

It was a risk. I knew it. But I also knew the people I faced, and I knew—hoped I knew—what they would do. Bending down, I rolled the jewel toward Mr. Keene. I aimed it carefully, so it would roll past Mrs. Keene. Mr. Keene lifted his talon off Dad's neck in order to reach for it—and Ryan's mother stepped in front and caught the Door. She cradled it in her sleeves, not touching it.

"Gretchen," Mr. Keene pleaded. "What are you doing?"

She began to retreat. Backward. Step by step. Toward me. "This has to stop, Thomas. Don't you see it's gone too far? And now our son . . . No more."

"But I did it for you," he said. "All for you."

Ryan's mother smiled sadly. "In the beginning perhaps, it was for love. But it hasn't been about love for a long time now. You've changed, Thomas. This power has changed you, and not for the better. I miss who you used to be. That is why I told Anabeth about the jewel. That is why I helped her try to steal it."

Ryan's mother was Mom's contact, I realized. She was the human who had helped Mom bypass the wyvern detection spell. She had interfered with their security cameras. She had given Mom all the intel she needed. She simply hadn't known about the final alarm on the Door—she'd been unable to see that part of the vault. He'd aimed the cameras away to hide how he was using the portal. He hadn't wanted a record of what he'd done to my mother, Maximus's wife, and who knew how many others.

"You betrayed me," he said. "We're family!"

And in that moment of distraction, I transformed and flew toward him, my claws extended, as my brothers breathed fire at Mr. Keene. Benden's flame shot out past theirs. As Benden's white-hot fire hit his side, scorching his scales, Mr. Keene launched himself into the air.

Soaring up, I chased him, shooting through the night sky. I felt the wind in my face, saw all three of my brothers in the air out of the corner of my eye.

He fled.

Larger and faster than us, he outdistanced us. When he was a pinprick in the distance, indistinguishable from the night stars, my brothers and I returned to the courtyard.

Transforming back into our human selves, all of us raced to Dad. He was clutching a gash on his arm but otherwise was okay. He smiled at me, a strained, lopsided kind of smile, but it still counted. "I'm proud of you, Sky."

Those words were like music from a solid gold piano.

"Now go save your mother."

I walked toward Mrs. Keene, who was still staring at the

sky, at the spot where her husband had vanished into the distance, and still cradling the jewel wrapped in her sleeves.

When I stopped in front of her, she blinked and seemed to notice me for the first time. She licked her lips. Swallowed. Tried to speak, failed, and then tried again. "Will you . . . will you bring my son home?"

"I'll bring all of them home," I promised.

And I put my hand on the Door.

I'd like to say the rainbow didn't hurt as much this time, but *ow*.

Blinking up at the roof of the cave, I wallowed for a moment in the familiar someone-hit-me-with-a-sledgehammer sensation. As the headache began to fade slightly, I realized I heard voices.

Loud, shouty voices, muffled by distance and a lot of rock.

At least two of them were familiar: Mom's and Ryan's.

"It's safe now!" Ryan was shouting.

Mom chimed in, "Listen to the boy! You can trust him!"

"Um, not to be overly critical . . ." Maximus. "But he doesn't know what happened back on Earth! His charming father could have the Door back in his possession. It could be guarded by another fire beast. You're asking these people to walk into what could be a death trap!"

"I'm asking them to take a leap of faith!" Mom said. "Like your wife did! Like you did! Like I did! Our freedom lies on the other side of this jewel!"

Other voices jumped in, and the cave echoed with shouted arguments.

Some wanted to charge in here and try the Door.

Others wanted to stay safe.

I could end this, if I could just stand up.

Wincing, I forced myself to sit. "Ow, ow, ow."

"Sky!"

Novi's shout brought the headache pounding back.

She dropped to her knees next to me. "Are you all right? Are you exiled again? Where's my brother? Is he dead? I knew he'd end up dead. Knew it was too good to be true. Knew—"

I stopped her. "Novi. He's fine. And I'm . . . Ow!"

"Oh! Sorry!" Fumbling in her pockets, she drew out the medicine that had fixed my headache on my first visit. I drank it greedily, and the throbbing receded.

The shouting, however, had gotten worse.

With Novi behind me, I hurried to the Hall of the Returned. Everyone was there. Or at least, you know, a lot of wyverns, mostly exiles and their families. It was packed. A few robots wheeled between them, holding bowls of soup that no one was interested in eating.

Ryan was standing on a table next to Mom.

I paused for a moment, admiring him.

"Don't trust me," he was saying. "Trust Sky! She can do it! She—"

Maximus cut him off. "—is standing right there."

Everyone turned to look at me.

There was total silence.

You could have heard a flame flicker. That silent.

And I knew I should make some kind of grand speech, but really, that's not my style. "Anyone want to go home?" I asked. "Real home?"

~

Not everyone wanted to go.

Maximus, for example, wanted to stay with his wife, and Angela said that even though she hadn't arrived here quite the way she wanted, she'd worked too hard to find Home to leave just yet. He did, though, leave her side long enough to say, "Congratulations."

I wasn't sure exactly which bit of it he was congratulating me for. "Thanks?"

"Your first heist," he clarified. "I'd say you nailed it."

Yeah, I guess I did, I thought. "Good luck with your life here."

He winked at me. "Don't need luck. I have love." And with that cheesy line, he sauntered back through the crowd toward his wife.

Others also chose to stay—they'd made lives here, or were afraid, or whatever—but there were plenty more who wanted to come with us. One of Ryan's uncles, the one who burned hamburgers at barbecues, was first in line. Plus a few wyverns I recognized as recent council members—one who supposedly left his wife and family for a life in Peru, another who had a very nice funeral. Several I didn't know. And of course, Mom and Ryan.

Stationed by the jewel, Novi handed out vials of the headache medicine. And one by one, we each touched the Door.

More rainbows.

More headache.

And then . . . more family.

All around me, families were reuniting and embracing, crying, staring, shouting.

Mrs. Keene let out a cry like a wounded bird as she threw her arms around her son. She sobbed into Ryan's shoulder as he comforted her. Ryan's lost uncle milled around the courtyard until a few friends converged on him, slapping his back and welcoming him home.

I started toward my family, but my path was blocked by a familiar pack of wyverns: my old friends. Emma, Emily, Jake, Topher, Rosario, and Carlos. Emma began, "Sky . . ."

I cut her off. "No, I don't forgive you."

Emma dropped her head. Carlos scuffed the ground with his shoe.

Then I sighed. "Maybe I'll consider forgiving you eventually. But Gabriela sits with us at lunch. And she's promoted to sole future maid-of-honor status."

Emma and Emily bobbed their heads simultaneously.

And then they stepped out of my way, and I ran toward Gabriela, Benden, and my brothers. They caught me in a tangled mess of a hug, and when we let go, all of us were crying. We all turned to Mom and Dad.

"Ew," Liam said.

Our parents were kissing, enthusiastically.

And then we—my brothers, my new friends, and I— threw ourselves onto Mom and Dad, folding them into a great bear hug. Or, you know, *dragon* hug.

EPILOGUE

I SET OUT TO steal a jewel, and I accidentally changed the world.

Gabriela says they'll have to revise the Wyverns Through the Ages poster. Someday, we may all have a chapter in a Modern Wyvern History course textbook. Like King Atahualpa and Sir Francis Drake. Because of us, it's public knowledge: the wyverns of Earth can still transform into dragons, and we possess an active portal to our home dimension.

And while the world—both worlds, really—adjusts to this new reality, we are taking full advantage of it. Skipping my mountain bike, I flew in dragon form to Gabriela's house.

I transformed back to human in her driveway and, after knocking my head on a wind chime, rang the doorbell. Both the chimes and the bell rang, and I heard footsteps and shouting inside. Gabriela's father hollered for someone to answer the door and her brother called back that he was busy and then her father yelled back something else, which I didn't quite catch because it was Spanish but must have been something like "do it or you're toast." Three seconds later, I heard footsteps thump toward the door, and the door opened.

Gabriela's brother glared at me. "Gabi, she's here again!" To me, he said, "You're copying her homework, aren't you? That's the only explanation for why you're hanging out with a loser like my sister."

Okay, so not everything is public knowledge. We kept Gabriela's part in the events of the last Reckoning a secret, to protect her privacy while she's a minor (my parents' words, not mine). When she's older, we'll tell the truth so she can take her rightful place in the history books, but for now only wyverns know.

"Send her up!" Gabriela called.

"Come down!" I called back. "They said yes! Novi's bringing it through!"

I heard a whoop, then what sounded like a stack of books falling down, then the thump of someone running down the stairs. "Gotta go!" Gabriela called to her family. At the door, she threw her arms around her brother. "They said yes!"

He looked as if he'd been hugged by a boa constrictor.

She flew past me, grabbing my hand as she ran. "Hurry up!"

Laughing, I let her drag me to her car. "You're sure you're not too excited to drive? Maybe you should give me the keys."

"Ha! Nice try." She got in and so did I.

It took us exactly five minutes and thirty seconds to drive from Gabriela's house to mine. It should have taken twice that. You can make good time if you don't use a brake. She tapped her hands impatiently on the steering wheel as I typed in our code to open the front gate and then zoomed in to park by the front door.

I'd been working on talking the council into letting Gabriela actually visit Home, but since the Door was only recently open to wyverns, there was resistance to sending humans through. Plus no one was sure exactly what the Door would do to a human body.

She seemed to like this consolation prize, though.

"I promise I won't scream and scare it," she said.

Scooting in front of her, I opened the front door before she barreled through it like a cartoon character in overdrive. She skidded to a stop. "Where is it?" she asked.

Mom came out of the music room, which was being transformed into a special room to hold the Door. She was wearing overalls, her hair was in a bandana, and a splotch of white paint was smeared on her cheek. Still, she looked like she'd walked off a photo shoot for a magazine on home decorating. She and Dad had decided to paint the walls themselves, on the theory that home improvement would give them a chance to work through the strain recent events had put on their marriage. She'd read that advice in some magazine, and Dad had agreed without hesitation—these days, he pretty much agreed to anything she said without hesitation. "Ah, Gabriela," Mom said. "How are you doing?"

"She's ready," I told Mom.

If she had been any more ready, she'd be vibrating. As it

was, she was hopping from foot to foot, more excited than a kindergartner at her birthday party.

Mom grinned. "It's in the kitchen. Just a visit, remember. You can't keep it."

Gabriela whooped and ran toward the living room.

"This way!" I called after her.

She pivoted and followed me into the kitchen.

The Door was on the counter, next to a plate of microwave pizza rolls. It was cradled in a velvet-lined box. Once Mom was finished remodeling the music room, it would have a more honored place in our house. But for now, we just kept it where we were hanging out. Glowing slightly, it drew Gabriela like a moth to a flame. "It's not here yet. Are you sure—"

The jewel began to pulse with rainbow light.

And then it was there, in our kitchen: a real, live unicorn, with Novi beside it. Its horn shimmered like the moon, its hide glowed as white as the stars, and its liquid blue eyes looked at Gabriela.

Gabriela screamed a shriek of pure joy. But the unicorn wasn't scared. Delicately, gracefully, and with all the dignity of a fabled mythical creature, it sniffed the pizza rolls.

"Its herdmaster said this one volunteered to come—it wanted to meet its first human," Novi said. She unstoppered a vial, drank its contents, and then gestured at the empty container. "Your wizard brewed us an even stronger headache medicine for portal travel. It might not be magic, but it's close."

Gabriela latched on to the first bit that Novi said. "It wanted to meet *me*? But I'm no one special."

"Yes, you are," I said. "After all we've been through, after all you did . . . yes, you *are*! And you were before any of this too."

To the unicorn, she breathed, "You really wanted to meet *me*?"

It whickered at her, a bell-like sound.

Hands shaking, Gabriela picked up the plate of pizza rolls. "Are you hungry? What do you eat? Anything besides sunshine and rainbows? These are . . . well, I don't know how to describe them. You probably don't have pizza in your world. But you can try one, if you'd like." She was talking so fast that her words spilled over one another. "Or maybe that's a bad idea. It might disagree with you."

I could have sworn the unicorn rolled its luminous blue eyes at her.

It then plucked a pizza roll off the plate with its teeth and swallowed it whole. We all stared at it. Gabriela made a tiny sound, like a bird's chirp. "Oh, I think I'm going to cry."

The unicorn, still elegant and radiant, let out a tiny burp.

Leaving Gabriela to bond with the unicorn, I led Novi through the house. She'd come with a second purpose, she said—to check on Worm, per order of her parents. I wasn't convinced that her parents had anything to do with it, but that was none of my business.

"He goes by Benden now," I told her.

"He'll still be my brother, you know," she said, "even if he's joining your family here."

We were working on legally adopting him, so he could

stay here as long as he wanted. Go to school. Even college. Mom and Dad were handling the rather complicated paperwork involved in adopting someone from another world. "You can share my brothers, if you want extra," I told her. "I have plenty."

And then Mom joined us and began clucking over Novi as if she planned to adopt her too. I wouldn't have minded gaining a sister, but Novi wasn't interested in leaving Home. She just wanted to be able to visit. I supposed it was just as well—given how devoted she was to following the rules, she would probably rat on me every time I snuck out my window.

While we'd been greeting the unicorn, Mom had changed out of her painting clothes and was now in her "casual" around-the-house clothes, which consisted of designer jeans and a perfectly ironed blouse, for tonight's get-together. Now that she was home, she seemed determined to wear every outfit she owned.

I stayed downstairs as Mom led Novi up to Benden's room. He'd already started making it his own, by burning designs into the walls with his breath. Actually quite pretty. I was thinking of asking him to decorate my door.

As I wondered what Novi would think of Benden's new living arrangements, I heard a car drive through the gate, and I peeked out the window. All thoughts about Novi, Benden, Gabriela, and the unicorn fled my mind.

Ryan was here!

And his mother too—my parents had invited her, and to my surprise, she'd accepted. Maybe she wasn't really an introvert; maybe she just hadn't wanted to leave the house while Mr. Keene was there.

Ryan's father was hiding in Europe. He'd even sent a postcard, which Ryan said was his father's way of saying he still cared, even though he'd nearly trapped his son in a portal dimension.

I raced outside.

Mrs. Keene smiled when she saw me. "Sky, you look lovely. Did you cut your hair?"

I *might* have spent a little extra time with the brush and styling gel this morning, knowing that Ryan was coming. "Just a new shampoo," I said. "You look well."

She did. There was pink in her cheeks, and she was *smiling*, which wasn't anything I'd seen her do for years. I hadn't realized how seldom she'd smiled when Mr. Keene had been there. I wondered how it had happened, how they'd gone from happy couple to miserable. From what I could guess, it had changed a little at a time. My eyes slid to Ryan, and then I had no more interest in worrying about his mother's failed marriage. We'd gone from good to terrible to everything I'd ever wanted.

Ryan was looking at me the same way he looked at his vanilla ice cream with red-hots, and I felt as if I were melting. My shoes seemed to have fused to the asphalt—I barely even noticed when Mrs. Keene passed by me into the house. She said something polite, a thank-you for us inviting her, and I think I said something polite back. My head was buzzing. "So . . . are we going to keep staring at each other dramatically, or are you going to kiss me?" I asked.

And then he crossed toward me in long strides, and my feet were suddenly able to move again. I met him halfway, and we were kissing.

It felt exactly the same as standing on the cliff looking

out over a valley of dragons. No, it felt like flying with other dragons, the wind catching my wings and forcing me higher. It felt—

"Okay, enough. That's my sister," Charles interrupted from behind us. "Everyone's waiting for you two."

We broke apart, but Ryan kept his hand intertwined in mine. We walked hand in hand into the house and into the TV room. It was time for movie night.

Tuck had made popcorn, lots of it, and drizzled butter and salt over it. "The trick is to steal the butteriest pieces," I told Benden and Novi, who were already on one of the couches. "But you don't want it to *look* like that's what you're doing; otherwise certain people get upset."

"Most buttery pieces are usually on top," Gabriela told the unicorn, and then she reached over and scooped out a handful of the best pieces. The unicorn ate delicately out of her hand.

"You've turned your friend into a thief," Liam noted. "Nicely done."

"You're welcome," I said to Gabriela.

She grinned at me, then smiled more shyly at Liam. He wasted zero time in crossing the room to sit next to her on the floor in front of the unicorn. She blushed, but looked happy. Tuck dimmed the lights, and Charles turned on the TV.

Along with the TV screen and the unicorn's horn, there was a third glow in the room: the Door. While I'd been outside kissing Ryan, my parents had moved it out of the kitchen—until its formal room with all the new security (to be paid for with a portion of our newly restored fortune) was complete, they were keeping a close eye on it. For tonight, it rested above the fireplace, secure on a pedestal that Dad had melted onto the stone mantel. Mom had put candlesticks next to it, so it would look merely decorative.

Novi pointed to the jewel. "You're keeping it *here*? In your living quarters? Shouldn't it be under guard when it's not in use?"

"It *is* guarded," Dad said. "It's here with all of us."

"We aren't going to hide it away," Mom told her. "Any wyvern should be able to travel through it of their own free will. It is no longer a punishment or a measure of control." She had a note of steel in her voice—I was fairly sure she'd used that tone to convince the council that the Door belonged with us. Novi nodded, accepting her word as authority.

Liam took the bowl of popcorn, offering it to Gabriela. I stole it back. Dad handed out sodas, while Mom found extra pillows for everyone who wanted them. As the previews began to play, I curled up on an empty couch. Ryan joined me. I snuggled against him, and he put his arm around me.

I am Sky Hawkins. You may have seen my name in the newspapers or on TV. I'm a wyvern, distantly related to King Atahualpa, Sir Francis Drake, and that guy who started the California Gold Rush. At the time of the last Reckoning, I led my first heist and gained my first hoard. It's here all around me:

Ryan, Gabriela, Benden, Novi, Mom, Dad, Charles, Tuck, and Liam.

My friends and my family are my treasure.

They are my gold.

ACKNOWLEDGMENTS

I'd like to thank all the pizza and chocolate I consumed during the writing of this novel. This book wouldn't exist without you. In particular, I'd like to call out a slice of balsamic tomato from Luigi's Pizzeria for being my muse. For me, every book starts with an "Ooh, I want to write *that*!" moment, and I had the idea for this book while I was eating pizza (with mozzarella, tomato slices, and balsamic vinegar—yum!) and talking about heist movies with my awesome family. Midbite, I jumped up and said, "I want to write *Ocean's Eleven* with were-dragons!" And then I ran off to write down the idea before it escaped like a thief into the night.

I'd also like to thank the Antwerp diamond heist, the Isabella Stewart Gardner Museum heist, and the security system at Fort Knox for being so fascinating. Also, the Svalbard Global Seed Vault, Cheyenne Mountain, and the Federal Reserve Bank of New York. And YouTube for the detailed how-to-pick-a-lock videos.

Thank you to my amazing agent, Andrea Somberg, and my wonderful editor, Emily Easton, as well as the other fantastic people at Crown Books for Young Readers and Penguin Random House. Without you, Sky would never have learned to fly.

And endless thanks to my family—I love you all more than dragons. Even were-dragons.

ABOUT THE AUTHOR

Sarah Beth Durst is the award-winning author of numerous fantasy books for children, teens, and adults, including *Conjured*, *Drink Slay Love*, and *The Queen of Blood*. She won an ALA-YALSA Alex Award and a Mythopoeic Fantasy Award for Children's Literature, and has been a finalist for the Andre Norton Award for Young Adult Science Fiction and Fantasy three times. Sarah lives in Stony Brook, New York, with her husband, her children, and her ill-mannered cat. You can follow her on Facebook, on Instagram, and on Twitter at @sarahbethdurst, or visit her at sarahbethdurst.com.